Controlled by Desire

JUSTINA STANIFORTH

Controlled by Desire

JUSTINA STANIFORTH

Published by Staniforth Publishing

To all the women out there who have always questioned
if they're worthy of that grand love
— you're more than that, you are everything!
Love starts with you Queen x

Content note – tropes, tags and content warnings

Tropes
Instalove, meet-cute, whirlwind romance, love overcomes tragic past, office romance, incapable of love, Happily Ever After, billionaire romance, opposites attract

Tags
MF, adult romance, instalove, quick burn, dom play, baby girl, princess, little one, sir, hard and fast, dominatrix, kinks, romance, contemporary romance, erotica, spicy, smut, alpha-male, dom/sub, spicy romance, steamy, HEA

Content warnings
Some content within this novel may be disturbing or triggering for some readers. Reader discretion is advised. Please be aware of your own triggers and limitations. Subjects include: trauma, loss, self-sabotage

This book contains graphic sex scenes that include elements of BDSM, exhibitionism, voyeurism, dom/sub and strong language.

Any character depicted in a sexual scene is at least 18 years of age. This book should not be used as a reference or guide for any sexual practices.

For those of you who wish to dive in headfirst, please remember this adult romance is a work of fiction and more than anything, have fun with it!

CONTENTS

CHAPTER 1 1

CHAPTER 2 10

CHAPTER 3 17

CHAPTER 4 26

CHAPTER 5 34

CHAPTER 6 41

CHAPTER 7 49

CHAPTER 8 59

CHAPTER 9 69

CHAPTER 10 79

CHAPTER 11 87

CHAPTER 12 95

CHAPTER 13 104

CHAPTER 14 114

CHAPTER 15 125

CHAPTER 16 133

CHAPTER 17 144

CHAPTER 18 151

CHAPTER 19 160

CHAPTER 20 170

CHAPTER 21 179

CHAPTER 22 186

CHAPTER 23 196

CHAPTER 24 203

CHAPTER 25 214

CHAPTER 26 223

CHAPTER 27 231

CHAPTER 28 244

CHAPTER 29 253

EPILOGUE...261

ACKNOWLEDGEMENTS 268

LEAVE A REVIEW...269

ABOUT THE AUTHOR 270

CHAPTER 1

SWISH.

THE CRUMPLED rejection letter I threw landed effortlessly in the trash can after making its way through the small basketball hoop hung on the wall.

"Nothin' but net!" I sigh, slumping back, letting my head fall against the couch as I squeeze my eyes shut.

Have you ever wondered where you'd be if you took the other fork in the road? If destiny hadn't dealt you the cards you hold? What if the people you loved hadn't left you? Would you be the same person, have the same personality, kinks or sense of humour? Or would you be someone else entirely?

My mind spun, falling swiftly into a world of what-ifs. Some days I couldn't pull myself out of the darkness where that small inner voice got louder and questioned all the whys. Why did you do that? Why would you say that? Why didn't you try harder? Why don't you just give up?

I huffed in frustration. "Shut up, shut up, shut up! Seriously, would it kill you to be positive, and give a little praise and self-love for once in your life?" I grumbled to myself, shaking my head in an attempt to dislodge the toxic waste sloshing around in there.

My thoughts wandered and her face came rushing back, as clear as the last time I'd seen her. Her kind hazel eyes smiled at me. I could feel the warmth on my cheek from where her hand cupped my face. I leaned into it, trying to hold onto an ounce of strength. If I let just one tear fall there'd be no closing the floodgates and the sadness would swallow me whole. She watched me intently, memorising my face as I memorised hers, especially that crooked smile that had a way of melting any foul mood I was in. But she was a shadow of her usual vibrant self and her bronze hair had lost its lustre. Somehow, above it all, the love and strength she'd always wrapped me in was still overpowering, bubbling at the surface.

'Show them who you are Charlie bear. Don't hide away. You are meant for big things – it's inevitable'.

Thump!

I shot up, brought back by the sound of the apartment door slamming and my housemate throwing her keys against the bench. Lizzie stalked into the lounge room, shopping bags dangling from her fingers. Her smile dropped as she eyed me slumped on the couch – defeat written all over my face.

"Oh no, not another one... How many does that make?" the usually bubbly and bouncy vixen asked, the edges of her mouth curving down.

"Twelve – I'm done. Seriously, I give up!" I said dramatically. "I'm obviously not meant to work in advertising! I'll be stuck working at the coffee house for the rest of my life," I flopped my upper body across the arm of the couch.

"That double degree, *with honours,* begs to differ. It's just been a shitty run. Buuuuttttt—," she let the word drawl out. "I'm positive your luck will turn around next week," she said smiling warmly. "Mark my words Charlotte May Drake, you are going to be the next best advertising exec in this city,... nay this country," she shot up, pointing her finger in the air. "And clients will be flocking to your feet just to have your name on their project!"

I couldn't help but laugh, "You've certainly got a way with words, I'll give you that. Mind sharing an ounce of that positivity?"

"Tut, tut… it's not just positivity Charlie. You know I'm just always right – I have a gift," she singsonged with a confident smirk plastered on her face as she closed the gap between us, pulling me off the couch with more strength than should be humanly possible in such a small petite package.

"Now, get up and put on this sexy little number," she raised an eyebrow, handing me one of the bags at her feet. "We've got plans – girls' night out! It's day five of our New Year's week of celebrations and you promised me a whole week of boogying our booties off and getting our flirt on."

Before I could object, Lizzie had her *Weekend Vibes* playlist blaring out of the Bluetooth speaker and was dancing her way down the hall towards my room.

I considered myself a plain Jane and a bit of a homebody. Don't get me wrong, I loved a night out with good company like most, but there's no denying I truly am at my most comfortable at home with my hair in a messy bun, no make-up on, and lounging around in sweats.

But I loved my dear friend, and the brightness she brought into my jaded life. And I loved the big city lights. So how could I pass up a night with my two favourite things – three if you counted the cocktails I was sure we'd be downing soon.

The mini dress Lizzie had chosen for me was gorgeous! A sparkly midnight blue backless dress that made my blue-green eyes and long dark curls pop. The low v-neck cut showed off just enough of my full C-cups to get noticed, but not enough to worry about wardrobe malfunctions all night.

At 5'6", I rarely wore high heels, preferring flats so I didn't tower over my 5'2" best friend. Well that, and I couldn't really let my hair down and dance the night away if I had to worry about sore feet and blisters. So I slipped on my favourite pair of Roman strap flat sandals and met Lizzie in the bathroom to apply the final touches.

Lizzie smiled and gave a twirl showing off her perfectly proportioned breasts and hips in a gold and white mini combo that highlighted her natural Ibiza-esque honey tanned skin. Her sandy blonde bob was perfectly styled as usual and her signature *Passion Red* lipstick completed the look. One that could easily adorn the front cover of a high-end fashion magazine. Although she came in a petite package, Lizzie radiated certainty and sex appeal without trying. She was confident, flirtatious and the right mixture of feisty and submissive. She was my polar opposite. Where she was assertive, I was meek. She was the yin to my yang. My perfect counterbalance.

"Smokin' HOT Lizzie girl!" I said fanning myself, applying a splash of mascara and a dab of tinted lip gloss to my face.

"Oh stop…." She giggled. "No don't stop! Seriously, go on," she motioned with her hands, giggling.

I rolled my eyes, nudging her with my bum. "If I give you any more compliments your head won't fit through the door," I teased.

"Ugh, fine. Are you ready then? Because those martinis are calling my name and I've got a feeling tonight's the night you are going to meet the man of your dreams."

I let out a long sigh.

No way in hell. I can't even focus enough to level up to a better job and better pay, let alone land the man of my dreams. Come to think of it, I'm not sure I actually had one… Well shit, had I been too preoccupied to even cook up my idea of the perfect man – how depressing is that!

Before I got bogged down in self-loathing again, the small voice inside my head sprung to life.

Oh Gods, yes! I want Mr Dreamy, even if it's just for the night. I want off this hamster wheel. Bring on excitement, bring on danger, heck bring on a mysterious man to spice things up.

A blush crept across my cheeks and my stomach filled with butterflies. "Calm down La Femme Nikita, we're not hunting tonight," I tried to cover up my betraying thoughts. "I just want a night with my special girl to drink and dance and forget about those damn rejection letters."

"Come on already, it's half-ten," I offered my hand. "First rounds on me." And with that Lizzie let out a squeal as she hurried to the front door of our apartment.

Our regular nightclub *The Sparrow* was just a few blocks away. As we rounded the corner the music, neon lights and smell of sweat and desire took over my senses. We walked towards the front door where the security guard smiled, a sparkle in his eye, and ushered us in.

"Lizzie, Charlie, lookin' fine ladies," Johnny flirted with his Southern drawl. "How many hearts you plannin' on breakin' tonight?"

"Just yours sexy," Lizzie shot back with a wink, leaning in to give him a kiss on the cheek as she walked past. It was hard to ignore how his hand lingered on her lower back or how he had to adjust his jeans when he let her go. It took a second too long for Johnny to take his eyes off Lizzie before he directed his gaze at me, nodded and cleared his throat shyly before looking away again.

The club was decked out in New Year celebrations glitter and gold, making it easy to forget what day of the week it was. Hell, it could have been mid-week and I'd still be transported to weekend madness in here. *Perfection!*

We walked slowly into the belly of the club. I could feel the music vibrating through my body, sending tingles up from my feet, up my legs, and all the way through my stomach and chest. There was something about it that flicked on that feel-good button and made me instantly feel electric and alive.

"This is exactly what I needed," I leaned into Lizzie's ear.

The dance floor was packed with bodies sliding against each other, but we skirted around the edges towards the bar and the tables at the back of the room. I could see Lizzie's ex, Eric, was busy working the bar we were nearing. As if he felt the invisible string between them, he looked away from the two girls he was serving and straight towards Lizzie. By the time we hit the bar he was waiting for us, an ear-to-ear grin and come-hither eyes focused on Lizzie. He leant forward across the bar to shout over the music.

"Damn baby girl, how come you never wore that when we were together?" he asked Lizzie, with a tortured look in his eye.

"What would have been the point? You would have just ripped it off me and let it crinkle on the floor," she giggled back. "Can we get two Cosmos please? Lizzie's shout," she said triumphantly before turning to scan the crowd.

"You got it babe."

Lizzie and Eric were together for two years before splitting six months ago. Their chemistry was still palpable. But in the end they figured out the only thing that connected them was the sex, everything else had faded over the years. Thankfully they had fallen into an easy friendship, and Eric still hung out at our apartment and had become protective over the both of us like a brother.

"So… how long are you going to drag Johnny along for?" I teased Lizzie.

"Who says I am?" she shot back.

"Hey, no judgement sweetie. You know I have no ulterior motives, I just tell it how I see it. The sexy beast of a man

6

wants a piece of you and he has since the moment you met."

Lizzie ignored me, grabbed her drink off the counter and downed it in a breath. "Let's dance!" she changed the subject as she began to move towards the middle of the dance floor. I placed a 20 on the bar, grabbed my drink and sank it down, and began following her out to the middle of the crowd.

I let myself go, cleared my mind of the past year and swayed with the music. Song after song I let my worries and self-doubt vanish, letting the music take over my body and soul as I fell deeper into the sea of dancing bodies.

I'm not sure how much time had passed but I needed a breather and another drink. I'd lost exact count, but it might have been Cosmo number four or five. I turned around to Lizzie and found her grinding her bum against a tall, tattooed guy I hadn't seen before.

I leaned in, "I need some air, want to come with me?"

Tattooed guy slid his arm around her waist and nibbled at Lizzie's ear before looking at me with a dangerous yet sexy-as-hell stare. "No, I've got all the air I need here," she smirked and leaned back into him, adjusting her body to lightly lick across his bottom lip. Turning back to me she said, "but if you want me to come with, just say and I'm all yours."

I knew Lizzie too well to be worried. She was in her element and although tattooed guy probably thought he was dominating the small woman in his arms, it was Lizzie who held the power. The women's self-defence class she taught every Tuesday didn't hurt either.

"Oh no no, you have fun… I'll just be over there if you need me," I said waggling my eyebrows and pointing towards the bar. Lizzie turned her body, wrapping her arms around his neck, bringing him in for a deep kiss.

I sat at a bar stool and motioned to Eric for another drink. Two drinks later Lizzie was still dancing and making out with tattooed guy. I swayed with the music, enjoying the feeling of my body getting lighter.

Thump!

I was pulled out of my tipsy glow as the guy standing next to me suddenly swung out in retaliation, his fist colliding with a guy behind him who had drawn first blood.

My stomach lurched and in a flash everything slowed down. I could see an elbow coming towards my head as he yanked his arm back to take another swing.

Oh God, I was about to become collateral damage, caught in the crossfire of a stupid pub brawl. Fuck my life.

I scrunched my eyes shut, pulling my arms up to cover my head. Waiting for the impact. At the same time, I was pulled backwards off the bar stool by a set of strong arms and felt a large solid body envelop me. The stranger lifted me away from the fight and towards one of the back tables. I swayed, a wave of nausea rolling through me. He sat, pulling me into his lap. His arms still wrapped tightly around me.

I felt dizzy. I felt dazed.

Shit, I think I'm going into shock.

I tried to steady my breathing while I kept my head tucked into the stranger's chest. My senses were returning, and I realised I was intimately sitting atop a strange man's lap, probably squashing him with my generous ass and thighs. But I couldn't help it, I didn't dare move. Instead, I drank in his animal magnetism, his strong muscled arms around me and let his hypnotizing scent distract me.

"It's okay princess, you're safe," he breathed in my ear, the deep husky tone of his voice creating an instant heat between my thighs as he gently brushed the loose strands of hair away from my cheek.

I risked a glance up towards his face only to be met with the most divine full lips and wicked smile.

Oh. My. Goddess. Hello Mr Dreamy.

Was I dreaming? Had I been knocked out in the fight? Who was this man and why was he still holding me tight against his body? All I knew was my heart was racing, pounding in my ears, and the red-blooded man in front of me was awakening long-dormant sexual desires.

CHAPTER 2

"UH… I'M S-SORRY," I stuttered as I tried to pull back too quickly. The world threatened to go black and spin on its axis. I wasn't sure if I was seeing glittering stars in my vision or if it was the flashing lights of the nightclub, but I put my hands against his chest to steady myself.

"Breathe Little Lamb," came that seductive voice again.

Sweet merciful Gods, his voice was like honey.

I tried to focus on whether the nausea had passed. After a second, I chanced a slow, deep breath. Then another. *Success!* The world stopped spinning and I felt the radiating warmth of his skin under my hands. My pulse sped up and my head flung back before my body floated higher and higher, light as a feather, and I was transported away.

I was surrounded by ink black silk sheets, lying atop a grand King bed in the middle of a generous bedroom. A fireplace crackled on the opposite wall. A soft light filtered in from a room somewhere to the side. The smell of leather and musk mixed with timber and flames, filling my nose and warming my chest. Warm strong hands glided up my thighs, across my hips, stopping at my ribs. My breathing strained at the sensation. I could feel the weight on my lower body increase as the dark-haired shirtless man crawled up my body. I looked down, trying to see his face but his hair fell over his eyes. His stubble gently scraped against my soft skin while the heat of his breath and tongue sent shivers from my toes to my nose as he trailed his way up to my breast, circling around

10

the mound before sucking my hardened nipple into his warm mouth.

Smash!

My eyes flew open at the sound of glass shattering and I was reminded that a club fight was still going on nearby. I could hear security taking control of the situation. I breathed deeply and focused on my hands in front of me, still holding onto a man's chest.

The crisp white button-down shirt he was wearing gaped open to his sternum. And under my hands — strong muscular pecs that I'd wager my week's paycheck led down to a deliciously toned stomach. This man obviously knew the ins and outs of the gym.

I tried pulling back again only to be met with the consuming heat of his stare. The most golden amber eyes shadowed with long, dark lashes pinned me to the spot. I jumped up and began fidgeting with my hands. "I'm so sorry. I don't know what happened," I laughed nervously. "One moment I was moving with the music and the next I was in your lap. I—"

"Hush Little Lamb," he said seizing my wrist and pulling me closer until our legs were touching. "It doesn't matter how it happened, but I can't let you go now."

Panic set in, I looked around the club, desperate to grab the attention of security, or Eric. *Someone.* The security guards had the brawling asshats held tightly between them, pushing them out towards the front door and no one on the dance floor had even skipped a beat. The music continued and from the corner of my eye I could see Lizzie and tattooed guy taking it to second base. I was on my own. I returned my gaze to his hand on my arm, then dug deep to find the courage to meet his eyes.

"Not without, making sure… you are safe Little One," a smirk pulled at the corner of his mouth.

He rubbed my hand between his big warm, rough hands, making circles with his thumb.

11

As if he'd flicked a switch in my brain – and my core – the panic vanished and something roared to life in me. I wanted to get to know him. More than that, I wanted him to know me. To know every part of my body. Every desire I'd ever pushed down into the dark corners of my mind.

Without another thought, I let myself explore his face. Intense eyes the colour of rich aged whiskey bore into me, and I invited them. His masculine features were enhanced by a chiselled jaw, cleft chin and rugged five-o-clock shadow. I tried to drag my eyes away, but I was transfixed and let my stare linger on his lips.

Fuck. Shit. Fuckityshit, what are you doing Charlie?

"Davies, grab us a bottle," he directed a man standing over his shoulder. This beautiful stranger had power and spoke with such controlled authority.

What would it take to see him lose control, to come undone…
with me beneath him?

"Come princess, sit with me," he snapped me out of my daydream.

"Charlie. M-my name's Charlie," I stuttered, sliding into the booth next to him.

"*Charlie*," he let my name melt in his mouth.

Dear Gods, he has to be a witch, a warlock. What is he doing
to me?

The warmth between my thighs grew into a wet heat, soaking my underwear. And those pesky butterflies made their second appearance for the night.

Tall, dark and handsome poured us both a glass of bubbly and took a slow, deliberate swallow, never breaking eye contact. There was an intensity that flowed out of him but softened with a hint of playfulness.

"What brings you to The Sparrow Charlie? Friend… boyfriend… Tinder date?" he quizzed, that grin never leaving his face.

I bit my lip, feeling an instant flush in my cheeks.

Shit. How should I play this? Like my usual honest, over-sharing self… or maybe take a leaf out of Lizzie's 'how to be irresistible to the object of your affection' guide? Maybe I could channel my bestie or at least try to fake the mystery and confidence she had… If there was ever a time you had my back inner self, this has got to be it.

With a dash of Dutch courage and a burning need to leave my boring life behind, I chose option C.

Staring into those golden pools, I tried to make it sound sexy, "You." But all I could hear was the fake coolness and shake in my lie.

Retreat, run away.

The little voice in my head had led me astray and now wanted to bolt for the hills.

Dear Gods, open up the earth and swallow me whole…

I shrank away, biting my lip again and looked down at my hands nervously pulling at the hem of my dress.

He leant even closer, firmly grabbing my chin, rubbing his thumb along it and up to my mouth, releasing my bottom lip from my teeth. Before I could say another stupid word to embarrass myself his lips captured mine. He softly teased my lips apart, enticing my tongue with his. His lips were soft and full, and I wanted to suck and bite them just to see if he would do the same to mine. To other parts of my body. I hesitated only for a second before deepening the kiss, rubbing a hand through his hair while the other gripped his shirt. The club's deafening music faded away and the world went silent. The only sound apart from the sliding of our mouths and tongues was the racing of my heart.

As though I weighed nothing, he lifted me onto his lap letting his hands roam up from my hips. One slowly travelled up my back, the other firmly grasping the nape of my neck. The heat in my core grew, bringing a shaky breath from my lips. I leaned my forehead against his, if only to make sure he wasn't a figment of my imagination. His grip tightened and I could feel his excitement grow.

His glare was filled with raw passion and need. I dived down into his mouth again, pulling his body firmly against my aching breasts. I could smell my sweet arousal, a mix of vanilla and peaches, and groaned at the thought of him smelling it too. He responded with a low growl as he moved his wandering hand around to tease the side of my breast, scraping his thumb across my swollen nipple. The bulge in his pants grew, straining against his zipper, pressing against my soft folds.

He cupped my face with his hands, pulling away to look into my eyes. His breath was heavy and uneven, "are you sure you want to do this Little Lamb? Because if we keep playing, I won't be able to stop myself. You will be mine."

I didn't need an excuse. As bat-shit crazy as this was, it felt good. It felt right. I didn't want to dissect my thoughts and actions. I wanted to let go. To be free. To live. I needed to live… if only for her.

I moved my hips against him and put my arms around his neck. I leaned in closer and whispered, "I'm yours," gently tugging his earlobe between my teeth.

I poured two cups of hot coffee, adding a dash of caramel to both as ordered before carrying them to the two women chatting at the corner table. I walked slowly back behind the counter of *Maggie's Morning Brew* and began refilling the coffee beans.

My thoughts kept wandering to the night before. I didn't even know his name. What kind of hussy did that make me? I shook my head trying to bring myself back to the present but it was no use. I could still smell him, taste him and feel the mixed pain and pleasure between my legs. I could still feel how he stretched and filled me, covering my body in sweat. The sweet smell of hot, raw, unadulterated sex. My cheeks flushed with the memory and my nipples hardened against my t-shirt.

'You don't know the power you have over me princess.
You are mine.'

"Coffee order," Trish hollered, bringing me back to reality. To the life I was destined to live – a barista who craved so much more. Oh God I hoped I was wrong, but some days just felt like there was no way out. Nothing better waiting on the other side. Not like last night. Not the tall, dark, handsome stranger that made me forget who I was.

'Little Lamb you are beautiful. You feel so soft, so warm,
so tight.'

Shit! I pulled my hand away as the hot milk bubbled over the edge of the pot onto my hand. I raced to the sink and began running it under cold water.

"What's with you today Charlie, have one too many last night?" Trish asked.

"Yeh something like that. Sorry I'll get my head on straight. Do you mind if I have a quick break to wash my face and grab a hit of caffeine?" I needed to snap out of it or I was never getting through my shift.

"Go on, I'll finish up this order. You go fix your hand… and your head," Trish smiled.

Trish had worked here since before I was born. She didn't own the store and didn't have any desire to move on to bigger and better things. She was happy right where she was and I envied her for it. But I knew I couldn't be happy here for much longer. I loved advertising and I had dreamt of working in it since I was a kid watching my parents do the same thing. I just needed to land an entry-level job in the field and work my way up. Maybe job application number 13 would be the lucky one…?!

CHAPTER 3

AFTER MAKING A handful of stupid mistakes making coffees and nearly losing a finger or two trying to grab food straight off the grill – *thank the lords for Tom's quick reflexes* – I ran out of the coffee house when my time was done, desperate to soak in the tub and download the night's events with Lizzie.

I had interrupted her make-out session before leaving The Sparrow last night, pulling her into the ladies' room to check in with her plans for tattooed guy and let her know I was leaving with Mr tall drink of water. When we moved in together while we were at university, we had made a promise, and we'd stuck to it ever since. If either one of us ever planned on heading back to a fling's apartment, we'd send the pinned location to the other. We may have been red-blooded women with primal urges, but we didn't have a death wish. So safety first…. Sex a close second.

After sneaking out of Mr Hot Sex's bed in the early hours of the morning, I had messaged Lizzie letting her know I was heading home for a few hours sleep before work. It had taken her all of five seconds to reply with a string of emojis.

Lizzie: (eggplant, peach, water squirt, high five, kiss, wink face)
Charlie: Detail exchange at 4pm!… I'll grab Chinese on the way home. xx
Lizzie: It's a date!

And Charlie….
  I am proud of you boo – you looked happy xx

I phoned in our regular order and flew into *Red Dragon's Palace* to grab our Kung Pao chicken, fried rice, and Wonton soup. The anticipation of reliving every detail of my bat-shit-crazy, but oh-so-amazing night for Lizzie had me giddy. I raced home head in the clouds, nearly knocking a woman flat on her back, and walking into oncoming traffic when I was sure the crossing sign was an emoji face winking at me.

I juggled the bags while fighting to get my key into the apartment door. It popped open as I staggered forward, spinning around to slam it shut with my foot. "Lizzie, I'm home," I called out while walking into the kitchen. I was welcomed with Lizzie's big cheesy grin, complete with bottle of wine in one hand, and two glasses in the other.

"Spill – and don't leave out a single detail," she squealed like a child on Christmas morning. "I mean it Charlie. Don't you dare fluff about like you did when retelling your tale with Mr small hands-small feet."

"Hey!," I shot back. "I danced around that debrief because it was bad enough the first time, let alone reliving it a second time with you. Oh God, so small….!," I giggled, shaking my head. "And thank you very much for bringing that memory bubbling back to the surface."

I joined her on the couch and began opening the containers, clumsily scooping a wonton into my watering mouth, letting the juices drip down my chin.

"Hey, no fair – start talking, *then* start shovelling food in, *after* I've got the first piece of the story to start drooling over," Lizzie huffed.

I teased her a little longer, slowly chewing the food down before taking a long, slow mouthful of wine.

Lizzie tapped her foot, crossed her arms across her chest and turned a funny shade of pink with annoyance. Her eyes widened, her brows raised and her mouth pinched together.

"Okay, okay, sorry…" I laughed. "I'm just trying to find the right place to start."

"How about at the beginning, like when did you lock eyes with him? Who made the first move? What's his name? And how many times did he make you come?" she pried.

"I don't know his name," I sighed, covering my eyes. "How crazy is that?! The insatiable need to devour every inch of each other's skin took over and then I panicked. *Of course* I panicked! And not wanting to be rejected the morning after, I did what any woman with an ounce of self-worth does…. I snuck out of bed and did the walk of shame before the sun came up, running out of there so fucking quick that I left without my panties."

Lizzie and I fell into hysterics.

"Well I'm glad my sex life amuses you," I chuckled. "I refuse to say another word."

"Hey, come on now, don't be like that. How about I go first? Because I've been dying to tell you about Scott," Lizzie readjusted getting comfy on the couch.

"Scott?"

"Yeh, you met him last night…" she continued, scooping out some Kung Pao chicken and fried rice onto her plate.

"Ahhh tattooed guy," I said between slurps of soup. "I mean I wouldn't say I met him, but I remember the possessive way he held you. The way you climbed up his body and ate each other's faces."

Lizzie went silent, her eyes glazing over as she recalled how he had come up to her on the dancefloor, engulfing her entire being in an instant.

"Hello… Calling Lizzie Ryan," I waved my hand in front of her face. "Where'd you go?"

"Hmmm?!… I think I'm in love," she exclaimed dreamily.

"What?" I spluttered, trying to catch my breath. "Was he that mind-blowing? *Fuckkk*, do tell!"

"Well not in love, but definitely lust," she grinned, stuffing a piece of chicken in her mouth. "There was a serious connection and I think there could be something there Charlie, he is… *perfect*. His eyes are the deepest chocolate, and his lips are sooo soft but driven by need, and his hands…. Oh. My. God his hands," she dramatically fell backwards.

"I'm guessing they're not small," I motioned with my hands.

"Haha, no they are not. They are just right!" Lizzie smiled.

"And the sex?" I quizzed.

"That's the thing. We didn't….. We fooled around and did everything else, but then we talked – for hours. About his life and mine, and he was so curious about me, not just my body. It's…"

"Who are you and what have you done with my friend," I interrupted, narrowing my eyes at her.

"I know, I know – but maybe he's the one who's going to change my wicked ways and make me want to settle down."

I couldn't help but smile. A deep smile that reached all the way from my mouth to my eyes and my heart. Lizzie deserved a man that saw past her gorgeous exterior and made her feel like the amazing woman she was. Not just a sex object. Someone who wanted to put in the time and effort to get to know the real Lizzie.

I let Lizzie continue replaying her night, filling me in on every detail, how they'd continued texting each other throughout the day and how they'd made plans for an official date tomorrow.

"He's picking me up from here at seven, you have to help me get ready and I want you to actually meet him this time."

"Like you even have to ask," I scoffed. "Honestly, I'm offended!"

Lizzie threw her arms around me and gave me the biggest bear hug. Pulling back she elbowed me gently, "soooo, spill the tea – did you silence that inner voice and allow yourself to be free? Did he hit a home run?"

"Yes, he rounded the bases several times and drove it home three…, no, four times," I boasted, completely satisfied.

"Eeeeeeep, I knew it. I could see that flash of freedom spark in your eyes last night before you left the club. I haven't seen that Charlie since uni and I've missed her," she smiled warmly. "So, keep it coming… tell me everything!"

I could feel my heartbeat creep up again as that familiar warmth in my lower belly and between my thighs returned. As if the mere thought of last night made every stroke of his hands, every flicker of his tongue against my skin come back to life, making the hairs on my arms stand on end.

'Fuck me – I don't know what you're doing to me princess… I can't control myself. I want all of you.'

I could feel his breath on my neck, hear his words driving me closer to the edge. I swallowed hard, shifting in my chair to bring myself back to the present. Lizzie's eyes explored my face but she sat there patiently waiting for me to share the closed captions with a smirk plastered on her face.

"He was – insatiable. I've never had a man want me as hungrily as he did. His hands traced every inch of my body. He worshipped *me*, *ME*… this not-so-little ol' me," I said smacking my thighs.

"He was so focused on me, on my pleasure – not his. It was in-cred-i-ble…, I've never experienced anything like that devotion, that… *enthusiasm* before."

Again, I was flung back, the memories hitting hard.

My fingers traced the rigid lines of his body, from the soft hairs that covered his chest, slowly moving further south to the V curving down from his hips. I could feel the weight of his form – the way he pinned me in place with his body, leaving me breathless beneath his bulk. How the soft brush of his lips covered my skin in goosebumps. How the sinister darting curiosity of his hot tongue and playful bites awakened sensations and left me desperately wanting more. So much more from a stranger who seemed to know my yearnings better than I knew myself.

I cleared my throat with another sip of wine and continued. "Before I was allowed to touch him, stroke him and taste him, he toyed with me for what felt like forever. He wound me up and repeatedly brought me so close to the brink right before denying my orgasm, over and over again."

"Umm Charlie, I don't know what your definition of worship is, but honey I think you're confused about a man's enthusiasm in bed…. And his incompetence if he can't get you to climax," Lizzie looked concerned.

"Hold your horses woman – I'm not done yet… As I was saying, he drove me absolutely crazy! But just when I thought I couldn't handle any more foreplay, and I was ready to push him off me, yank my clothes back on and storm out of there – leaving the sadistic prick high and dry I might add – he moved his tongue up to my clit, lapping and sucking while his fingers darted deep and fast inside me, driving me over the edge with such purpose," I shared with a Cheshire smile.

I couldn't help but laugh as I pulled my legs up to my chest and hid my face on my knees. "Who even am I? I don't do one-nighters – not like this. Not this intense!" I sighed.

Lizzie's expression went from worry to wonder. "Jesus Charlie, who the fuck is this guy?"

"He was possessive *and* powerful, but he didn't scare me Lizzie. I felt… safe." I surprised myself, letting those words escape my mouth. "Shit, I even felt like I belonged to him – mind, body and soul. Truly free to explore him and be explored with no shame. And Christ his size… It was made for me. I mean, have you ever felt stretched and tested, but your body just knows how to adjust and any discomfort just melts away to pure pleasure?"

"So why run away?" Lizzie questioned cheekily. "I would have woken him up for some morning delight!" she said, her eyebrows dancing playfully.

"Because!"

"Because…?" Lizzie pressed.

"Because… oh God I don't know. What if he didn't like what he saw when he woke up? What if he wanted to send me home after he was satisfied but was too much of a gentleman? What if he has a wife and I'm a homewrecker? What if—"

"I'm gonna stop you right there before you destroy your *amazing* night of memories. He wanted you, and by the sounds of it, bad! He loved every goddamn second with you. And even if it was all for one-night-only, what a helluva night. Hot, hot, HOT!" she said fanning herself dramatically.

Lizzie continued to creep forward as I recalled the things he had done to me, the acts I found the courage to play out, that made him groan harder, drive deeper and growl that I was his.

'Mine.'

After we both divulged every wicked desire and action from our nights and made our way to the bottom of two bottles of wine, we lay on the lounges together in content silence.

It didn't take long before the world became blurry and I was dragged down, deep into the land of dreams, down into a world with Mr Dreamy.

The fire crackled next to me, bathing me in warmth and light. I was hypnotised by the flames, unable to look away. 'Lie back and lift your hips,' his silky voice ordered. I did as he asked. He knelt in front of me and lifted me higher, placing pillows under my bum, tilting my hips up in line with his thick member. I tried to look at his face but he leaned in closer, putting his arms around my legs and began kissing the inside of my thigh. My eyes fell shut at the heavenly feeling of his tender kisses.

23

He licked from my knee up to my soft folds. One of his hands released from around my thigh and skirted around my entrance before a finger slid inside. I gasped at the welcome feeling. He moved in and out slowly. When my juices started to lap in his palm, he entered another finger, stretching my inner walls. His mouth moved up from my thigh to my aching clit. He licked and sucked, matching the rhythm of his fingers. The intensity built, my breaths became ragged and I couldn't hold in the moans any longer. He answered with a guttural groan, quickening his speed. 'Oh God, I'm close'. He pulled his mouth away for a second, "Cum for me princess, cum now," before returning his attention to my throbbing clit. Stars formed behind my eyes and the pressure built until I exploded, bringing with it the most intense orgasm. As I basked in the after-glow I tried to still my panting and open my eyes to see Mr Dreamy. But sleep had other ideas and swallowed me whole.

CHAPTER 4

BRRREEEP! BRRRREEPPP!
BRRREEEP! Brrrreeppp!

I was jerked awake by the shrill ringing of my phone.

"What. The. Fuck…." I groaned. "It's too early – and it's Suuuundaaaaay!" I grumbled reaching to find my phone on the table.

I squinted an eye open trying to make sense of the numbers on the screen I held up in front of my blurry vision, but they were alien to me.

Who the hell was calling me this early?

Anyone who knew me at all knew not to awaken the sleeping beast, especially on a sleepy Sunday.

"Mmmmake itttt stooooppppppp!" Lizzie begged from the other lounge.

I let my arms fall back above my head, willing my brain to wake up faster and decide whether to answer or let it go to message bank.

I took a long, steadying breath and hit the answer button bringing the phone back up to my ear.

"Hello," I said in the friendliest timbre I could muster. But it fell flat. There was no hiding the irritated tone that bled through.

"Ms Drake?" a soft woman's voice answered.

I quickly cleared my throat and tried again. "Yes, this is she. And it's Miss, not Ms."

"I apologise for phoning so early Miss Drake, my name is Jane Ellis and I am calling from *Crescent Incorporated*."

My head spun, a little from the booze still floating around in my system, and a little because the name was unfamiliar to me. *Crescent Incorporated… Crescent Incorporated.* I tried desperately to recollect if I had agreed to do something for this company, or worse – had I crossed paths with someone important, pissed them off and was about to be sued?

Shit, if this is some so-called charity organisation fishing for a donation, someone was gonna get the not-so-friendly side of Charlotte Drake!

Jane's perky voice continued, "We would like to schedule an interview tomorrow morning, 9am if you're available?"

I stumbled, feeling dazed and confused. *Did I apply for a job with Crescent Incorporated?* Okay, there had been quite a few lately, but how the heck did I forget that I was waiting to hear back from one more company? *I must be losing my mind.*

I sat up straight, capturing Lizzie's attention. "Ah yes… of course I can make that work. Do you mind sending me through the details?" I chanced asking a stupid question. She was going to see straight through me and know I was completely unprepared for the job opportunity, whatever that job was.

But she remained professional. "Of course, sending it now. See you tomorrow morning Miss Drake." With that, the line went dead. A second later, a message flashed up on the screen with the heading **Interview confirmation – Crescent Incorporated**.

I let my hand drop into my lap, frowning at the phone and its now black screen.

"Who the heck was that?" Lizzie asked, stretching out her body before rolling to sit up facing me.

"Ummm, that was Crescent Incorporated. I have an interview tomorrow morning."

"Crescent Incorporated, I don't remember you mentioning that company. And with a name like that you'd think I'd remember it well, with my bias for all things astronomy-related."

"Mmm. It's not ringing a bell for me either, strangely enough. But this girl's not gonna say no when an opportunity comes knocking… or in this case, calling on a Sunday morning." I smiled.

"That's right baby girl," Lizzie said, her morning husky voice coming across more sexual than supportive. "Must be quite the dedicated staff to be making work calls on a Sunday though. That, or you're about to audition for some slave drivers," she teased.

"Zip it you," I leaned forward slapping her leg.
"Ouch!"

I made my way to the kitchen for my second extra-large cup of coffee, towelling my hair dry as I entered the room. I flipped my hair back and threw the towel across the back of the chair. Sitting across from Lizzie I pulled my phone from the bathrobe pocket, plopping it on the table face down.

"Feel a bit better after soaking your thoughts away?" Lizzie asked, sliding a steaming mug of freshly brewed coffee towards me.

"The best! There's nothing a hot bath can't solve," I confessed, lifting the mug up to blow on it before taking an eager sip, moaning in satisfaction as the instant delight warmed me up from the inside out.

"Ha, I beg to differ."

"And I call bullshit. How could you possibly disagree that a blissful soak in the tub doesn't make all your worries float away?" I rebuffed.

"Oh come on, don't tell me you've never been that horny that a little DIY in the bath doesn't quite take the edge off but instead makes it 1000% worse, and leaves you aching for the real thing," she said rolling her eyes back and biting her lip.

"No," I shot back, "But now I'm wishing I didn't know that about you since we share the same bath, you little nymphomaniac."

"You can talk," she smirked, waggling her brows.

She wasn't wrong. My latest escapade had given life to a side of me that had been hibernating until now. And just the thought of it had me tingling for a repeat performance.

Lizzie returned her focus to breakfast, nodding and taking a large bite of smashed avocado toast. Somehow she always managed to miss her plate with the falling crumbs covering most of the table instead.

"So, what's the plan?" I asked as I played with a small pile of crumbs between us.

"Shopping of course. I need something for my date tonight, and you need something for this new sexy, confident Charlie and the wonderful opportunity that awaits you tomorrow morning!" she said between bites. "So, tell me, is the interview for the same type of position as the other recent job apps… or is it something completely different? I need some hints if I'm going to find you the perfect thing to wear," she asked as she stood, scraping the pile of crumbs onto her plate before heading to the kitchen.

"Umm I assume so, but to be honest I don't actually know. That woman Jane sent me a message after she called, let me find it."

I turned my phone over and tapped it to life, clicking on the message from Crescent Incorporated and began reading it aloud.

Interview confirmation – Crescent Incorporated
Dear Miss Drake,
We are pleased to offer you an invitation to interview for the position of **executive assistant** *at* **Cresent Incorporated**

advertising agency.

*Your scheduled interview will be held at 9am, this Monday at
Crescent Incorporated head office – 136 Varick St, New York, NY.
If you have any questions, don't hesitate to reach out. We look
forward to meeting you.
Sincerely,
Jane, on behalf of Mr Crescent and associates.*

"Executive assistant... *What the fuck?!* There's no way I would have applied for that, heck I don't know how to be a personal assistant for a junior manager, let alone one at the executive level. There must have been a mix-up," I stuttered, panic beginning to show on my face.

"Give yourself the benefit of the doubt Charlie, you definitely have the skills to be someone's PA, shit this is just a stepping stone before you have your own PA, right?!" Lizzie countered. "It doesn't matter if this is a happy coincidence. What is it they say? When one door closes, another one opens," she smiled warmly.

"Or, behind every closed door might wait a thief of minds and a collector of souls," I rattled off one of my favourite Odd Thomas quotes.

Lizzie shot me a warning look, "Nope, I don't believe that for one second. And my saying is so much better. Just believe in yourself missy-moo, because I believe in you."

She was right. It probably was one of the last jobs I'd applied for in sheer desperation when everything else was blowing up in my face. It was probably a dose of anxiety-driven amnesia. I could do this. I knew the advertising world backwards and forwards. I couldn't count the hundreds of hours I'd spent with my parents as they worked on campaigns, made creative breakthroughs, and then when we saw the finished product in magazines, on TV, billboards, or the side of a bus. If I couldn't start as an advertising assistant, then a personal assistant could still be my foot in the door.

"You're absolutely right," I said with renewed hope. Let's go find those perfect outfits!"

Thud thud!

Lizzie froze on the spot with the knock at the front door.

"He's here, oh my God, what do I do?" she grabbed my arms, begging with wild eyes.

I giggled, "First, you breathe." And she did.

"Then you give me your best power stance." Again Lizzie did as I asked, placing her hands on her hips, standing up tall and raising her head, channelling Wonder Woman.

"Then… you slowly but deliberately walk to the door and let in the man you are dying to go on a date with. Now scoot – don't make him wait any longer," I teased, lightly slapping her bum in the direction of the front door as another knock sounded.

I sat back on the couch with my interview prep notes, listening to the pair flirt like a pair of high school sweethearts.

How cute. And a little unpredictable. I couldn't have imagined Scott would have a gentler, nervous side after the confident show he put on Friday night with Lizzie.

Lizzie pulled him towards the living room, stopping just in the doorway.

"Scott, this is my Charlie. I mean my housemate Charlie," she said nervously. "Although she's more like a sister – the kind you'd give your life for and she for you, rather than the annoying one that just steals your clothes and makes your life a living hell," she rambled.

Overhearing their wholesome hallway courting, I was expecting Scott to look wary, as though he was about to go through the seven rings of dating hell with the onslaught of inappropriate questions and threats from the scary housemate. But as I looked up to meet his warm, welcoming

31

eyes, there was no hesitation in them. His smile was genuine and one that showed his keen interest and excitement to be here, holding the hand of the girl standing next to him.

"Nice to officially meet you Scott," I beamed.

"Likewise," he said with a honeyed tone.

I'd be lying if I said his voice didn't float across my body and make me blush a little. No wonder Lizzie had decided to talk all night with this man, rather than just jump his bones. His voice sounded like sex, and he looked like a fabulous mix of devil and angel. His long sandy blonde hair was tied up in a man bun. A tattoo peeked up from the top of his shirt, stretching up from his broad shoulders to the curve of his neck. And just as Lizzie had described, I was in danger of getting lost in those deep chocolate eyes of his. *Hubba hubba.* I chanced a quick glance at his hands – yep, big hands all right, before moving my focus to Lizzie and smiling in approval.

"So kids, where you off to tonight?"

Lizzie tilted her head up to look at Scott for an answer.

"A little dinner, a little wine, then I thought we might wander through the Twilight Markets and see where the night takes us," he said to Lizzie. "But if you have other ideas, I'm open to anything you'd like to do."

There it was, that underlying confidence and sexual promise. I knew exactly where Lizzie's mind went to. So did mine.

Lizzie nipped at her bottom lip and started backing towards the front door, gently pulling Scott with her, "No that sounds great actually. We better make a move."

"Nice to meet you Charlie," Scott bowed his head towards me before turning to follow Lizzie.

"We'll catch up tomorrow after your interview okay... Good luck honey," Lizzie shouted back just before the door slammed shut.

CHAPTER 5

I HAD WOKEN well before my alarm clock, nerves frying every cell of my body.

Five a.m. – that's just fucking cruel. Come on Goddess Fortuna, if there was ever a time to have your girl's back here and sprinkle a little bit of fortune and luck my way, now would be it.

I sighed and rolled from my side, sprawling flat on my back in the middle of the bed with my arms outstretched, staring at the ceiling. Lights from a passing car shone through the gaps in the curtain, dancing flashes of different shapes and sizes across my bedroom. My head swam with all the possible questions they'd shoot at me, but it sounded like a babbling, incoherent mess.

What is it about interviews that make you question your abilities, your understanding of the English language and your life choices?

Gods help me – maybe there's still time to cancel? No way I'll be able to sound intellectual in gibberish. And I'm not sure I can handle one more rejection.

Lizzie hadn't returned home last night, but she had sent me a message with her pinned location when she'd reached Scott's place after their date. With the apartment so quiet, my thoughts and self-doubt were screaming at me in surround sound. I needed to get in the right frame of mind if I had any chance of impressing Mr Crescent and Co.

I sluggishly rolled to the edge of the bed, pushing myself

up to sit. I planted my feet flat on the floor, clenching and releasing my toes, feeling the soft rug beneath them. I stood slowly, reaching my hands high above my head before closing them together and bringing them down slowly to rest in front of my chest in a prayer pose. I closed my eyes and focused on my breathing.

In, 2, 3, 4. Hold…. Out, 2, 3, 4. Pause.
In, 2, 3, 4. Hold…. Out, 2, 3, 4. Pause.

I repeated the meditative breathing exercise five times before releasing my hands and letting them fall limp at my sides. A few shoulder rolls and I was feeling a little calmer.

I still had four hours until my appointment. Enough time to find my Zen. Through the dark I made my way to my ensuite before flicking on the duller of two bathroom lights. I turned on the shower, standing directly under the spray, letting it wash away any lingering cynical feelings. I let the steam envelop me and repeated my mantra over and over.

I release negativity and open myself to positivity.
I release negativity and open myself to positivity.
I release negativity and open myself to positivity.

Feeling a little clearer of mind, I dressed in my new 'built for success' outfit, as Lizzie had put it. Navy tailored pants that made the roundness of my bum look extra perky, a matching blazer with the arms folded up to mid-forearm, navy heels that I fell in love with a bit more each time I put them on, and a simple collared cream blouse to bring it all together.

I tried to get my long curly mane under control for 15 minutes before giving up on the idea. The universe had me over a barrel with this wild hair, but I couldn't complain – it was the same as my mother's; rebellious auburn curls enhanced by blue-green almond eyes, peeking through the strands. And I would always be grateful for the quick glances at my reflection where I could feel her looking back at me. Staring too long into her eyes always captivated me as though

I was deep in a coral reef, surrounded by the magical aquamarine shades highlighted by the sun streaming through the ocean's ebb and flow. The colours swimming together effortlessly.

"Miss you ma," I whispered, looking away from my reflection.

"Okay, out it is," I said with determination, running my fingers through the roots to give it a little bit more body, before flicking my hair back and forth to sit in place wherever it fell.

I stood in front of the mirror, did a few slow turns to check every angle and landed in a Wonder Woman power pose.

Damn! I... look... good! Actually, scratch that – I AM good. And I am the perfect person for this job.

I grabbed my purse and checked it for the USB drive that held my advertising portfolio – better to have it, just in case there was an opening to show them that I could do more than just be a PA. I clipped it shut and spun around, heading out the door.

With two hours to go I grabbed a tall cappuccino, extra shot, and a bagel from the coffee house down the block and headed to Washington Square Park to compose myself before my interview. I sat at a bench seat that basked in the morning sun, letting my self-doubt and worries drift away as I watched people busy themselves with their morning routines. I've always loved people-watching, and early mornings are always the best time to watch the chaos unfold. Runners are focused on their stride with music in ears. Groups of kids walk playfully together, joking and laughing on their way to school. Men and women heading to the office hurry along, coffee in one hand, a phone in the other. A million ants busying themselves, all with their own agenda, but part of the bigger picture – all just trying to get through life, together.

I'm sure I looked goofy, sitting by myself, looking out at the passersby with a big smile plastered on my face. But I didn't care. This was one of my happy places and it helped calm my mind, every single time.

There were still remnants of Christmas and New Year's decorations still scattered in various shop displays and along sidewalks. It was so magical, my absolute favourite time of year, and it made me happy like a pig in mud. Hell, if Lizzie let me, I would keep our Christmas decorations up all year. *Party pooper!*

Time slipped away in the blink of an eye. As the sun moved its way higher in the sky, making its appearance through the gaps in the tall buildings, I could feel the warmth move up my body and settle on my face. I let my eyes close, enjoying a sensation I can only imagine feels like being surrounded by love and happiness.

When I looked at my watch it was already 8.30am. Half an hour to walk the two blocks to Crescent Incorporated and arrive early for my interview.

Ha, screw you critical inner voice. No time for you to destroy my confidence or give any more power to self-sabotaging thoughts – Charlie 1: Inner voice 0.

For the first time in a long time, I felt truly good about myself. Whatever the reason, I was grateful. Be it the downtime in the park to realign my chakras, the best friend a girl could ask for who had a way of pulling me out of my slump, or the night of all nights to remember with Mr Hot Sex.

That familiar heat low in my belly made a sudden return.

Shit! Don't think about that – not nowwwww….

I stopped in my tracks, shaking my head as though the movement would dislodge the vivid images from behind my eyes, and took a slow, deep, steadying breath.

Focus... I open myself to positivity.

In control again, I walked around the last corner towards Crescent Incorporated. *Holy shit!* I craned my head back looking up at the skyscraper in front of me, shocked by how large the company must be to need such a huge tower. One more slow measured breath out and I stepped through the front door. I quickly assessed the enormous foyer and the business men and women shuffling around, then continued moving towards the front desk with as much confidence as I could muster.

The woman behind the desk gave me a practised smile. "Can I help you?"

"Good morning, I'm Charlotte Drake. I have an appointment with Mr Crescent at 9am."

"Ah yes, Miss Drake" she said, clicking a few buttons on her computer. "Here, take this visitor pass and head to the elevators to your right. Swipe the card and ride up to the Penthouse." She held out the pass in one hand and motioned towards the elevators with her other outstretched arm.

I hesitated before taking the pass. "Th-thank you," I stuttered.

Penthouse.... What alternate universe have I stepped into? She may as well have told me to head to the bridge on the Starship Enterprise.

The elevator panel showed 34 floor buttons, and above them a button labelled 'C-suites' and above that 'Penthouse'. I swiped the card across the reader and clicked Penthouse.

Ding! Ding! Ding!

The elevator made its way up swiftly. The floor numbers climbing on the display – 31, 32, 33, 34, C1, P. I drew my attention from the numbers to my reflection and quickly tamed a few strands of hair I could see threatening to fly away.

Ding!

The doors opened to a spacious lobby. Scanning the room, it was obvious this company was doing well for itself. A large Mahogany and cream chaise sat to my left. Another two generous-sized cream armless suede chairs at my right, a small Mahogany table between them. And directly in front of me was a generous white desk with a fresh-faced, pretty and petite, well-dressed woman behind it. She had to be around my age. Then again, I couldn't see a single line on her face, unlike mine, so maybe she was fresh out of senior high… That or she was a Botox fan.

She stood as I approached, "Miss Drake, so glad you could make it." Her soft gentle voice ringing a bell.

"Jane?" I questioned, returning the smile.

"Yes, Mr Crescent is expecting you. Right this way," she gestured back towards a short hallway to the left of her desk with grand double office doors waiting at the end. I followed, discreetly wiping my sweaty palms on my pant legs. "Call me Charlie."

Jane gave a quick knock at the door and then waited a few seconds. I didn't hear any noises from behind the door, but Jane reached forward, twisting the handle and pushed it open.

"Charlotte Drake, this is Luca Crescent," she said as she stepped aside to let me walk past her. I smiled at her once more before refocusing on the person in the centre of the room.

My heart skipped a beat, then swiftly stopped beating altogether and jumped out of my chest, falling to the floor with a thump.

Fuck! Why is Mr Hot Sex standing in front of me?

CHAPTER 6

MR HOT SEX stood leaning back on the front of his grand desk, ankles crossed, and hands in his pants' pockets. He looked taller and fitter than I remembered. How was that humanly possible in only a few days? His broad chest strained against his shirt with every inhale, and I was sure I could see the faint outline of his nipples wanting to bust free.

Damn, damn, double-damn. This man is unbelievably handsome.

The sight of him literally took my breath away, and I worried if I couldn't remember how to breathe soon, I was going to pass out right in front of him.

He had the sleeves of his white business shirt rolled up to mid-forearm. A flash of those fit arms roaming down my chest, landing on my hips, squeezing firmly, controlling my movements with each deep thrust filled my mind and I swayed a little. I stumbled a step backwards and felt the edge of the office door against my back. I gulped and opened my mouth a crack to suck in more oxygen before trying to reclaim my poise. I straightened up, took a step forward and cleared my throat. His gaze hadn't left my face since I walked through the door and I'm sure he didn't miss my mini-heart attack.

Very suave Charlie.

The smirk on his face widened and his eyes darted to Jane for a moment, "Thank you Jane, that will be all for now." She accepted his direction without question and with a slight nod of her head she stepped out of the office, closing the door as she went.

I stared at the closed door, frowning with confusion. *What the hell is going on?*

"Eyes on me Little Lamb," his deep gravelly voice ordered.

I wanted to ignore him. I wanted to storm out of his office – away from this blindside. I wanted to hide. I *wanted* to jump on him and feel the vibrations of his moans under my tongue and the growing hardness of his body against mine.

Fuck, fuck, fuck!

I shut my eyes for a split-second, remembering the feel of the sun on my face earlier and how I had felt good about myself. I took a measured breath and slowly returned my attention to him, determined to hold onto the newfound confidence he had helped bring out in me.

"Luca," I tested his name on my lips, enjoying the feel of how it sounded and the glint in his eyes it aroused.

Feeling a little more strength roll through me, I took a small step toward him. "Luca Crescent…" I said slowly. "And here I was thinking you must have been a nameless fallen angel, sent to rock my world before moving on to the next unsuspecting woman."

He didn't move. He didn't speak a word. Was he testing me with that stare and that seductive grin?

Smug bastard.

"Why am I here? It's obviously not for a job interview," I sighed. "And how did you find me?"

Luca pulled his hands out of his pockets and pushed off the desk, dropping his head and letting his dark locks fall forward around his face. Raising his head again, he brushed his hair back into place causing his arm muscles to tense and began gliding towards me. He was slow and calculating with his movements. He stopped directly in front of me, close enough that I could feel the heat radiating off his body, and drink in his heady scent – a decadent mix – part woody, part aged leather, part rum spice… and 100% pure masculine man.

Luca's eyes trailed across my face and hair before dropping down to take in the rest of me. He reached for my hands, uncurling my entwined fingers, and pulled me towards the chair in front of his desk.

"Sit. Let me explain," he said gently. I did as he asked, conscious that from his angle above me he could probably see down my blouse where the buttons met. That little voice sprung to life as I set my shoulders back, showing off my ample bosom.

Remember what these feel like Mr Hot Sex? I know you're a fan – so gawk, but don't touch.

He took a step back as a low groan escaped his throat, then backed himself into the chair next to me.

That's right, you're not the only one that can summon up steamy memories Mr Crescent.

He sat leaning forward, elbows resting on his thighs. He looked down at his clasped hands as though trying to find the words. I could feel my brows furrow as I watched him. What was this hesitant side of him? This streak was new, unfamiliar. And it made my hard exterior soften. The silence stretched out, slowly killing me.

Say something!

I leaned forward to gently squeeze his arm, letting my hand linger for a moment, feeling electricity course from his arm through my fingers.

"Luca, it's just me. Just a woman who shared a moment in time with you. Surely that means we can talk like adults," I coaxed.

He raised his head, eyes lingering on my breasts now clearly visible through my gaping top, before those golden amber pools stared into my eyes once again. I let go of his arm and sat back, my heart threatening to pound out of my chest.

"Charlie, you're here because I want to offer you a job, and… because I wanted to see you again. Little Lamb you left me in the middle of the night, without a word. Without these," he purred, pulling my panties from his pocket.

I felt the blush rise up my neck and cover my entire face. Why would he keep them? Why would he have them in his pocket? At work! I reached out to grab them but he pulled back, returning them to his pocket. "Mine," he growled.

A memory came bubbling to the surface. Luca driving deep into me with his arms wrapped possessively around my body. His body firm against my back, my head leaning back against his shoulder. My panties down around my ankles. His hot breath against my ear, the words 'mine' mumbled into the crook of my neck.

"Okay sure, why not. Couple of things though," I replied, trying to remain calm but letting curiosity get the better of me.

"Firstly, why would you offer me a job? You don't even know what I do for a living. And secondly, you still haven't told me how you found me. Shit, I didn't even know your name until five minutes ago, how could you possibly know my surname or find my phone number?" I asked, my voice rising an octave with nervous laughter.

"No more games Luca," I said.

He smiled wide, letting his pearly whites shine. "I seem to remember you like games Little One," he teased, running his hand across the stubble on his chin and licking his lips.

I didn't respond. Instead, I leaned back in the chair, crossing my legs and folding my arms across my chest, closing myself off from him. He may be the sexiest man I've ever laid eyes on and one that makes me want to rip his clothes off, but I felt like I was being played and I needed him to answer my questions. Now.

"I own The Sparrow, and after our fucking amazing night together I went back to speak to my bartender Eric. I noticed you and your friend spoke to him as though you knew him well.

"You sneaky ass. Guess it pays to have connections and investments," I mused.

"It has its benefits," he smirked. "Well we chatted and he mentioned you were trying to land an advertising assistant position. He gave me your name and number. But don't be mad at him princess, I'm sure he only did it for fear of losing his job," he joked.

"I hope you're joking," I shot back. But I couldn't hold back a small smile any longer. He certainly had a way of getting me to let my guard down. Alarm bells should be ringing, right? Surely this was a sign of a playboy. Someone so confident that they could get anyone and anything they wanted. So why was I so drawn to his authoritative aura?

"If you haven't read the room yet princess, I like you. I like when you do as I say. When you beg for more. The feeling of that tight pussy," he purred.

My mouth dropped open.

"I told you that night if we kept playing, you would be mine princess," he shifted in his seat, his body moving painfully closer, but not touching. His stare penetrating my soul.

"I don't know what to say," I whispered. "I mean sure, you liked our sexual connection – for the love of the Gods, I did too. But you don't know me Luca. Not really. I can't be your booty call, working as one of your executive's assistants, and expected to drop everything to come running for you when you need a little *release*."

"Mine," he said bluntly.

"What?" I frowned.

"*My* personal assistant," he said matter-of-factly. "Work and play can be separate things Little One, but they don't have to be."

He reached out and unfolded my arms, taking my hands in his. "I need to keep you safe. I won't force you to do anything you don't want to Charlie. Just think about my offer – if you want the job, it's yours. If you need me to help you… release any tension, just say the word," he grinned, rubbing small circles on my hand.

Oh fuck – just imagine, I'd be the talk of the company. New girl gets a job for sleeping with the boss. Slut – I can hear them now. No way! Well, maybe. No! But may—…, shit what was I thinking?

"Umm, can I have a few days to think things through?" I asked in my sweetest tone.

"Fuck Little Lamb. You don't know what just the sound of your voice does to me," he leaned his mouth down to my hand, biting the top of it gently but with clear intent behind it, letting his hot, wet breath linger as he exhaled heavily.

I couldn't help but giggle. I needed to put some space between us before we both jumped in headfirst, again. I didn't know what I was going to say to his offer, but I knew I needed to get out of there right now. Every second I was this close to him was a step closer to giving in to my dark desires. To thinking with my pussy, not my head.

Would that be such a bad thing? Hey, shut up you traitorous little voice you.

I stood, letting go of Luca's hands reluctantly. I grabbed my bag and took a hurried step towards the door. He stood, slowly following.

"So I'll call you soon, after the blood returns to my brain and I can make sense of everything you've said," I stirred, turning to open the door before I changed my mind.

"Charlie," Luca's fingers wrapped around my arm, stopping me in the doorway.

I turned, surprised at his closeness. He held out a business card towards me. "I'm glad we met. You are… something else," he grinned. "This is my personal cell number. I'll be waiting for your call Little Lamb."

I looked up into his hypnotic eyes, smiling as my heart skyrocketed again. I grabbed the card, but not before he hesitated, holding it a second longer while our fingers brushed past each other. I placed it in my bag and then stood tall, raising my head and pulling my shoulders back. I straightened my blazer and turned, walking out of his office.

I'm not sure if I held my breath on purpose, or if it was my body's subconscious way of trying to ensure a little self-preservation since his fucking amazing scent surrounded me. Either way, it was enough to help me walk out of his office without faltering. But I was going to have a long hot soak in the tub the minute I got home. Lizzie was wrong – a little manual override would definitely take the edge off.

Ha! You. Are. Screwed. Charlie! – Charlie 1: Inner voice 1.

CHAPTER 7

I WAS SURROUNDED by the deepest, darkest blackness. I could feel myself blinking, eyes searching my surrounds, desperate for a hint to where I was – but my mind struggled to believe my eyes were already opened. There was no hint of light, no glow illuminating anything around me. The complete darkness threatened to suffocate me, to swallow me whole and erase me from existence. Panic was setting in. I tried to move, tried to run, but I was stuck on the spot. The ground began to drag me down. Shit! Was I trapped in quicksand? No, it wasn't possible. My mind raced a million miles an hour, desperate to remember where I was and how I'd gotten here. My chest was being squeezed by an invisible force, any second and my heart was sure to explode from the pressure. The pain increased in intensity. A shrill scream escaping my lips as I tried to shake myself free. I could feel the warm wetness of tears streaming down my cheeks but still the void hid all. 'No! Someone help! Please help me!' I could hear the words but they didn't sound like mine. Were they in my head or had I managed to murmur them. 'Wake up.' A soft angelic voice different from the other broke the deafening silence of the consuming nothingness. 'Charlie, open your eyes'.

I shot up out of bed, covered from head to toe in a cold sweat. Warm tears coated my cheeks and my breathing was laboured. The morning sun's rays were peeking through the curtains, but the warmth hadn't reached the apartment yet to take the winter chill out of the air. The bedroom door flung open and a panicked look was plastered on Lizzie's face as she scanned the room, a baseball bat held in both hands.

"Charlie, what's wrong? You were screaming."

"I was? I'm sorry," I sobbed. "I'm okay. I'm fine, it was just a nightmare," I tried to reassure her. *And myself.*

I patted the bed next to me and lay back down, blowing out slow breaths. Lizzie walked over, dropping the bat on the floor and climbed in next to me, rolling to her side in my direction. I could feel the weight of her stare on me but couldn't pull my gaze away from the glint of sun creeping across the wall. My breathing had returned to normal and I found myself trying to remember details of the nightmare that had just cast me out. I turned to Lizzie. She was staring intently but waiting for me to speak first.

"It was the same as I used to have when we met," I smiled sadly.

"Oh honey. I'm sorry. What can I do to help?" she said, rubbing my arm gently, sidling closer.

"Nothing. It's not a relapse, I promise. It was just a one-off shitty nightmare. I couldn't even see their faces this time. It was just blackness. A void of nothingness. And I was stuck," my voice trailed off remembering this latest nightmare, and the many that had come before it.

I met Lizzie on my first day at university. Both freshman and lost on campus, we were drawn to each other as though destiny or some divinity was looking after us that day. As luck would have it we were fated to be roommates, and it couldn't have been more perfect if I'd planned it myself. Like PB and J, there was something wild and strange that drew us together for the perfect coupling. What can I say, that bitch was my ride or die, and I was hers.

I lost my parents when I was 15. If it wasn't for my beautiful, selfless, humanitarian-of-a-sister Lola, I would have been sent to live with a great aunt or uncle or ended up in the foster system. But Lola did everything in her power to make sure we weren't ripped apart and took on the responsibility of raising and caring for me. She was only three years older than me but had always had her head screwed on straight. I remember my mother always referring to Lola as my *little mama*, always there for me when she was out of town for work.

'While I'm away you look after each other Charlie bear, okay. Your little mama will watch over you. She will protect you, and you her. I love you baby girl.'

When I met Lizzie, she slotted right into our little family unit – and just-the-two-of-us became a party of three. No one would ever replace my mother, but I know there's no way I would have made it past those horrible years if it wasn't for my little mama and my de facto sister Lizzie. They became the two halves of my broken heart, with them I was whole again.

But as if losing your parents isn't cruel enough, the powers that be saw fit to test me again, you know, to find out what my *real* breaking point was. *What a fucking cruel joke.* Lola was diagnosed with brain cancer in my last semester of uni but she didn't tell me until I graduated, because that's the type of bloody angel she was. We fought it with everything we had for 10 months before she was stolen from me and I was thrown down into that deep dark hole again.

Lizzie didn't leave my side. She held me, rocked me, and looked after me while wave after wave of nightmares consumed me, tempting me to give up on it all. After my parents died, I would dream about their plane going down night after night, waking with the sounds of their screams in my head. But after Lola died it became a combination of losing them all together, all at once. The overpowering loss ripping me apart. Darkness swallowing me whole. Hearing ma, dad and Lola screaming in pain, crying out for help. But not being able to reach out for them. And it played on repeat in fucking high definition.

Eventually the dreams came less often. In fact, it had been

months since I'd had one at all. And it wasn't a feeling of sadness or dread that had triggered it now – well not that I was aware of.

###

It had been two days since my encounter with Mr Hot Sex. *Luca*. I had told Lizzie every detail and voiced every 'what if' my mind came up with, but I still didn't know what to do about his offer. Time for Plan B. I'd made plans to catch up with Eric tonight and see what clues I could gather from him. And from his initial reluctance to meet up, something was telling me he knew exactly what I was going to ask him.

But first I had to get through my shift at work.

It was just after the lunch rush when Trish came and begged me to do a little overtime because Maxine had called in sick. Knowing I was falling a little behind on rent I accepted the extra three hours. I would still be able to make my favourite gym class and catch up with Eric, so there was no harm in helping Trish out. But when I say time dragged, I meant time, fucking, dragged! With two hours to go I swear the clock started ticking backwards. 3:30. 3:29. 3:28. *Shoot me now!*

Maybe accepting a new job is exactly what I needed. Back in an office environment, surrounded by the excitement of ad campaigns, brainstorming sessions and a hot-as-Hades boss. *Shit!* Why did the one job offer have to come from Luca? Why did I give in and sleep with him that night?

Because you were drawn to him like a giant magnet, and because he wanted you just as much as you wanted him.

God how I wanted to feel his hot breath against my neck again. His firm hands roaming across my body. The vibrations of his deep gravelly voice moving through my core. But no good ever came from office romances. Did it?

Well… I mean it could be the best perk of the job.

Don't be stupid Charlie, this could destroy any chance of being taken seriously, of ever working towards becoming an advertising exec in your own right.

Ting!

The bell above the door rung as the customer opened the diner door, bringing me back to the now and saving me from spiralling again. I glanced at the clock, 4:42, well how 'bout that. A few little daydreams and time finally moved its sweet ass again.

"Hi, how can I help you?" I asked with a smile.

And. That's. A. Wrap! *Finally.* I locked the front door of the shop and went to the back office to switch into my favourite navy leggings, gym tank and joggers. One final round to make sure all the machines, lights and appliances were turned off and I grabbed my bag and headed out the front. Store door locked – check. Security roller screen pulled down and deadbolted – check. 5:45, not bad. Plenty of time to run two blocks to the gym and make my class. I was always up for a little light cardio to warm up, but 15 minutes might be pushing it a smidge. And damn there go the naughty thoughts again, finding steam all on their own. I knew exactly what type of cardio I'd like right about now, but that was not an option. Even if the proposition was there on the table and he was offering to be my fuck buddy.

Shit! Nope, not gonna give in that easy. An hour of boxing and body combat will have to do to work off this pent-up energy.

###

An hour later I stopped by the corner store on the way home to pick up a few extra ingredients to whip up a quick post workout dish for me and Eric. I was seriously craving a yummy beef and squash marinara pasta dish to soothe the soul. And like ma always said, a man's heart is through his belly. So if I had any chance of getting Eric to spill the beans, it was going to be through a good meal and drop of wine.

Dinner was simmering on the stove and Eric had just messaged saying he was 15 minutes away. I made a dash for the shower for a quick rinse but the minute the hot stream covered me, time stood still and I was lost in the magical way the heat relaxed my aching muscles. In what felt like only a few minutes, I could hear Eric's voice travelling down the hallway.

I flicked off the shower. "I'm in here, sorry, I'll be out in a minute. Pour us a glass of wine would you?"

"Sure babe. Take your time," he hollered back.

Dressed in sweats and bed socks, wet curls left out to air-dry and a stomach growling for a feed, I walked out to the kitchen to find Eric relaxing on the lounge, wine in hand, watching a re-run of *Friends*.

He really was a sight for sore eyes. His mousey-brown locks were long enough to fall into his eyes, but always gelled back when he was working. And his dark chocolate eyes held an intense fire that threatened a screaming good time. No wonder he made more in tips at the bar than his wage. If it wasn't for how gentle and caring he really was, I'd warn every girl to stay the fuck away or chance losing their soul.

"Ready to eat?" I said while serving us both a generous helping.

"Abso-friggin'-lutely" he laughed, slapping his leg in hysterics watching Ross yell at Rachel and Chandler to pivot his new couch.

"Fuck I love this episode," he chuckled.

"Who doesn't?" I said, handing over his bowl and taking

a seat next to him.

"Where's Lizzie tonight?" he questioned, not bothering to look at me. Even though they were happy just being friends, it was obvious she still had a piece of his heart. Probably always would.

"At Scott's. But enough about her, tell me, what's happening in your love life? Who's the flavour of the month? Or are you still seeing that Amber chick?"

"Nah, we ended things a few weeks ago. If it's meant to be it shouldn't feel like so much fucking work just to find time to see each oth—" he broke off, falling into a fit of laughter as his attention went back to the screen.

More screams of "pivot" from the TV had him in hysterics.

I turned and watched the scene play out, laughing madly at the sheer stupidity.

"Sorry, sorry, you have my full attention now, I promise," he said smiling a minute later, hitting the mute button on the remote and readjusting himself to face me. "He's just such a funny fucker."

"Where were we?" he asked.

"Amber." I said, scooping a spoonful of pasta into my mouth.

After filling me in on how he and Amber had split, and with a little prying about who would keep his bed warm now, he gave in, spilling about a regular at The Sparrow that had caught his eye and had been flirting with him for the last two nights.

"Sounds to me like this girl is seriously trying to grab your attention baby boy," I waggled my eyebrows at him.

"Yeh, maybe," he blushed. "I'm back at work on Friday night and if the tempting little red-head is there again I'm going for it – a turn around the dancefloor or a quickie in the back room, I'm up for either," he leaned forward squeezing my thigh.

"Ha, you're the best and the worst, you know that right?"

I laughed. "But I love it."

I walked our bowls back into the kitchen and brought the bottle of red back with me, refilling both our glasses.

My turn.

"Speaking of The Sparrow," I took a sip of wine. "When were you going to tell me you gave my deets to your boss, hmm?"

"Oh shit, I'm sorry Charlie. The way he spoke about you, it sounded like you kinda knew each other. He's not causing you trouble is he?" he said looking concerned.

Do I let him sweat a little or let him off the hook? He did tell a stranger who I was. But there's no way he would intentionally put me in a bad situation.

I squinted over my glass, sitting with the silence for a moment.

"No… it's fine. I'm not mad at you Eric," I smirked. "I was just surprised to hear from him."

"Woah, back the fuck up. I'm missing something here aren't I? Hold on. Oh shit, did you guys fuck?" he said unapologetically.

The uncomfortable heat crept up from my chest to my neck and cheeks before I even had a chance to open my mouth to reply. The way his deep voice wrapped around the word *"fuck"* made my insides flip and a wave of nausea, desire, and embarrassment hit me hard. I looked back to the TV trying not to squirm under his gaze.

"Ah ah, no way. You're not getting out of this missy," he said excited, flicking off the TV. Eric crawled his hands forward on the lounge as if stalking his prey. "Spill" he growled, snapping his teeth at me.

"Down boy," I giggled, pushing him back against the couch.

Without giving away too many sordid details, I rehashed the MA-rated version of my debaucherous night, hinting at the unforgettable delights and watching Eric's eyes get wider with each recount. He shifted uncomfortably a few times, readjusting his pants, which only heightened my growing desire and enticed fits of giggles out of me freely. I then brought him up to speed with my re-introduction to Luca in his office and the offer he put on the table.

"So, what should I do?" I finished.

"You don't want me to answer that doll."

"Yes I do. Come on Eric, you're like a brother, I know you wouldn't tell me to do something you thought would hurt me. I'm asking, no begging, for a little brotherly-advice."

"Take the fucking job Charlie, this is your in, the opportunity you've been waiting for to kick off your advertising career. And it sounds like the sex is negotiable. If you want some extracurricular activities on the side, take it and enjoy it. If not, use him for a foot in the door. A start to a new career. Luca Crescent is a powerful man. A powerful man with money and contacts."

"Yeh and a player to boot," I cut him off.

"I don't know."

"Yeh, I'm sure," I rolled my eyes.

"Well I can't speak to what he does behind closed doors, but I've never seen him with any woman at the club."

I frowned at him, shaking my head gently.

"Honest Charlie, you know I don't lie to you."

"But listen," he continued. "Don't make your mind up tonight. Sleep on it. And do what *YOU* feel is right," he emphasised.

Fuck. I sure as hell knew what felt right — that Greek God between my legs! But would being anywhere near him kill my career before it even had a chance to get off the ground? And how much self-control did I really have? Fuck. Fuck. Fuuucckkkkkk.

CHAPTER 8

I WAS ON auto-pilot for the rest of the week.
Wake up.
   Eat.
      Go to work.
         Go to the gym.
            Shower.
               Eat.
                  Sleep.
                     Repeat.

Lizzie and I were passing ships in the night. The detail of our conversations limited to quick text messages. When she wasn't busy working, she was spending her waking, and sleeping, moments with Scott. I was happy for her, honest. But I missed her and how she could make everything feel alright. Calm the worry beast. But we had made plans to meet at The Sparrow tonight. Firstly, to catch up over a drink and dance. And secondly to try to get a sneak peek of Eric's flirty girl.

Nothing I tried on felt right. The sparkly blue dress felt too much. The little black dress felt desperate. The slinky emerald piece made me look nauseous.

"What is going on?" I huffed, falling back on my bed dramatically.

My inner voice was playing dirty tonight and not in a good

59

way.

Why bother going tonight? Lizzie will be with Scott and Eric will be ogling his little red head. You'll be the fifth-wheel. May as well just stay in. Save yourself the trouble.

"Aaaghhhh!" I yelled in frustration.

Oh shit, hopefully the neighbours didn't hear me and call the cops.

And now I was laughing deliriously. What the actual fuck was happening with me?

Focus. Breathe. Lock the crazy away Charlie!

I took a long, slow, deep breath in. Then blew it out even slower. A few more and I was ready to get up and try on the red halter-neck chiffon jumpsuit Lizzie had left me as a "miss you" present yesterday.

"Damn that girl has a gift," I smiled, twirling back and forward watching my reflection in the mirror. The backless number had a way of sitting perfectly on my hips. I picked up my phone, took a pic and sent it through to Lizzie.

Charlie: Thank you my goddess. It's perfect (smile)
Lizzie: (…)

The three dots flashed up, but then disappeared. I rolled my eyes thinking how they were probably having a quickie before going out. In our brief catch-ups she hadn't been shy to rave about how randy Scott was. How every time their hands, arms or any part of their bodies brushed past the other, sparks ignited and they were jumping each other's bones.

"That'd be right," I giggled to myself.

I finished getting ready with a glass of bubbly to keep me company.

Ding!

I searched the bed for my phone to read the new message, finally finding it underneath the pile of discarded outfits.

Lizzie: Get your beautiful butt here already. There's fashionably late, then there's this.

I glanced at the time on the screen, 9:30. What was she whinging about. We said we'd meet 9-9:30. So I was right on schedule according to the universally-accepted timing for women.

Charlie: Don't get your panties in a twist. I'm on my way.
Lizzie: What panties? (wink)
Hurry – Eric's flirty girl is here. He needs his wing-women.

I grabbed my clutch bag and keys and headed downstairs while ordering an Uber.

###

The music was pumping into the street when I stepped out of the car. Johnny was at his usual post at the door. He turned in my direction, immediately putting an arm out to push a few people waiting further back to make room for me to enter like a celebrity. Having a regular club and knowing the right people certainly had its perks.

"Mmm, mmm, mmmmmmm" Johnny smirked, shamelessly looking me up and down.

"You've taken my breath away darlin'. I don't know if I want to fuck you or marry you," he said grabbing my hand gently. "I'll treat you like a goddess from your head to your toes."

"Johnny, you and I both know you'd only be settling for me while my girl walks this Earth," I giggled, leaning in to give him a kiss on the cheek. Oh. My. God! His chest was solid muscle under my hand. *Yummy!* Guess that's part and parcel of being the head of security for a high-end club. "But thank you for making me feel like a goddess all the same," I smiled.

"Always darlin'," he grinned, pushing the door open for me to enter.

I scanned the room as I walked in, instantly spotting Eric leaning across the bar twirling a strand of the redhead's hair around his finger. Poor girl never had a chance – she was putty in his hands.

I was nearly bowled over a second later with Lizzie running and jumping at me, wrapping her arms around my neck. Stumbling a few steps back, I found my balance again before wrapping my arms around her too.

"Eep, I've done it again," Lizzie squealed loudly over the music.

"What's that? Climbed me like a tree?" I laughed.

"Yes, but also, I've found the perfect outfit that makes your beauty shine bright baby girl. Seriously if I didn't like men as much as I do, you'd be in trouble," she teased, planting butterfly kisses all over my cheek.

"Should I be jealous?" came a voice from behind me. I shot around, my heart landing somewhere in my throat. Relief washed over me seeing Scott smiling at Lizzie and me.

Lizzie let go of me and seductively swayed her hips as she walked up to her waiting man. "You'd be a fool not to be."

Scott bent down. His hands sliding from her hips around her ripe peach, lifting her up against his body and devouring her mouth.

Hot, hot, hot! Hmmm, maybe voyeurism is my new thing.

Considering that just over a week ago these two were taking things slow with long night chats and getting-to-know-you dates, something had changed because there was no stopping these two little bunnies now.

We grabbed a drink and headed for the dancefloor. And Scott, bless his cotton socks, danced with both Lizzie and me, spinning us around each other and indulging in a bit of dirty dancing. I could feel the eyes of others in the club and you know what, I freaking loved it. Scott easily pulled off the part of the stud with a girl on each arm, a tattooed version of Patrick Swayze.

Eric was on the early shift so came out to find us when he was finished behind the bar. And always the gentleman, he came with a round of drinks to share. After giving the lovebirds some time alone and dancing with me for a song or two, Eric dragged me towards the tables near the back bar where I could see the girl with flaming red hair watching his every move, surrounded by a group of friends. She was a pretty little thing. Petite like Lizzie, but with ivory skin like snow. Eric stopped us shy of the tables, staring at the redhead the whole time. He gave the smallest *come hither* movement with his head, a crooked smile tugging at the edge of his mouth. I nearly fell over backwards when the little redhead began walking towards us as though in a trance.

"Woah. She's got it bad," I leaned in whispering.

Eric put out his hand and pulled her into his side. She was quite a bit shorter than me, meaning she fell into his side easily, as if he could tuck her under his wing. And if she wasn't here drinking at a nightclub I would have sworn she was in her late teens.

"Lucy, this is Charlie," he said smiling.

"Hi Charlie, it's so nice to meet you," she said meekly. "I've been so afraid to speak to Eric the last few weeks seeing him here with you. I was sure you were a couple. But when he told me you were his sister, I've got to admit I felt so relieved and just knew I had to try to get to know him."

She was so fresh and bubbly that it made me a little jealous. Was she super friendly or just a little infatuated with my *brother*.

I smirked at Eric, quickly raising my eyebrows at the curious introduction.

"Hi Lucy, I love your hair and that outfit is gorgeous," I smiled warmly.

"Thank you. Yeh it's a wild crazy mess most days," she said, pulling at a few spirals sitting at her shoulder and letting them bounce back.

"Don't worry, us curly girls have got to stick together. Come sit and tell me about yourself," I said pulling her towards an empty lounge to our side, away from her onlooking cackling friends. I didn't have to do much prying, Lucy was a talker. And she seemed so at ease with Eric at her side, whether he played with her hair or rested his hand on her thigh. It was obviously way too early to guess what would grow out of this budding romance, but if I had to go off first impressions, there was some chemistry and something else I couldn't put my finger on, or something I hadn't experienced myself. But there was something so natural about them, they genuinely looked comfortable around each other. I couldn't help but smile just watching the pair.

The DJ transitioned into a new song causing Lucy to jump in her seat with excitement. "I love this song, come dance with me?" she batted her eyelashes at Eric.

Eric looked up at me as they started scooting out of the booth. He reached toward me as Lucy pulled him in the opposite direction.

"No no, you two go on without me. I'll finish my drink and be out soon."

I grabbed my phone out of my clutch to check the time. 12:30. I wonder how much longer Lizzie would expect me to hang around now that we'd caught up and I'd been Eric's wing-woman. Warm hands gently rolled up my shoulders, thumbs rubbing up my neck, brushing my hair to the side.

I shut my eyes enjoying my muscles release. "Mmm, that feels amazing Lizzie, a little deeper on the shoulders though."

Hands moved from the nape of my neck back to my shoulders, alternating between gentle and firm squeezes, rolling my head to the side with the movements. A hot tongue ran up my exposed neck to the base of my ear.

"Lizzie cut it out," I laughed, pulling forward to turn around and face her.

"Luca," I gasped. "I, I thought you were Lizzie. What are

you doing here?"

His glare was intense as he slowly made his way from behind the lounge to the seat next to me. My eyes never left his – drowning in the pools of honey staring back at me. My mouth dropped open but I couldn't speak, and if my legs still worked I would have pushed myself further back into the lounge rather than being able to feel the heat radiating off him. His plump lips were pulled into a tight line and I could see his jaw strain as though he was clenching his teeth shut. He looked mad. Shit, I've never seen him like this – what did I do? Was he angry at me?

"Say something Luca," I whispered.

But he just continued staring at me. His eyes traced up and down my jumpsuit, landing on the halter neck he had just had his fingers on. His Adam's apple bobbed as he swallowed hard and I remembered the feeling of it in between my teeth last week. The feel of his stubble against my lips and other body parts. Was he trying to get a reaction out of me? Well, he wasn't going to. Two can play at this game.

I lounged back raising my arm up to lie across the top of the booth, crossing my legs so my body leaned in towards him. He had a collared midnight black shirt on tonight, sleeves rolled up showing off his forearms. He mirrored my posture, leaning back, raising both his arms to lean across the top of the bench seat. *Fuck!* All that did was pull his shirt taut against his strong chest and it was becoming increasingly hard not to appreciate the beauty in front of me. As my eyes lingered on his chest my attention was pulled up to his beautiful face as his expression lightened into a sexy smirk. My stern composure faltered, and I couldn't help but throw my head back in amusement.

Luca stretched his arm along the lounge, rubbing the top of my hand.

"You haven't called princess." The strokes of his thumb turned into familiar circles.

"I'm sorry, I've just been going back and forward in my head. And I still don't know what I should do. But I understand if you need to find someone else to fill the EA position."

He put a finger against my lips, stopping me in my tracks. His thumb traced a line along my jaw stopping on my neck's pulse point.

"Luca."

In one swift movement his lips crushed against mine. I parted them without a second thought, inviting his tongue to taste me. He accepted, softly darting and sucking at first before increasing the intensity. I could taste the whiskey on his tongue and it warmed my tastebuds, sending the scent to linger at my nose. His hand moved from my neck, wrapping around my hair, pulling me closer. The hot rigidness of his body touched my soft curves making every nerve ending in my core ignite and I forgot every earlier thought to stay away from this man.

I had never felt a pull like this before. There was something about Luca that made me lose all self-control and inhibitions. I rubbed my hands up his chest letting them wrap around his shoulders and settle at the nape of his neck. I pushed and pulled his soft hair through my fingertips. He met my eagerness, letting his free hand wrap around my body, gently scratching down the length of my spine, cupping my backside, and moving to the underside of my thigh where his squeezes became firmer and more needy. His mouth did the same, and I knew my lips were going to look like a swollen bruised plum when we parted.

As if he could read my mind, he pulled back an inch, his hot breath hovering above my mouth as he leaned his forehead against mine. "Your move Little Lamb. I've played my hand and I'm not going to force you into something you don't really want."

"Make your decision and let me know," he exhaled, kissing the tip of my nose, before standing up and walking away. I watched him stride through the club, Davies following closely behind, before they both disappeared through the crowd. I dropped my head into my hands, leaning forward on the table.

"Dear Goddess, help me. Just tell me what I should do," I whispered to myself under my breathe.

My mind was swimming, I could still smell him, taste him, and feel the heat of his body.

Shit, did he just leave me high and dry? Dick!
Luca 1: Charlie 0.

CHAPTER 9

I WASN'T IN the mood to continue partying after Luca left me sitting there, shocked into silence. I left Lizzie, Eric and their dates on the dance floor and headed home at about 1:30, my mind swimming more now with renewed fervour and apprehension. I felt pulled in opposite directions. My heart and body pulled toward the incredible chemistry with Luca, and my head pulled in a direction seeking a path where my future and career were built solely on my proven ability and expertise. Not my honeypot.

But why was I fighting what felt so right, so natural? My frustrations were growing, why did life have to be so damn complicated?

Charlie, you are being crazy! Why are you doing this to yourself? Pull yourself together and stop catastrophising. Do you really think Luca is trying to make this an unsolvable puzzle? Or is it purely coincidence that you were drawn to each other at the same time you were trying to kick start your career, and he has the means to do that?...

Damn Little Voice had a point. Maybe Crescent Incorporated was a place where both of those worlds could collide.

It was nearly three a.m. when I dragged myself to bed, exhausted by it all. Thank the Gods exhaustion was on my side tonight and I fell into a slumber in between one crazy thought and another.

###

The tweeting of nearby birds brought me back to consciousness. I was lying almost completely flat on my stomach, face buried into the pillow at an awkward angle. Opening one eye I could see the warm glow of the morning sun streaming in. I tried straightening and rolling onto my back. Ouch, that crick in the neck's gonna hurt all day. *Great!* I slowly climbed out of bed and went for a warm shower to see if that would relieve some of the strain in my neck.

My dreams had been confusing and blurry. As if I was plunged deep in the sea, swirling around with the whipping waves. One moment I was back in the club with Luca, a prisoner trapped in the stare of his hypnotising golden eyes, sitting in silence staring at each other, no words said, no movements made.

Then I was whipped to the side, back to my catch-up with Eric. I watched him smile at me, so caringly and genuine. I listened curiously as he told me to jump right in and *'take the fucking job and the amazing sex on the side'*. His advice left my stomach doing little flips. It made my heart skip in my chest and those hard-love words formed a smile on my face.

I was barrel-rolled into another memory of meeting Luca in his office after that first night together. How he smirked at me. How he looked into my soul. How he exuded raw power and desire. My breathing was ragged as he stalked closer to me, circling me like prey, like a lion on the hunt. Growling *'mine'* into the crook of my neck, his breath leaving a hot mark beneath my ear.

My memories were a dangerous place to be. They always flicked through time giving me whiplash, like someone was sitting at the control panel pressing random buttons.

In an instant I was dragged back, as though a hook was yanking me back from the pit of my stomach and then I was kneeling beside my beautiful Lola in bed. *'You are meant for big things Charlie bear. It's inevitable'.* She struggled to get the words out, but it didn't stop her squeezing my hand and finding the strength to get her point across. *'Don't destroy your future. Grab onto every opportunity, every possibility – with both hands, and don't let go.'*

As I walked toward the kitchen, absent-mindedly brushing my hair, her words echoed in my head. *'Don't destroy your future'.*

Don't destroy my future. Is that what I was doing? Was I self-sabotaging? Was my sister speaking words of wisdom from beyond the grave, still doing her best to lead me in the right direction? Spurred on by her voice and words, I started to put together a pros and cons list. A list of possibilities that could happen if I said yes to Luca.

The sound of keys unlocking the front door caught my attention. I quickly hid the list I'd been compiling under a book next to me on the dining table as Lizzie walked in. She eyed my hands on the book before offloading her bag onto the table and taking off her heels, balancing on the back of the chair.

"Is the coffee pot still hot?" she asked.

"Yep, just made a new one," I smiled back. "Where's Scott this morning?"

She grabbed a mug from the cupboard above her head and began pouring her coffee. "Home. We're not joined at the hip you know. We can spend a day apart," she looked over her shoulder at me and rolled her eyes.

"Ha!" I blurted out. "Since when? I've hardly seen you these last couple of weeks. Actually, I was thinking of sub-letting your room."

"Don't you dare," Lizzie spun around to face me front on. "I do love spending time with Scott, but I think I'm starting to realise we jumped into this hot and heavy and I need *my space,* to unwind and debrief without him."

"And if you think you can get rid of me that easy, thou doth not know mineself at all," she feigned deep, dramatic hurt, leaning against the kitchen counter, the back of her palm resting on her forehead.

I tried to maintain a straight face, but it was no luck, she had me chuckling and feeling super grateful that she didn't have plans to leave me anytime soon. "So how much of your time can I take today to bounce a few things off you. I need your advice Lizzie."

"I'm all yours babe. Come on, let's make some brunch and move to the lounge room to settle in," she said, walking behind me and wrapping her arms around my shoulders in a bear hug.

We spoke about everything from the last few weeks. Discussing how much had changed in such a short time. How Scott had blindsided Lizzie, flipping her world on its axis when she wasn't looking for anything new. She still wasn't sure where the relationship was heading, but for now they were enjoying getting to know each other and the perks that came with the honeymoon-stage of a relationship.

I told Lizzie about my catch-up with Eric and his words of encouragement to take the leap. At the mention of his name it was plain as day, she still held a flame for him too. I was sure they would eventually find their way back to each other. There was something so organic and beautiful about them as individuals, but together it was fucking magnificent. If only they could see it too. One day, I was sure of it.

"So how come you decided to leave the club early last night? Did you get all up in that maze of a head of yours?" Lizzie questioned.

"Yes, and no," I coyly answered, grabbing our empty plates and walking them back to the kitchen. "Are you hungry for something more filling or interested in a liquid lunch? I'm thinking Mimosas!" I said, shimmying and swaying my hips to imaginary music. If I was going to relax and be open to Lizzie's feedback I needed my defensive walls to come down a little, and bubbles always helped with that.

"Ah, a girl after my own heart. You had me at Mimosas," she laughed. "You pour and I'll find some tunes to create the right atmosphere."

With delicious cocktails in hand I took a deep breath and prepared to replay last night's surprise encounter.

"I kissed Luca last night," I blurted out.

"What? And you're only telling me now. Did you leave with him last night? I didn't see him waiting for you."

"No, I didn't leave with him. I was getting to know Eric's new girly and they headed to the dancefloor. Next thing Luca had his hands over my shoulders and neck. Shit, I thought it was you coming over to see how I was."

Lizzie laughed aloud at that, nearly spraying her drink all over me.

"Hey, control yourself woman, it's not funny. Why would I think it was him, you always rub my shoulders, and you know I love it."

"True, but are you saying my small hands feel like his big hands?" Or were you just trying to fool yourself?"

"I, uh, I didn't think about that. Just the feeling of it. Until he licked my neck that is."

"Charlie! Oh. My. God. Then what happened?"

"He sat, we eyed off, he looked furious at me, and then his stupid sexiness made my eyes wander and he grabbed me and we made out," I blushed. My mouth was dry and I was a little scared what words would come out if I kept on talking. I took a slow sip of my drink and waited for Lizzie to process. She looked a little confused, and frowned looking down at her glass. "So, hang on, let me get this right. He massaged your neck, won at a stare-off, then made out with you and you *didn't* go home with him. Does that mean you decided to have nothing to do with his job offer?" she asked.

"He said he had waited for my call and that he's put his moves on the table. He said he isn't going to force me into something I don't really want, and that I had to make my decision. But—"

73

"But what Charlie-girl?"

"I don't want him to think he is forcing me into something I don't want. God, I do want him. Desperately! But I just don't know how to mix work and pleasure. Or if I even should."

Lizzie grabbed my free hand, and for a second I could feel Lola in her grip. "You won't know if you can have the man and the career *until* you try. Call him Charlie. Ask him to meet up today, in the daytime, somewhere neutral and open so there's less chance of jumping each other's bones. And then *talk* to him."

My eyes focused on my hands while I processed Lizzie's advice.

"Talking. You know it's that thing where people discuss their thoughts, opinions, and dreams with someone else," she said sarcastically.

I rolled my eyes, throwing a pillow at her. "But what should I say?"

"Say yes. Speak your hesitations. Speak the truth and start living the life you deserve. You owe yourself that Charlie," she smiled with her eyes, lips and whole body. What would I do without my de facto sister? Be a shadow of myself, or nothing at all. That's what.

My hands shook as I dialled Luca's number. A single ring later his deep voice answered.

"Charlie."

One word. Two syllables. But *soooo* damn sexy.

Fuck.

A moment of silence as I remembered how to use my voice.

"Hi Luca. Are you free to meet up today? We should talk."

"Yes, I'll get my driver to pick you up and bring you back here."

"No," I answered, a little too forcefully. "C-can we meet and go somewhere? Take a lap around the park maybe?"

"Sure. I'll be there in an hour," he said without hesitation or disappointment.

"Do you want the address?" I asked.

"Princess, I know where my girl lives. I'll be there in an hour."

The line went dead and I was left shocked, smiling, but shocked.

Almost an hour on the dot later, there was a knock on the apartment door. I was sitting on my bed, pulling my shoes on and could here Lizzie answer the door. "Hi Luca, it's nice to meet you, I'm Lizzie," came her sweet-as-sugar voice. "Come in."

Oh shit, why was she inviting him in. I struggled with the second boot, nearly tumbling off the end of the bed in my haste to get up and stop him seeing my apartment. Ma always said you can tell a lot about a person from how they live. What would my small, basic home say about me? I stood looking around the room for my phone and bag. I leaned across the bed to grab my phone perched on the far pillow.

"Princess," came his honeyed voice. Way too close! Shit, he was in my room.

I lost my balance, falling on my side on the bed. *Great, that's all he needed to see now, my clumsiness.* Trying for composure I scooted to the edge of the bed to stand and was met by his outstretched hand. I hesitated for a second before accepting his help.

"Thanks. You didn't need to come up, I could have met you downstairs. I'm sorry for keeping you waiting."

He took a step back, standing in the door frame. Maybe he could sense my nerves or maybe I was making him feel uncomfortable.

"You didn't keep me waiting. I wanted to come up," he said scanning my room briefly.

"I like your place," he said through crooked smile.

"Thanks, it's not much, but it's home and we love it," I said blushing. *Oh God. Why was I rambling?* "Umm, ready to go?" I began moving towards him, motioning towards the front door.

"I'll be back soon," I shouted out to Lizzie from the hallway. She popped her head around the corner, smiling. "Nice to meet you Luca. Hope to see you again soon."

"Likewise," he called over his shoulder as I nudged him out the front door.

We walked a block or two in silence, looking up on occasion meeting each other's eyes. I felt like a school girl. Not a confident 23-year-old woman who was capable of screwing a man's brains out.

Fuck. Get your shit together Charlotte, take the lead, you've got this.

We crossed the road and headed into Washington Square Park. It was filled with people enjoying the sun's warmth. Not quite warm enough to remove winter coats, but enough to strip off scarves and gloves.

"So Luca, tell me something about yourself," I started the conversation.

"Hi, my name's Luca and I've been clean for 234 days," he smirked.

"Hah, hah, very funny. I'm being serious. I know you're a businessman with a few companies and ventures under your belt. I know your tall, dark and handsome. And—"

"An unbelievable lover," he interrupted, raising an eyebrow.

"Fair. I won't disagree. Although one night is not much to go off," I flirted back.

He didn't reply, but flung his head back letting a deep moan escape his mouth. "We can fix that Little Lamb," he went on, a cheeky sparkle in his eyes.

"Maybe," I replied. "But I want to get to know you, if that's something you'd be okay with. I can't deny the intense chemistry we have, but I'm not a casual girl Luca, I am worth more than that."

"Yes, you are princess, and I want to get to know you too."

He stopped, looked down and grabbed my hand before beginning to walk again. A smile crept on my face and butterflies flew in circles in my belly. And he wasn't lying. Although he chuckled often, seeming amused with my line of enquiry, he answered every question I shot at him without hesitation. Where he grew up, where he went to college, when he started his business empire, what his hobbies were. The only question he skirted around was when I asked if he was close to his parents. He didn't refuse to answer, but he deflected, bouncing the previous question back to me. I wasn't going to push it, heck I wasn't ready to talk about my family either, and buggered if I was going to be the one who led us down the path to awkwardness.

"Yes," I suddenly said, looking up into his eyes.

"Yes what?" he frowned questioningly.

"Yes, I'd like to accept the offer to be your EA. I've worked hard to get to where I am and I'm ready to learn so much more about advertising, under your guidance. And I'm not saying yes to a booty call whenever you want, but I'm saying yes to trying this new chapter and seeing where it takes us – no pressures, and no strings attached, right?"

"Right. No strings. Like I said princess, I won't force you to do anything you don't want. And I mean it. Let's see what happens, of its own accord," he brought my hand up to his mouth, placing a soft kiss on my knuckles.

"I'll speak to Jane tomorrow and get her to send through the paperwork. When can you start?"

"Oh, ah, well I really should give Maggie and Trish two-weeks' notice so they can find a replacement and I can help train them up. Is that okay?"

"Of course, Little Lamb. Two weeks it is."

CHAPTER 10

TRISH HAD ORGANISED a little send-off for me on the weekend at a local karaoke bar and it was a little bittersweet. I was excited to step into the corporate world, but I had spent the last couple of years with the Maggie's Morning Brew crew and they were a family of sorts. Although I knew we would still see each other, I was sad to be saying goodbye to being their co-worker. Call me a sap, but with the losses I've had in my life, I couldn't help but yearn for family. And the Brew Crew had become that in a comfortable, familiar sort of way. Getting ready to step into the next chapter of my life, I guess it was only fitting that my farewell party ticked off something from my bucket list. And as much as singing in public filled me with anxiety, I actually freakin' loved it! There was something so empowering and freeing belting out *'I will survive'* on a little stage with my tribe cheering me on and singing along.

###

Jane had couriered me a starter pack a few days after Luca and I had our walk in the park. A yellow envelope filled with documents; contracts, a position description, pay details, request forms for ID cards and IT accesses. Since returning it all a week ago I had filled my time with training my replacement, shopping with Lizzie for a couple of office outfits, and refreshing myself on advertising 101.

Now here I was, standing outside Crescent Incorporated's head office bright and early on a Monday morning, ready to take the first steps into this new adventure. Walking into the foyer I could see Jane talking with the security guard near the front desk. Actually, at second glance, I think she was flirting. Yep, definitely flirting. Although I didn't know her from a bar of soap, it looked as though there was too much giggle in her answers, a fair bit of batting of eyelashes and even some nervous playing with hands as he leant in closer to her. Jane looked up as I approached, straightening and taking two steps away from Mr Buff.

"Charlotte, it's great to see you again," she smiled. "I thought I'd bring you your ID badge in person, rather than leave it with the front desk. Come, let's head upstairs," she said holding out my security card.

"See you later Jane," said Mr Buff in a gruff yet heady tone.

"Y-yes," Jane replied, clearing her throat. "See you later."

Once we were alone in the elevator, heading up to the Penthouse offices, I couldn't hold back any longer. "What was that?" I said softly, smiling at the now-blushing Jane. "There was some serious tension in the air."

Jane laughed nervously, "no, no. We've just started chatting recently, but he's not a man of many words and I couldn't tell you if he fancied me or thought I was a babbling looney."

"I think it's the former, but who am I to say, I've been here all of two seconds and I'm already prying inappropriately," I rambled. "I'm so sorry."

Ding!

"Think nothing of it, I actually appreciate some female companionship and banter," Jane replied, stepping out into the lobby. "This place is way too testosterone-heavy," she giggled.

Jane spent the rest of the day showing me the ropes, giving me a tour of not just the penthouse, but also other floors and introducing me to so many new faces. I'd be lucky to remember a handful of their names. In a nutshell, my job would be to organise Luca's schedule, arrange meetings, business trips and assist with any ad campaigns he was leading, including liaising with internal and external designers, photographers, web creators, and various staff in other departments to get the job done. No pressure!

The Penthouse sat up on level 36, but the view from the large floor-to-ceiling windows was magnificent and felt like we were on top of the world, overlooking the cityscape and the Hudson River. On our level there were three executive offices and a massive boardroom. The hallway to the left of the front desk led to Luca's office suite. And to the right of the desk was a longer hallway, leading to two slightly smaller offices which belonged to advertising executives Brad Cavanaugh and Stephan Hewitt, with the boardroom closest to the front desk. Jane and I shared the long desk. She sat to the right and was EA for both Brad and Stephan. When I asked why they had to share an EA, she just shrugged and said "I guess that's the perk of being the big boss, you get your own EA". I'd make a mental note to ask Luca about it later. He wasn't in the office today, so it would have to wait until tomorrow.

Jane and I went down to the C-suites for lunch, taking advantage of their generous kitchen area, which was not unlike a cafeteria in that fresh food was supplied every day for all staff, and according to Jane, Friday's also had the added bonus of happy hour drinks from five to seven. Of course, there was fine print attached to that which Jane summed up as you were officially off the company's clock and there was an expectation that you didn't behave inappropriately with colleagues. Well fuck me sideways and call me a letterbox. If that wasn't asking for office romances to happen, I don't know what is.

I liked Jane, she was an open book and it didn't take much to get some gossip or someone's back story out of her. She appeared quite confident and capable, and very comfortable in running an office. In fact, she had a way with words, a Midas touch that had others going out of their way to help her. During our short tour to the other floors, six people had offered to do little tasks for her when I thought she was just having an innocent conversation about campaigns and research she was doing. Damn, the girl was good. I'm going to have to keep my wits about me or I'm sure I'll find myself doing Jane's work for her too.

While at lunch Jane told me about the power players. Luca Crescent was the king of this kingdom. Jane outlined his business empire and rattled off names of businesses, big companies and clubs he owned. It was hard to imagine how someone so young could have done so much already. Hmmm, how old was Luca? I knew he had to be older than me, but surely not by much. Shit, I hoped not, I never imagined myself sleeping with someone old enough to be a father or uncle.

"I wonder how old Luca is? He looks so young to be so successful and the head of a million-dollar company," I tried to sound nonchalant.

"I think he's 27 or 28. But he lives and breathes work. You'll find you do a lot of your check-ins with him virtually. It seems like he has to up and leave for business deals across the country and overseas at the drop of a hat."

"Oh really. Good to know," I replied, feeling a little sting in my heart.

"Sometimes Brad or Stephan go with him, but they all have their own accounts to look after so it's not a regular occurrence that they're all out of the office at the same time."

"Mmm, yeh right. So does he come from money? Is this a family company?" I continued my line of questioning.

"I've tried to find that out for the past year, but he's a vault. Word on the street is he is a self-made millionaire, but it wouldn't surprise me if there's a long line of business empire grooming in there. Don't you think he just oozes high society and an impressive pedigree?" she giggled.

"I suppose so," I chuckled back. "What about Brad and Stephan?"

"Well Brad does come from money, as does his boyfriend. He's always taking extra-long weekends to spend at their holiday house in Long Island. It's a gorgeous place. He invited a few of us out there last Independence Day long weekend and I didn't want to come back. It was decadence at its best."

"And Stephan?"

"Where do I start," she paused for effect. "Stephan is a player. Every week a new chick calls for him. He thinks he's God's gift to women, honestly. The man is gorgeous and he flipping knows it," she shook her head.

"And what about you Jane? Any hot interoffice flings to boast about?" I smirked, waggling my eyebrows. Aiming for nosy rather than jealous.

She looked around to see if we were alone. Shit, this must be juicy.

"Well it's over now, but there was one-hot-month not too long ago where one of the execs had me every which way he wanted. I mean, no complaints here. It was completely consensual, but sweet baby Jesus, he seriously blew my mind," she revealed, lounging back in her chair, fanning herself.

"Sounds hot. Dish, who was it?"

Jealousy was threatening to rip out of my skin and choke her where she sat. She has to be talking about Luca and I'm just another stupid conquest to him.

"I can't say. I really shouldn't have said anything, especially not in these four walls. Don't worry he's out of my system and we're both professionals and are able to work together."

"Oh come on, don't leave me hanging girl, I won't say

anything, I swear," I tried to sound friendly, like we'd known each other for years.

"Well–".

"Miss Ellis, Mr Cavanaugh wants you back upstairs if you're finished with lunch, says he can't find the notes for his next meeting," a young guy who looked like an intern interrupted.

"Thanks Teddy, we'll head back now. Did you want to pop up now and grab those papers we were speaking about earlier?" she smiled, standing and motioning for me to follow.

"Actually, that'd be great," he said like a little puppy dog happy to have someone to play with.

Fucking fuck fuckity fuck.

Seriously, could the kid have interrupted at a worse time? I walked quickly trying to keep up with Jane's speedy pace towards the elevators. She was busy for the rest of the afternoon and I wasn't able to interrogate her again. But I'm not one to give up easily. I'm sure I'd get it out of her eventually.

Luca wasn't in the office for the next two days. He sent through a few emails giving me a few tasks to keep busy with while he was away. He also sent through text messages to my phone. On day one he checked in to see how I was settling in.

On Tuesday he texted again.

Luca: Sorry I'm not there for your first days. Should be back in town in a day or two.
Charlie: Don't be silly, you're a busy man running multi-million dollar companies and I'm sure you have many incredibly important things to do without worrying about me settling in.
Luca: Have you been asking around about me Little Lamb?
Charlie: No.
    Maybe. Just trying to get to know you.
Luca: Then ask me your questions, I'll tell you everything you want to

know.
Charlie: Deal.

On Wednesday, my phone pinged before I'd even finished getting ready for work.

Luca: Woke up this morning with a certain curly-haired princess in my thoughts.
Charlie: I hope those were good thoughts.
Luca: The best.
  And the naughtiest.
  Charlie: Thanks for the reminder. I'll try not to get distracted today.
  Any special instructions?
Luca: If I want to talk work, I'll email. Texts are for you and me princess.
  Today's instructions… every time you answer work calls and say my name, I want you to picture my tongue on your body.
Charlie: Luca, I can't.
Luca: Charlotte, I wasn't asking.
  I promise you'll enjoy yourself.

Oh boy, what was I getting myself into?

CHAPTER 11

I'D SPENT THE most part of a week watching and studying Jane. She was a doer and good at her job. No wonder she could organise not one, but two business executives. Even if it was because she managed to get tasks done with others offering to help her out. Whatever works, right? She flitted around the office, and I couldn't help but giggle as she jumped in the elevator to head down to HR. What can I say, she was beautiful and clever. And everyone seemed to be a fan, even Brad and Stephan. Hell, I remember how Luca had smiled at her when she escorted me to his office the day we officially met by name. He smirked and gently told her that'd be all. He had said it warmly, more than just a boss to an employee.

Hold the fucking phone… Holy shit! I fucking knew it… Luca was the exec who Jane had hooked up with and had hot, crazy sex with. Of course. Why would I be someone special to him? He was just ready for his next plaything, and obviously he enjoyed keeping his sex buddies in-house – nice and close for ease.

Fuck! What. An. Idiot.

Now don't get all up in your head again Charlie girl. You didn't come here for the man. You came for the job. You're here to start making a career for yourself. Breathe. Learn. Be professional. Prove your skills.

Yeh that's right, Jesus. I've never been controlled by desire before.
And I'm not gonna start now!

Exactly. You CAN work with him, and with her. Just smile and
get the work done, then go home and forget about them. You don't
need to hook up with him again. He'll move on to his next conquest
before you know it. And there's plenty of other fish in the sea for you.

Ouch. That thought actually hurt my heart a little. But it
also brought me back to reality. Luca was a powerful man
that was used to getting what he wanted. He said he wanted
me, wanted to get to know me. Yeh, like fuck he did – he was
just enjoying a free ride for a while. And I bet he didn't hold
on to his playthings for very long before he got bored. The
room was getting a little fuzzy and shrinking around me. My
breathing increased and a flood of nausea hit me hard.

Oh God, not a panic attack. Not here. Not over a fucking man
I just met.
Focus Charlie..... Breathe. In, 2, 3, 4. Hold.... Out, 2, 3, 4.
I release negativity and open myself to positivity.
You. Can. Do. This!

Jane had jumped from a meeting with Brad and a client,
to one with Stephan and a group of suits who clearly had
money to burn. I took advantage of the time by myself to
refresh on the latest programs and applications, and learn
their filing system.

Ding!

Luca: Sorry. Business deal dramas. Won't make it back this
week. Will have to rely on those dreams to keep me company a little
longer.

What did he expect me to say? I had replied to his emails and he already had me working on tidying up files for a recent campaign. The fire in my belly from earlier was still roaring and I had no interest in being fucked around, only to be tossed aside and kicked to the kerb. I didn't have another job to fall back on. I needed to make this work.

Okay Charlie, keep it civil and keep it short.

Charlie: Thanks for letting me know.
Luca: Thanks…. Charlie, what's wrong?
Charlie: Nothing. Busy filing.

Brrinnngg! Brrinnngg!

Shit! Luca's number popped up on my screen. My heart pounded and my stomach jerked. Dear God, why was he trying to call? What was wrong with emails and messages? If I heard his honeyed voice there was a good chance I would let all my angry thoughts float away. Nope, nope, no. And with him gone until Monday I could work on out-of-sight, out-of-mind. Isn't that how it goes? My phone stopped ringing, sending him to voicemail.

Ding!

Luca: Answer your phone.
Now Charlie.

Brrinnngg! Brrinnngg!

Great. I hadn't even lasted a full week. Ciao! Adiós! Au revoir! This had to be a new record for me. My mind zoomed around as I stared at my ringing cell phone. Do I stick to my guns and keep it professional, void of emotions? Would he be able to hear the irritation in my voice? How could he think we were still at that flirting stage when he was just using me?

"Hello?" I answered, almost at a whisper.

"Princess, what's happened?" a hint of concern pulled at his words.

I cleared my throat, praying to the Gods to keep me cool, calm and collected. "Nothing at all. I've been learning how to prep for client meetings and it's been super busy around here. Not that you don't already know that Luca, I mean Mr Crescent, it's—"

"Mr Crescent, now I know you're pissed off," he fired back, a mixture of anger and amusement in his voice.

"I—ah, I forgot my place for a second. Jane has instructed me on correct protocol and titles. I apologise Sir."

"Princess, you are mine. My EA. You call me Luca. Or Sir, I like how that sounds," he purred. "But let's reserve that for when you're begging me to make you cum. Others, they can stick to formality."

Why was he still talking to me so boldly, still flirting in his messages and now on the phone, as though I wasn't sitting in his office under watchful eyes. Could I have been wrong? No. We'd had one amazing night, a hot as fuck make-out session, and a walk in the park. That was not enough to make a man stop looking elsewhere, well at least not the men I've known before. As if my brain had just caught up to my apocalyptic imagination, I felt stupid, judgemental and a little like a drama queen. This man was going to be the death of me. One minute I felt like a strong, sexy, confident woman, and the next I was second-guessing everything.

Fuuucccckkkkkkk!

"Little Lamb, I know you're still there, I can hear you breathing."

"Ye—yeah, I'm here," I stuttered.

"So, how many phone calls did you take?" he asked playfully.

"Wh—what?"

"How many times did you say my name?"

Oh shit, too many. And not enough. I spent a large portion of yesterday picturing his tongue gliding across my skin, all over my body, deep in my body. It had got me so worked up that even last night's spin class hadn't worked off the ants in my pants so I stayed an extra hour for the yoga class too, only to race home and take care of business myself with Luca screaming in my thoughts. And now he was going to know. Kill. Me. Now!

"Ummm, five or six," I lied.

"Do I have to remind you I have access to all of the cameras in my building princess. Let's try again, how many times did you picture my tongue on your sweaty, naked body?"

"You don't play fair Mr Crescent," I chanced calling him by title again. But this time with promises behind it. "Fine, 18. And by that stage the memories were burnt behind my eyes. So thanks for that."

"And what did you do about it?"

God, I knew it. He was going to make me say it. "I took a couple of classes at my gym, worked out my frustrations," I tried to skirt around the darker truth.

"And?"

"…And nothing," I lied again.

Wow, this guy had some serious confidence, or maybe he'd bugged my bedroom and bathroom, and phone. Ha! As if, calm down Charlie, your life isn't a Netflix dark romance.

"Come on princess, we're getting to know each other, aren't we? Remember our deal."

My head snapped up with the feeling of eyes on me. I had been so oblivious, head in the clouds and my phone that I hadn't heard Jane step out of the elevator and walk over to me. She had a stack of files in her arms and was standing opposite me, leaning over the desk.

"What you doin'?" she singsonged.

Shit, how much had she overheard? Did she hear me say his name?

"Ah thank you for the update, I will have to get back to you on that other matter when I know more. Goodbye," I abruptly ended the conversation, hoping Jane would leave it alone. I just hope Luca wouldn't fire me, maybe I could suggest he punish me in another way.

I spun around to face Jane. "I'm sorry about that. I won't take personal calls during work hours," I blushed, opening the top desk drawer and placing my phone face-down in it.

"That's fine Charlotte, we all have lives outside of here. The bosses understand that. Just don't spend all your time on it," she winked at me.

Ding!

My phone echoed in the drawer. I turned my chair back to my computer screen ignoring it and began to tap on the keyboard. Jane plopped the papers down next to my arm and rounded the desk before spinning to face me in her chair and rolling closer.

"Answer it," she smiled.

"Oh no, it's fine. I'll answer it after work."

"Come on Charlotte, don't be coy with me. Are you hiding a boyfriend from me?" she giggled.

"No, definitely not," I laughed a little nervously. "It's just a friend."

Ding!

"Fine, tell me when you want, or keep him a secret. No skin off my nose. But whoever it is, don't leave them unread. That's just cruel girl," she said, rolling back to her side of the desk.

I finished typing my sentence, clicked send on the email then slowly opened the drawer to retrieve my phone. I didn't want to look too eager and put any more thoughts in Jane's pretty little head. I was going to have to play it safe around her. If Luca was her ex, or if not, I didn't want to give her any reason to make my life hell.

Luca: We'll continue this later when you can talk.

And tell Jane she can do her own paperwork, you're my EA, not hers.

I looked up and around the office with wild eyes, trying to spot the cameras he was watching me on. Sneaky devil. Where the hell were they? Mental note, no office shenanigans. I might like it rough and wild, but I was not into being the next hidden sex tape sucker. That shit goes viral quicker than #catsoftiktok memes.

Luca: Breathe princess. I'm the only one with video access.

I turned off the phone screen and pushed it to the side. I wonder if Luca has cameras in his office. Surely not. I bet a man like him values his privacy. Then again, the way he didn't think twice before pulling me onto his lap and sucking the air right out of my lungs at his nightclub made me think he had a little more kink in him than I thought. I bet he loved a bit of voyeurism and exhibitionism. Just the thought of it had me playing with the neckline of my shirt and biting my lip as a smile crept across my face.

Ding!

My phone screen lit up with a single message. I glanced over it, seeing two small words that made my stomach jump and a familiar heat return between my thighs.

Luca: Fucking gorgeous!

Quite the wordsmith. Oh hells bells. Let's be honest, I didn't care if he was the next Shakespeare or not. So long as he was ready for some Netflix and chill when he was back in town. And for my sake I hope that was asap!

CHAPTER 12

FRIDAY AFTERNOON FINALLY rolled around and I. Was. Buggered. A full week of learning new things had me mentally wiped out. Jane tried to get me to stay after work for happy hour saying it would be the perfect opportunity to meet some of the company cuties, but I just didn't have it in me. Instead, I promised her a raincheck and to be honest, I didn't know if that was ever something I could do with this thing between Luca and I still clear as mud. I flicked a message through to Lizzie on my way home, my safety net check-in to let her know my plans for a quiet night in. A minute later she shot back a reply.

Lizzie: (thumbs up). I was thinking… a girl's night out tomorrow, somewhere new, what do you think?
Charlie: I'm keen, just need to catch up on about 20 hours of sleep first (tongue out wink face)

I was surprised to find Lizzie at home, waiting for me in the lounge room, sans Scott. Netflix ready on the TV and Chinese takeaway boxes and red wine waiting on the coffee table. I kicked off my heels and headed for the couch. But Lizzie stopped me in my tracks, grabbing my shoulders and turning me around, shooing me away for a hot shower before I was allowed to collapse on the couch. Bossy boots.

We caught up on the week's events only half paying

attention to *Sweet Home Alabama* playing in the background.

"Have you heard from Luca again since Jane caught you on the phone with him?" Lizzie asked.

"No," I huffed. "And to be honest, when he said we'll talk later and told me he was watching me on the security cameras, I was sure we would get into a bit of dirty talk or phone sex later that night."

"Did you try calling him?"

"Well, no. But–"

"Ah ah ah," she shushed me. "This isn't the 1800s, our foremothers fought for the right to be equal for a reason. You are a strong, sexy, smart woman. If you want something, make the move."

I knew she had a point, but she was annoying me. Just because she was super confident and loved dominating her men, it didn't mean I did. Submitting to Luca made me feel wanted and powerful, as backwards as that sounds.

I didn't want to bicker, so I turned back to the movie. But I could feel Lizzie's eyes on me.

"I know Lizzie," I eventually spoke. "But he likes to take the lead, and I like that he does. I don't think that's giving up my power. Anyway, it doesn't matter now, he's out of town and you and me have plans this weekend," I smiled.

"Scott doesn't want to come out?" I asked, grabbing the bottle of red to refill our glasses.

"You know he's always up for the club scene, but I just need a little break."

"What's happened? Are you okay? Did he do something?" I sat up straight.

"No, it's not like that," Lizzie hesitated. "I'm just feeling a little stuck. Like we're just on repeat, every day. And maybe I'm a little bored."

My mouth dropped open. I thought they were going strong, I mean she'd spent most nights at his apartment since they met. Hadn't she?

"Bored… I thought you said sparks ignite every time you

touch. And just look at him, sex on a stick, seriously," I said, biting the tip of a finger.

Lizzie laughed, failing to slap my leg when I moved too quickly out of her reach. "Yes, he *is* gorgeous, and yes, the sex and orgasms *are* good. But it's always the same thing. The same moves, the same positions. It's just lacking that surprise and excitement. Does that make sense?"

"Mmm it does, but can I ask if you've spoken with him about it, taken the bull by the horns as you would have me do, and initiated that something different that you want?"

"Of course I have honey, it's me Lizzie God-damn Ryan," she broke into a fit of giggles. "I think I scared the shit out of him when I sat on his face. It took all of 2.6 seconds for him to roll us over so he was on top and in control again."

"What did he think you were trying to do? Suffocate him. Death by pussy?" I laughed. And that was all it took to get us rolling around cackling like two crazy girls on their way to the psych ward.

After a morning run, Lizzie and I wandered through the grower's markets grabbing fruit and veg for the next week. Lizzie had brought home some of her work so spent a few hours reading through a draft novel of an up-and-coming author she had signed with the book publishing house she worked at. I spent the afternoon reading up on Crescent Incorporated's history and its latest clients.

It was just after eight when Lizzie and I started getting ready for our night out, complete with orange blossom margaritas in hand. Dressed to impress, Lizzie showed off her tiny waist and ample breasts with a sunset-coloured cut-out mini dress, her blonde bob styled into beach waves. I was feeling renewed and pretty positive after my time with Lizzie this weekend, which gave me the boost I needed to wear the revealing number I'd had hidden at the back of my cupboard for far too long. The glittery red, low-back cami bodycon mini dress was an absolute showstopper, one I hoped I could pull off. If I'm being honest, it didn't leave much to the imagination, but I didn't care, it made me feel sexy, confident and powerful. And I was beginning to like that feeling, it was addictive.

Lizzie still hadn't told me where we were going, keeping me in the dark for a 20-minute train ride and an uncomfortable block walking in heels. She pulled me by the arm, excitement seeping out of every one of her pores.

"Where are we going?" I begged.

"You'll see, we're nearly there. It's just up here," she said, tugging me up a narrow alley that looked as though it would be our final resting place, as in tortured and murdered. Dead. I tried slowing her down, tried pulling her back towards me. But the little firecracker was driven forward with anticipation, there was no stopping her.

She stopped at a dark navy door, hesitating for a split second before rapping her knuckles on the door seven times.

"Lizzie," I whispered.

The door creaked open and a burly, bearded man I'm sure led a biker gang, motioned us inside. I followed slowly, and closely behind Lizzie, never letting her hand go. At the end of the hallway another man stood, opening a dark maroon curtain for us to enter as we approached.

Holy mother-fucking fuckballs. She's brought me to a BDSM club. What the fuck? Ooh, what are they doing over there?

Lizzie led me around the club slowly, shocking me into silence. There were so many things going on, as though different scenes were unfolding, each with different stars, different kinks, each with their own audience. So many people having sex for everyone to see. Across the room a man was tying up a woman with a red rope with what looked like incredibly intricate knots. Near them a man sat on a chair, a woman kneeling in front of him with his cock deep in her mouth. Her arms were tied behind her back and another man fucked her from behind.

My head was spinning. I had only heard stories about places like this before but to see it with my own eyes I was overwhelmed with a whole new bag of feelings. Fear mixed with excitement, nerves, curiosity, lust and rapture.

I leant into Lizzie as she stopped to watch a woman whip a man chained to a cross. "I thought these clubs were for members only. How are we here, and why?"

She turned to me, a grin plastered across her face. "They are, but you can be invited by a member, and we were," she squealed, squeezing my hand in hers. "What do you think? Isn't it amazing," she said, looking back as the woman brought the whip down across the man's chest.

"Come on, let's go and thank our host," Lizzie pulled me toward a bar near the back of the room.

"Wait, our host, Lizzie I don't want to have sex in public, well at least not tonight. Stop, please," my voice raised an octave higher with alarm.

"Charlie, it's not like that. There is nothing that happens here without complete consent. And we're here to watch tonight, not join in. Okay. Trust me," she smiled, rubbing her thumb against my cheek.

I let her lead me again, taking deep breaths in a desperate attempt to calm my breathing and racing heart. I could see two men, hidden half in shadows ahead of us and there was something familiar about the bigger guy.

"Lizzie, Charlie, I'm glad you could make it ladies," Johnny grinned, rising from his seat to come and greet us.

"No fucking way," I smiled, a small giggle escaping my mouth before I could stop it. "Johnny you invited us to–," I hesitated I didn't even know what to call it, "this place?"

"*House of Himeros*," he corrected. "Yes, I did. Lizzie said you ladies were searching for something more. What's more than this?" he smiled, making butterflies go crazy in my belly.

"Lizzie, Charlie, let me introduce you to my friend Mike," he said as a shorter, and not quite as broad man stepped forward, grabbing Lizzie's hand, planting a kiss on it, then doing the same to me.

Wow, if a smile and eyes could talk, his would be screaming that he wants to bend us both over and fuck us until we forgot who we were.

Mike walked us over to the bar. Leaning his arm onto it, his collared shirt pulling tight across his chest, revealing a hint of a tattoo across his heart. "Ladies, Johnny here tells me you are strictly watching tonight, so let's get you both a wristband and a drink."

"Sorry, do you mind elaborating?" I asked, hoping it wasn't a stupid question.

"Some people come here to watch, others to play," he raised his eyebrows. "If you come to play, you don't drink – you come into this with your full senses not dulled by alcohol or drugs, and you consent to the experience. Of course, everyone has their safety word and can change their mind at any point."

He grabbed two glasses of champagne handing them to us before sticking a red wristband on each of us.

"But if you don't want to play, and instead you want to watch, you can drink and relax, enjoying your surroundings in another way."

"Any questions ladies," Johnny said, running his hand through his hair, causing the material to pull against his bulging bicep.

"So many," I giggled.

Johnny and Mike were open books, like walking encyclopedias on BDSM. But they never crossed the line. I knew Johnny would always be a Southern gentleman, a flirt who was super smooth with the ladies. But hiding underneath I'm sure was a man who could be tamed for the right woman. Now though, it was evident that right woman would probably have some serious kinks and the pretty little blonde next to me had them in droves. They only had eyes for each other tonight. And although there was no touching, kissing or heavy petting between the two, I'd bet my first born there would be in the near future. Lizzie just had to decide if she was ready to move on from Scott.

Mike seemed like a good guy too. He was sure of himself in body language, words, and the ladies loved it. A few girls sitting at the bar kept looking over to our table with fuck-me eyes directed right at him. Some brazen women even propositioned him right in front of me. But he was quite the charmer. He gave me all his attention while Johnny and Lizzie chatted up a storm, making me feel like the only woman in this club, when clearly, I wasn't. I'm almost 100% sure he was flirting with me, and 1000% sure he wanted to play with me, right here in front of an audience. Heck, he'd said it in almost those exact words. I didn't know if I wanted to do any of the things I had witnessed tonight. And if I did, I didn't know who I wanted to do them with. My tipsy mind begged to differ though, picturing Luca doing *all* the things to me, but maybe behind closed doors. Or not.

We left the club a little after two a.m., Johnny and Mike putting Lizzie and I safely into a cab, refusing to let us catch a train home. Johnny handed over some cash before telling the driver our address. I didn't like handouts, but after the events of tonight and the number of drinks I had under my belt, this was one offer I was happy to accept.

Safely home, and snuggled in bed, I couldn't help but laugh to myself, the scenes of the night replaying in my head. "And to think I started the night thinking the dress I wore was too revealing, ha! I think I was one of the most covered up women in the House of Himeros," I giggled to myself as sleep pulled me down. The last thought flickering behind my eyes was Luca standing over me, cracking a leather whip across my aching pussy, growling deeply, *'beg me Little Lamb, beg me to let you cum'*.

CHAPTER 13

I SLEPT LIKE a log until the morning. And I probably would have slept longer if my bladder wasn't screaming at me to get up and empty it. "Shit!" I mumbled, shaking my head as I caught my reflection in the mirror. My hair was a wild bird's nest and the apparent waterproof, smudge-proof mascara of last night was now streaked over half of my face. "Fan-fucking-tastic."

I desperately needed a coffee, but it was going to have to wait until I scrubbed this mess off in a hot shower. With the room now filled with steam, memories of last night's scenes were slowly resurfacing. I still couldn't believe how erotic it was, watching complete strangers living out their fantasies. Butterflies fluttered around my belly, goosebumps spread across my skin, and throbbing heat pooled between my thighs. *Fuck me!* No wonder the porn industry was worth around $100 billion.

I wrapped the towel around my body then tried to detangle the mountain of curls, clump by knotty clump.

Thump, thump, thump!

I stopped shuffling around the bathroom making noise, straining to listen if I heard a bang outside, or if the noise came from me in my frustration.

Thump, thump, thump!

Shit, I wasn't imagining it. I looked around the bathroom for a dressing gown, but it wasn't hanging in its usual place.

"Lizzie, can you get that?" I called out. No reply. "Lizzie!" I said a little louder.

Thump, thump!

"Okay, coming, coming, hold your horses," I huffed, pulling the towel as low as I could risk to cover my bits, without flashing my tits to the unexpecting knocker. I opened the door a creak to look out.

"Luca, what are you doing here?" I spluttered, opening the door a little wider to see him leaning forward, an arm raised against the door frame, eyes to the floor.

His gaze travelled up my body achingly slow. He took his time moving up my legs to where the towel started, up to the outline of my hips, and hesitated on my cleavage straining against the top of the towel and where my wet curls lay, leaving drips of water to roll down my shoulders, chest, and down the valley between my breasts.

"You've been a naughty minx, Little One," he mumbled, his tongue peeking out to lick his lips.

"Wha–, I, ah, huh? No, I haven't," I stuttered, searching my memories of last night. I had watched a lot of sexual acts and asked a lot of questions, but I didn't do a damn thing, I was sure of it. And how could he possibly know I went out last night? I stood in silence, watching him, waiting for any hint of what he was referring to.

"Are you going to let me in Charlotte?" he purred my name, and my body reacted. The playful tone was still underlying, but I felt like I was getting in trouble by the school principal, when my full name was used. Oh… Maybe that was it. Had I fucked up at work already?

Opening the door, I wrapped an arm across my body, holding the towel firmly in place, and took a few steps back so he could walk by without having to squeeze past me. No need to make this any harder than it already was. Even a foot away, his woody, spiced rum scent filled my senses, travelling down my throat and settling in my chest. *Dear Goddess, why did he have this pull over me?* I was having to fight my willpower to not lean in and lick across his Adam's apple and up to his pulse point.

He walked in, then stepped backwards, pushing the door shut with his back. Leaning against it he lowered his head again, tucking his hands into his front pockets. My mind was flipping around in my skull, I didn't know Luca well enough to be able to read him. What the hell did this body language mean? And why wasn't he talking or looking at me?

I stood in silence, waiting for him to talk. His rugged good looks were raw and primal today. He stood there in loose, worn jeans and a white tee, his hair falling forward into his face. I was hypnotised by the muscles tensing in his jaw. He looked pissed, like he wanted to punish me. And I wasn't mad about it. Nope. I was fucking turned on.

Holy heck, one night at a BDSM club and I'm entertaining all sorts of kinks. Who the hell am I?

"When did you get home?" I breathed. My voice sounded mousey, guilty even. I cleared my throat and tried again with a bit more oomph. "Did you get the business deal sorted?"

Luca stalked slowly towards me, moving with power and confidence, his gaze like one of a predator daring to meet my big eyes, watching his every calculated move. I took a step back as he neared. Then another, stopping when my back met the wall behind me.

He raised a hand toward my face, rubbing his knuckles up my cheek before tucking loose strands of wet hair behind my ear. "I'm not here to talk work." His smooth baritone voice dripped with sex appeal. "If you wanted to explore your deepest desires you should have called me Little Lamb."

Hold the phone, he seriously couldn't be talking about last night. How the hell could he know where I went... unless... he was there. But he was out of town. And so what if he was... he doesn't own me. Right now all he is to me is my boss.

Ha! Keep telling yourself that Charlie.
"Whoa, you might wanna pump the breaks there Mr

Judgey. You seriously can't tell me what I can and can't do with my desires." I could feel my irrational defence system come to the fore and I had no control over it. My mouth had a mind of its own. "This hot and cold shit doesn't fly with me Luca, I'm not Jane," I huffed, crossing my arms tightly across my chest, trying to create some space between us but failing miserably, instead pushing my breasts up against his strong, warm chest.

His brows furrowed and he pulled back for a second before leaning in even closer. "What does Jane have to do with any of this—".

"Oh please," I interrupted, getting annoyed with his denial. "I know all about the hot office romance and the month of sexcapades. And I don't care. What you do with your time is none of my business," I spat between gritted teeth, pulling away from him. "But I'm not interested in being the next notch on your belt to joke about with the other execs. I'm sure you can take your pick of any other woman out there." Oh God, I'd gone too far, but I couldn't stop the words before they spewed out of my mouth. My eyes heated and I could feel the tears threatening to well up and betray me.

Luca stared at me with a look of confusion plastered on his face.

"It's fine Luca, you don't owe me anything."

"Stop Charlie. I don't know what you've heard, but it's bullshit. I've never touched Jane. But it sounds like someone else is fucking around on work time." He looked pensive, " I have my suspicions and I'll deal with them later."

Oh no, maybe I hadn't thought this through. I didn't consider Jane was with someone else in the office and could be reprimanded over it.

"I–uh, I don't want Jane to lose her job, she is an amazing EA, more like an office manager really," I said laughing nervously, full of regret and self-loathing.

"I'm not going to fire her Charlie," he smiled, moving to cup my face. "You need to know that I don't want her, and

I would kill anyone that spoke about you like just another conquest. You're my special girl." Before I could reply or come up with another lame excuse, Luca leaned down, pressing his lips against mine. He swiped his tongue across my bottom lip, teasing it open and I welcomed the sensation. His sweet taste and prickly stubble against my cheek was driving me crazy and my body reacted like a girl in heat.

I leaned into his hard body, wrapping an arm around his neck with the other brushing through his hair, grabbing a handful at the nape of his neck. I deepened the kiss with all of my unspoken desires, spurred on by the feel of his large hands moving to my ass, lifting me off the ground, his growing hardness pressed firmly against my lower belly. I pulled away, sucking in a breath. "Lizzie's home, maybe we should take this out of the hallway."

"Yes, ma'am," he grinned, a dark glint in his eyes. He sunk his mouth to that sweet spot between my collarbone and neck, kissing it lightly before nipping it with a sting that struck me to my core, but wouldn't leave a mark on my skin. He walked towards the bedroom, still holding me up against his body like I weighed nothing and I was his for the taking.

Me Jane, you Tarzan.

I couldn't help but giggle. This was a man that knew what he wanted and for some crazy reason, right now he wanted me. And dear Gods, I wanted him too. More than my job, more than food, hell – more than air itself. Okay maybe a slight exaggeration, but it wasn't far off.

He slammed the door behind us with his foot, stepped over the pile of last night's clothes and lowered me onto the bed, coming down on top of me with his full weight.

Fuck yes.

I reached down to the hem of his shirt, pulling it up and over his body, throwing it to the floor with the rest of the abandoned clothes. He came down, again taking my mouth with his hot darting tongue. A hungry moan escaped me and he reacted instantly, grinding his hardening length into my pussy. There was way too much material still between us and it needed to go. Now.

Reaching down to undo his button, Luca stopped me, grabbing my hands and bringing them up above my head. He pinned both of my hands under one of his, and held firmly around my wrists. As if he was reading my mind, he lifted his body, tracing his other hand down my arm, across my breast and grabbed the towel where it was tucked in across my chest. "This, has to go," he grunted, as he unwrapped it, leaving my body bared to his every dirty thought and act.

He took my breast into his mouth, flicking and sucking before pulling away to swirl the hardening peak of my nipple with his tongue. My groans grew needier, and I wriggled trying to release my hands. Needing to drag my nails down his back, to pull his head into my chest. But there was no release. His head moved to the other breast, his free hand moving between our bodies as his fingers slid down my wet slit. "Oh. My. God. Luca, yes," I moaned, squeezing my eyes shut.

He kept devouring my breasts, giving each nipple attention as his hand at my mound got to work. He entered one finger, then another, moving to the same rhythm of his masterful tongue. He entered a third finger, pumping in and out, while his thumb made small circles on my clit. First slowly, but building with speed and intensity. My breathing became ragged as my body verged on the edge of an orgasm. My back arched with excitement. "Don't stop. Don't. stoooo—" Spots swam behind my eyes as I exploded, my breathing steadying with the waves of ecstasy. Luca slowed his rhythm, letting my climax ride out. He released my hands, moving lower, letting his hands glide over every mountain and valley of my body. "Mmmmm. Your turn cowboy," I flirted.

"Not yet Little One, I haven't had my fill just yet," he breathed against my stomach. Covering it in soft kisses and long sensual licks. The mixture of hot and cold licks, kisses and gentle streams of breath had my stomach flipping, then flopping. Before my brain could comprehend the sensations, he had buried his head between my legs, licking up my slit before diving in with his tongue. "Fuck Charlie, you taste so good."

My legs buckled, only supported by his strong shoulders and arms wrapped around my thighs, pulling me firm against his hungry face. My hands moved to his head, his soft hair falling between my fingers. He moved his hand back down to my pussy and began finger fucking me while he sucked my clit like a lollipop. "Jesus fucking Christ," I cried out. "Stop, or I'll cum again." My body was pulsating, quivering under his touch. He released my clit for a second. "Cum for me Little Lamb, cum now," he growled, then dived back down to take what was his. His stubble scraped against my softness. A few more energetic thrusts and I was flying over the edge again. He pulled away, crawling up my body and kissed me deeply, letting me taste my own juices on his mouth.

I wrapped my legs around his waist, rolling him onto his back. I sat up and tugged his jeans off, adding them to the pile of discarded clothes. He was commando, no underwear or boxers in sight. *So, fucking manly! So, fucking hot!* "My turn," I smiled, wrapping my hand around his impressive cock. I struggled to get my hand around its full size, but that didn't stop me fisting it firmly and stroking him from root to tip with an eager hand. I upped the rhythm, watching his head roll back and enjoyed the deep moans escaping his throat before leaning over to tease the tip with my tongue.

I swirled around and around, licking the salty pearl off his tip and sucked him in deep. His hands came down to my head, moving me up and down as he pushed all the way to the base, butting against the back of my throat. Hot tears lined my eyes as the Kraken-of-all-cocks threatened to take my air supply. It took a second to remember how to breathe through my nose before I was able to relax as I swallowed him in, feeling powerful as he fucked my mouth. I could feel his body tense under me and his moans grew deeper. He stopped me in my tracks, pulling me up to look at him. "I want you to ride me princess. Be my good little cowgirl," he ordered, sitting up as he pulled my mouth to his, groaning as he tasted himself on my lips and tongue.

I straddled his lap, kissing him deeply as he wrapped his strong arms around me. I took a second to pull away, leaning across to the bedside drawers, pulling out a condom and rolling it down his shaft. Leaning in I licked across his throat and that Adam's apple that teased me earlier, nipping his earlobe between my teeth. In answer, he lined up his cock at my entrance and lowered me down slowly onto him.

Sweet. Baby. Geezussss.

And as amazing as the sex was, the intimacy as he stared into my eyes was something new, something fucking electric. My heart hitched in my chest and I flung my body against his, resting my head and mouth on his shoulder before those stupid tears welled up again. The pace grew as we both rode towards climax. In this position, he was so fucking deep inside of me that the angle was hitting my g-spot – that or it found a brand new spot of ecstasy. I felt my body building, every nerve ending on high alert. My body trembled and my pussy clenched his cock tightly as I came, screaming in complete satisfaction. He thrust deeply a few more times before growling his climax into my hair.

It took a few minutes to untangle our bodies and fall onto the bed. We lay in pure bliss, completely spent, bodies covered in sweat, ragged breaths filling the space between us. Luca rolled towards me, raising up on his elbow and kissed me gently. "You're coming back to mine."

I began to speak, but he stopped me, putting a finger to my lips. "Don't pull it apart baby girl, you said you'd give it a chance to get to know each other… Pack an overnight bag, and I'll send my driver to pick you up after lunch."

My mouth dropped open. "So you're fucking and fleeing then Mr Crescent?" I smirked, squinting my eyes at him and

111

crossing my arms across my chest.

His deep, lazy laugh made those butterflies in my belly awaken. "That's a new one," he chuckled. "But no, I won't fuck and flee you, princess. You're mine. I'll go organise dinner and you," he kissed me on the nose, "debrief with Lizzie. I bet she's either left the apartment embarrassed by the noises coming out of this room, or she's lying there hot and bothered, waiting for all the sordid details," he teased, waggling his eyebrows.

"The latter, definitely the latter," I giggled.

CHAPTER 14

I'D HARDLY CLOSED the door behind Luca when I was jumped from behind. Lizzie spun me around lightning fast, grabbing onto both of my arms, jumping excitedly on the spot, silently screaming in approval. Or praise. Or bewilderment. It was hard to tell. "Oh. My. Fucccckkinnngg sex goddess," she squealed. "Charlotte May Drake, you got some 'splainin' to do woman."

I couldn't help but laugh like a horny schoolgirl in love. Ah, lust. I meant lust.

"Guess we're back on," I chuckled, skipping to the lounge with Lizzie. I filled in the gaps for Lizzie, although to be fair, she had a play-by-play of her own with the paper-thin walls in our apartment. And I wasn't even embarrassed.

"See," she huffed sadly.

"See what?"

"That's what Scott and I are missing. The impulsiveness, the raw desire, the need to explore each other and trust someone enough to give that control away." There were no right words to ease her troubles, so I sat, listening, rubbing her leg and squeezing her hand in mine. "I need to tell him; it's been fun, but we both want something different out of this. But enough about me. I'm sorry Char. No more pity party – gah, I'm not that girl, I can't believe I just rained on your parade... I am so freakin' happy for you boo." Her whole face smiled as she leaned in to give me the biggest hug.

She always gave the best hugs.

"So, what now, huh?" she asked.

"Well, actually, his driver will be here in a couple of hours to pick me up. We're having a sleep over," I squirmed, hiding my face in my lap.

"Fuck yes girl, I'm totally here for it," she winked.

My blood was pumping in my ears as we pulled to a stop outside *'Crescent Towers'*, complete with a swanky doorman out the front.

What the actual fuck. I need to do my homework. Surely he can't own these apartments as well? Jane never mentioned real estate as part of his empire. How is this my life right now?

My door opened, and Luca's driver, Enzo, stood to the side. "We're here Miss Drake." I hesitated, shutting my eyes briefly to take a steading breath, before stepping out onto the kerb. I followed as Enzo led me inside to the elevator. We stood in awkward silence waiting, watching as the numbers counted down until the doors opened in the lobby. Enzo again held the door open for me. I entered but he stayed where he was, instead leaning in to swipe an access card and pressing the Penthouse button. "Are you not coming up?" I asked. "No Miss Drake, but he's expecting you. Have a good night," he smiled softly, nodding his head before stepping back and letting the doors close.

He was right. The doors opened right into the entry of Luca's apartment and there he was, standing there waiting for me, like a scene straight out of Fifty Shades of Who's Your Daddy? And all I wanted to say was, *'Please daddy, take me right now, six ways to Sunday'.*

He stood there looking pensive, but the glint in his eyes gave him away. Shirtless, leaning against the wall with his strong arms crossed under his pecs, he wore low-slung grey sweatpants which dipped dangerously low to expose that deliciously cut "V" at his hips. My eyes wandered for too long and I could feel the blush race up my neck and that tingly hollow knot in my stomach. I was stuck to the spot, both hands tightly holding onto my overnight bag in front of me for dear life, in danger of racing closer and eagerly stroking down his chest and fisting that gorgeous bulge in his pants.

"Come on princess, dinner's ready," he flirted, pushing off the wall and turning to lead the way. I followed slowly, eyes darting around his spacious open-plan apartment. Luca sauntered into an enormous kitchen, straight from the Master Chef set, grabbing two plates and setting them on a dining table set for two. But I continued forward, walking to the full floor-to-ceiling windows and the incredible view of the city lights laid out in front of me. "You've got a thing for windows and natural light don't you?" I smiled, looking over my shoulder at Luca as he walked towards me with a glass of wine in each hand.

"Little Lamb, you have no idea… but you will," he gave a wolfish grin, handing me a glass. "But first, I need to feed you, replenish those energy reserves."

"Replenish. Why Mr Crescent, it sounds as though you have some wicked plans for this evening," I teased, biting my lip. Luca rolled his head back with a moan. "You keep talking like that princess and I cannot be held responsible for filling your mouth with my cock instead of food," he paused. "Your choice," he breathed, stepping into me and grabbing my hip firmly, "what'll it be?"

I swayed a little, releasing my lip to lick my now parched mouth. He had me hooked. I was addicted to Luca Crescent, his dominant nature, and the pure sex God vibes that he oozed. Before my mind went down the slippery slope of debauchery, my hand splayed on his bare chest. "Food first… then dessert," I promised, gently scratching my nails down to his stomach, before walking around him to the dining table. Don't get me wrong. I wasn't being a dick tease.

I had every intention of letting him have his way with me, fill every hole in my body, and I was going to enjoy devouring every inch of him. But I needed to control some part of this, whatever *this* was, even if that meant pushing back a little and topping from the bottom.

Although the table could easily seat at least eight, Luca had my place set at the head, with him sitting closely to my right. He served up a generous size of some fantabulous seafood pasta dish with a side of greens. He wasn't lying about replenishing my energy stores. There was enough food to feed a small army. At least with food in my stomach, the two glasses of wine only gave me a warm buzz around the edges. Conversation flowed easily and light-hearted jokes and flirting were second nature, like we'd known each other a lifetime.

With dinner finished, plates stacked in the dishwasher and a new bottle of fresh bubbly pulled out of the wine cooler, Luca stalked around the kitchen island, grabbing my hand and rolling his thumb across my knuckles. "Let me give you the grand tour princess."

Holding my hand he led me through the main entertaining areas, a home gym fitted out with top brand equipment, a guest bedroom, bathroom, and a spacious home office complete with bookcases covering every wall and a luxurious chaise lounge I could picture myself curled up on, reading one of the many paranormal or dark romance novels on my TBR list while he worked at his computer.

A curved staircase near the entrance led to an immaculate bathroom and two more rooms; the first a guest room that looked untouched, and the second, yep, his bedroom built for sin. It was the size of my whole apartment. *Damn!* I stilled in the doorway, dropping his hand to watch him walk across the room. More floor-to-ceiling windows filled this room, but one side had blackout blinds half drawn. A large king bed took centre stage, covered in crisp ivory sheets that had to be million-thread count. They were begging to be touched and who was I to ignore such a plea? I floated straight towards the bed, slowly reaching out to run my fingers across the sheets. Yep, silky smooth. *Double damn!* Towards where Luca stood were two walk-in closets and a spacious private bathroom with his and her sinks, a generous-sized bath and a massive shower with dual shower heads and a built-in bench seat.

Oh dear Gods, we are gonna have some serious fun in here.

I couldn't hide the smirk as *all* the dirty thoughts flooded my mind. Luca wrapped his arms around me from behind, watching me through the mirror. "You like princess?"

"Do I like? Ah, is the sky blue? It's the nicest place I've ever seen. In my *entire* life," I admitted. His guttural snigger vibrated at the nape of my neck, his hot breath sending a chill across my body. "It's yours for the taking Little One, but I think you really need to try the shower, see if it's up to your standards."

He stayed at my back, his hands untucking the hem of my cami from my high-waisted dress pants, slowly lifting it up my body, over my raised arms, and over my head, leaving my braless breasts free in the breeze. Nipples already peaked with excitement, his hand massaged my breast, flicking and pinching my hard nipple while his other hand came up to my throat, gently squeezing. Not enough to take away my air, but enough to take my fanny flutters to a whole other level. This felt like the breath play I'd watched at that club and it had me slick, ready for more. *So much more.*

His hand left my needy breast, dipping into the front of my pants, fingers slowly opening me, rubbing against my slit, circling my clit. "Fuck you're so wet Little One. Does this turn you on?"

"Y–yes."

"Tell me what you want princess," he groaned, dipping two fingers into my pussy, pushing them deeper, making my legs squirm.

"Please Luca, give me more," I whimpered.

"More what?"

"More… more everything," I panted, rocking my head back on his chest, grinding my bum against his growing erection. Suddenly he was gone, hands pulled away, the warmth of his body missing from my back. I opened my eyes, feeling empty and alone. Luca stepped around me. He'd lost the sweatpants and was on full display in all his beautiful God-like glory. Stepping into the shower he turned on the double shower heads and stepped under the stream, placing both his hands against the back wall, letting his head slump forward. His muscles rippled across his back, and his toned ass was screaming to be bitten. Without turning he ordered, "pants off Little Lamb and come here". *You don't need to tell me twice.* I tucked my thumbs in at the hips and yanked down my pants and underwear in one move.

I stepped behind Luca under the shower spray and was instantly impressed with the water pressure and the space available to fool around in. Rising up on tiptoes, I gently kissed across his shoulder blade, slowly licking down his spine and moving my hands lower to squeeze his ass cheeks. "Please Sir, can I have my dessert now?" I begged, leaving little kisses over his sweet cheeks. Luca growled above me, "Say it again," he commanded.

"Please Sir. I want your cock deep in my throat."

He turned, his stiff length level with my face, and brushed my hair back off my face. I grabbed the base and licked around the tip before sucking him in, feeling his impressive girth scrape my teeth. Moving him further down my throat, I sucked and slurped and gagged, desperate to taste all of him. It was messy and frantic, but it didn't turn him off. Instead, he only grew harder in my mouth. "I want you to play with your clit with your other hand," he moaned. The combination of his pleasure and mine had me climbing fast, warmth spreading in my core. I sucked in a breath around his cock, spiralling as my fourth orgasm for the day hit hard. Luca stilled, body jerking before he was filling my mouth with his release.

He pulled out gently and I caught the drips off my chin, pushing them back in my mouth, swallowing it all down. He tugged me to stand, planting a sensual kiss on my lips. His hands scraped through my hair, bringing me closer to him, deepening the kiss. Spinning me around he moved me backwards until my legs were against the bench seat. Lowering me to sit, he broke our kiss, whispering in my mouth, "My turn for a sweet treat."

He sunk down in between my legs, sprinkling hot kisses on my knees and working his way north as his hands traced around the outside of my thighs, lifting one leg over his shoulder. His mouth was hot, his tongue like silk on my clit while his growing stubble gently scratched across my pussy. The opposite sensations were waging a small war inside me. The pleasure mixed with a little pain wasn't enough, I wanted him deeper, rougher. I wanted him to shatter me into a million pieces. Completely fucking own me.

"Baby, I need more," I huffed, fisting his hair.

"What do you want Little Lamb, say it."

I opened my eyes, looking down into the golden pools staring up at me from between my thighs. *So fucking beautiful.* "I'm yours Luca, I want you to own me. I want you so deep inside me so we don't know where you end and I start. Take me, destroy me, I want to scream your name as I fall apart."

He gave an evil smile and stood in an instant. I squealed as he lifted me with him, spinning us around so he was sitting on the bench seat, me straddling his lap. "Are you on the pill baby girl? Because if you are, I am tested and clean."

"Not the pill, but I have the birth control implant," I leaned in, needing to kiss him again. "And I'm also tested and clean. Know that I want this Luca. I want you inside me, skin to skin," I moaned, biting his bottom lip.

He palmed my breasts as he lowered his head to suck and flick my nipples. He licked up to my neck, gently biting that sensitive spot below my ear. He notched himself at my entrance with one hand while the other wrapped around me. "Slide down baby." I lowered myself, moaning at the feel of him completely filling me. I moved up and down, rocking my hips into him, matching his thrusts. His base rubbed against my clit making the heat at my core swell. His hands at my hips pulled me down firmer as he drove up into me. I could feel him in my stomach as the tension built. Long and slow movements mixed with quick deep thrusts. Time became a blur as the intense pleasure spread across my body.

"Fuck. Luca, I'm close."

He sped up, growling as he moved like a jackrabbit. "Oh. My. God…. Luca, I'm cum—" my words were broken off as my clit vibrated and the waves of my orgasm crashed around me. He growled his own release, jerking and slowing his movements as we fell apart, together. I went limp, my body falling against him, shaky and warm and completely spent.

We cleaned up, throwing on bathrobes before moving to Luca's bed. It felt like a pile of clouds and I was sure I'd never be able to pull myself away from the heavenly feeling. We lay in the afterglow, completely at ease with each other and the silence. The events of the day and the world-shattering sex rolled through my mind, my bones, and across my skin. Luca's eyes were closed, his arms folded behind his head. "Luca?" I whispered.

"Mmmm."

"What did you mean earlier today when you said I'd been naughty and I should have called you if I wanted to explore my deepest desires?"

His eyes slowly opened, staring at the ceiling. But he stayed silent. "Luca, no more games, if we're gonna try, we've got to be all in or not at all." He rolled to his side, leaning his head across his arm, stretching a hand across my stomach. "I know you went to House of Himeros and I was offering to explore those kinks with you, if you wanted to do more… than just watch."

"Wait, what? How could you possibly know that, and

how the fuck do you know I just watched. God, don't tell me you have someone watching me, do you?" I sighed, a frown drawing my brows together.

"Baby, it's not like that," he huffed.

"Well, what is it like then Luca?" I asked, pushing myself up to sit facing him.

"House of Himeros is one of my clubs, and my boy Johnny from The Sparrow frequents the House on a regular basis. He mentioned he had a killer night with two voyeurs. It wasn't until he said your name that I just about fell off my fucking chair, my naughty little minx," he said with a bop on my nose.

My mouth fell open and my eyes fell to the bed as my mind raced. How could Lizzie and my Johnny, be Luca's Johnny? If that was true, surely we would have seen Luca at The Sparrow a dozen times or so before on our nights out. "Breathe, princess. You're not being tracked, followed or stalked. And I'm abso-fucking-lutely up for some kink play whenever you want. In private, at the club, hell, at the fucking office," he grinned, leaning forward to playfully bite my thigh.

The thought had me squirming for more. But a few too many nights streaming adult romance-come-crime thrillers had taught me to keep my guard up or risk becoming the next true crime hit. But my Luca didn't have those stalker vibes and I just needed to re-learn how to trust again and let myself be vulnerable. I looked back at him as he stared at me through his dark eyelashes. "I know, sorry, I know you're not stalking me," my expression and tone softened. "I think I'm just in shock. It's just, how did we never meet before that first night at your club? Lizzie and I have been chatting to Johnny for at least six months."

"The universe wasn't ready for this powerhouse," he smiled, lying back to face the ceiling. "Now come lie with me, time for rest Little One."

I lay back down, snuggling into his side, in the crook of

his arm. Breathing in his woody warmth.

The universe – heck, I didn't know if I'd ever be ready for this atomic bomb of chemistry between us let alone the universe. But right now I was happy and I was going to enjoy that feeling I've been missing for too long.

"Sleep now, then we explore desires, boundaries, and kinks later," he teased sleepily.

I shut my eyes, a giddy smile spread across my face as I imagined all the delicious things we would try together.

CHAPTER 15

I WOKE THE next morning to a growing heat in my core and a handsome-as-fuck man between my legs, tongue-fucking my still-aching pussy.

I've died and gone to heaven. Or hell. Whichever it is, I'll happily stay if this is how I get to wake up every damn morning! As Hades is my witness.

After some morning delight we showered and dressed for work, stealing glances at each other, filling the air with teasing smiles and silent promises for more hot sex later. Enzo picked us up in front of the building and made the way downtown to Crescent Incorporated. We might have shifted this relationship into overdrive, and I wasn't even sure if we could put that label on it yet, even if it felt so... natural. So right. But there was still a part of me that needed to stay guarded, to protect myself from any more heartbreak. The pessimist in me was waiting for the rose-coloured glasses to fade. And there was nothing worse than a shitty rumour mill to break something that was just building its foundations. So, I took a step away, creating a little distance between us as we walked through the foyer towards the elevators.

Walking into the Penthouse office space, we were met with a toothy grin from Jane. "Good morning Mr Cresent. Charlotte," she smiled. Luca nodded, returning pleasantries as he walked around the front desk towards his office. Jane's eyes darted towards me and her eyebrows raised, getting lost somewhere between her fringe and her hairline. "How was your weekend? Do anything interesting?" she singsonged.

"Not really, just the usual," I tried to sound bored.

"Hogwash, there's something flicking between you and Luca," she insisted.

"Don't be silly Jane, we just rode up the elevator together. So kick those thoughts to the kerb right now," I rolled my eyes, trying to sound nonchalant.

I put my head down, and bum up for the rest of the day, determined to prove my place in this company, and it wasn't just to be the boss's friend with benefits. Luca left soon after arriving, his calendar filled with back-to-back meetings with various clients, so there was no chance to add fuel to the gossip fire raging inside Jane's pretty little head.

I returned early from lunch to see Stephan pacing back and forward in the meeting room. I knocked gently on the glass door before entering warily. I was still finding my feet here and I didn't want to get on the bad side of any execs. "Mr Hewitt, is there anything I can help with, or get for you?"

He sat in one of the boardroom chairs, leaning his chin on his clenched fists. "Not unless you have a fresh idea on how to sell yet another brand of headphones to the 15-25 demographic," he grumbled.

I hesitated for a second, wondering if this was stepping over a line, pushing the boundaries of an EA, particularly an EA to another exec. But the prospect of stretching my rusty advertising muscles had me excited.

Just handballing ideas with Stephan isn't overstepping. No, it's helping the company out. Being a team player. I'm sure Luca will understand that. Use it as a learning opportunity.

"Happy to brainstorm with you, if you'd like?" I raised my brows, questioning. "Wanna tell me about the client's outline and what ideas you've vetoed?" I smiled, taking another step closer.

"Why not?" he snorted. "Maybe I need a new muse or a fresh set of eyes," he gave a crooked grin, gesturing for me to take a seat next to him as he spread out a pile of papers across the table. We spent the next hour talking through a handful of ideas before one sparked a twinkle in his eyes. Feeling in my element, I sketched a rough storyboard on his tablet as we padded out the idea. "You've got some talent there, Charlotte," Stephan complimented, nudging my shoulder with his. Looking at my watch and noticing how much time had passed, I handed the tablet back shyly. "Thank you," I smiled. "And thank you for letting me brainstorm with you. I better get back to it though, make sure I haven't missed any messages from Mr Crescent," I pointed my thumb towards my desk.

"Of course. I'll let you know how I go with the creative directors on the storyboard."

"That'd be great, I'd love to see where you take it. But Mr Hewitt—."

"Stephan," he interjected.

"Stephan," I smiled meekly. "It was all you. I just filled in the gaps, so no need to speak about any of this with Mr Crescent, or Jane," I begged with my eyes.

"You did more than fill the gaps Charlotte, but I'm happy to keep this our little *secret*," he said a little too seductively, throwing in a wink for good measure.

Oh hell no player. Don't even. Run Charlie, run.

Despite Luca's requests for another sleepover, I hesitantly declined. I needed new clothes, to debrief with Lizzie, and to let my tender lady bits rest for a night. But by Wednesday night Luca had me desperate for sexy time, getting me hot and bothered with his indecent text messages in lieu of a physical release. We had planned to get together on Tuesday, but Luca was called away for an overnight trip to Washington. And on Wednesday, Lizzie had left me a dozen voice messages and two dozen texts, begging me to come straight home and game plan with her. Turns out her game plan was all about how to take things to the next level with Johnny now that she'd ended things with Scott.

Luca: I am dying over here princess. I am starving for my favourite sweet dessert.
Charlie: You're not the only one. I've been dreaming about that luxurious bath of yours.

Do you have bubbles and flavoured massage oil or should I pick some up?
Luca: Fuck...

Pack your overnight bag. Enzo and I will pick you up for work tomorrow morning and he can take your bag home.

We rode to work together, and if he didn't have Stephan's ad campaign to attend with the clients first up, I know he would have taken me in the back of the car, no cares for fucking up our clothes, hair, or my makeup. And I wouldn't have said no either. Instead, he held my hand, rubbing circles across the top with his thumb. Leaning in, his breath hot on my neck, he whispered, "I need to touch you, feel what's mine."

My breath hitched and my heart did a weird *thadump-dump,* jumping in my chest. I turned sharply, our noses almost touching. "But what about Enzo?" I whispered. "His eyes are on the road Little One... and I have a feeling you're curious if being watched or caught out will give you the thrill you desire." The devil smiled at me through his features and I swear I could feel an orgasm crawl closer just from the thought. "Shut your eyes, princess, focus on my touch."

Leaning away, but eyes still watching my every breath, he nodded at me, slowly moving his hand from mine, and rubbing slowly down my skirt. I gulped and closed my eyes as he asked. His hand skirted around my knee, spreading my legs just wide enough to slip his hand up the inside of my thighs. Without hesitation he palmed my pussy, rubbing the silky material against my growing desire. The feel of the silk against my throbbing clit, a mixture of heaven and hell. Just like this man next to me.

As my breathing increased, he pulled my panties to the side, letting his second and fourth fingers part me while his middle finger teased my entrance, dipping inside. Curling that finger he rolled it against my aching clit before moving it back down and entering me in one smooth movement. *Geezusssss.*

My eyes shot open and straight to the back of Enzo's head. His gaze was still straight ahead but I was desperate to know if he had spotted me in his rearview mirror. *Oh Goddess.* Tingles spread through my lower belly and straight down to my pussy. The brushes of Luca's fingers on my sensitive nub felt like the quick flutter of butterfly wings. I arched my head back on the headrest looking over to Luca as I bit my lip to silence the moans desperate to leave my mouth. "Keep those eyes on me, princess," he groaned. "Strangle my fingers with that tight cunt." *God I loved his dirty mouth.*

He adjusted his hand to enter another finger, dancing them around inside me, feeling like he was reaching every wall, every nerve ending. He circled my clit and pumped his fingers without mercy, sending me over. I sucked in a breath, devouring the warm feeling spreading as I slowly came down. I raised the back of my hand up to my mouth, biting on a knuckle, smiling at Luca behind it. He pulled his fingers out, bringing them up to his mouth and licking them clean. "That's my good girl," he whispered. "Now slip out of those panties and give them to me. They're mine now." As if a puzzle piece just clicked into place, I was struck with an epiphany.

I think I have a praise kink. Well shit...

###

Jane and I brought in jugs of water and coffee to the boardroom, before taking our spots standing in the corner near the door, out of the way, but on hand should the executives need us. Stephan took centre stage for his presentation, flanked by Luca and Brad sitting on opposite sides of the table nearest to where he stood. Four clients sat silently, waiting to either be impressed or disappointed and ready to walk away with their millions. My body tensed with nerves. Stephan had shown me the finished storyboard and hadn't diverted from my suggestions. I thought it was great. But I wasn't the client. If this went down like a lead balloon, surely I'd get the blame.

Oh God Charlie, just breath. You're the fly on the wall,
remember?

Stephan pulled his presentation off without a glitch, as if spinning golden thread with his words. He was good, I'll give him that. The clients were happy. The execs were happy. And Luca was gleaming like a proud father. Once hands were shaken and contracts signed, Jane led the clients out to the elevators as I began to clean up. "Great pitch Hewitt. I loved it, and the clients loved it. Well done," Luca congratulated Stephan, patting him on the shoulder. "Gotta say though, it was a little different than you're usual stuff. Did you collab with Cavanaugh?"

Stephan's eyes darted to me briefly. "What are you trying to say Crescent? That I can't come up with the goods by myself?" he chuckled. "Back off dude, it was all me. Just took a step back and looked at it from a different angle."

"Okay, okay, snappy, I was just asking," Luca joked back. "You came through with the goods. Now let's keep the clients happy and coming back for more."

I know I'd told Stephan to keep it between us, but I couldn't help but feel annoyed seeing the pitch play out in front of me. He didn't need to offer details about my help, but Luca had noticed the difference in this campaign. He could have mentioned we brainstormed a few ideas.

You can't be annoyed Charlie, you told him to keep it hush hush.

God I know, but I want, I want…. I want Luca to be proud of me too.
Ha! And there it is again. I'm hooked on being his good little girl. Luca 2: Charlie 0.

CHAPTER 16

THE LAST COUPLE of weeks had been chaotic to say the least. Luca, Brad and Stephan had all taken on new clients, keeping Jane and I busy lining up schedules, meetings, and updates with the creatives, financials and production teams. Luca had pulled me into his office a few days ago under the guise of missing a file for a meeting the next day, only to fill my mouth with his silk tie and bend me over the back of one of his chairs, driving me to O-ville as his tie drowned my moans and screams. It was only that luck was on my side and Jane was picking up the prints from another floor that she didn't see me strut out of his office on a post-sex high.

I stayed at Luca's place a few times over the past fortnight, and he'd convinced me to leave a few overnight supplies there, 'just for convenience' he'd said. A toothbrush, deodorant, a spare outfit for work, you know, just the basics. We indulged in my bath fantasy, and he worked my body with flavoured massage oil before trying a new kink on me in the kitchen, going down on me and driving me fucking wild, edging me over and over again with orgasm denial. I fucking hated it, but more than that, I fucking loved it. And I know I'm part of the minority who actually loves sucking D, but I really do. I can't get enough of his incredible cock. It's beautiful, and perfect, and made for me.

On my nights at home, Lizzie and I chatted about her

progress with Johnny. Not surprising at all, but she really likes him and wants it to be more than a hot one-nighter. If you ask me, the writing's been on the wall for a long fucking time, she just wouldn't listen to me. She says they still haven't jumped into bed, but they've taken their courtship to a whole other level, returning to House of Himeros to explore her voyeurism curiosity. Part of me really wanted to go with them and bring my sex-toy-on-legs along for the ride, but I was having too much fun one-on-one with Luca and didn't want to test our limits just yet. Hell, I don't know if he's the jealous type – probably not, seeing how confident and in control he always is. But I kinda am, and I didn't want to bring out the green-eyed monster and scare him off with my pettiness if he was invited into someone else's play. Which let's be honest, of course he fucking would be, my own Himeros, God of sexual desire. And if he is Himeros, then I want to be his Goddess Hedone, the one to give him every ounce of pleasure humanly possible.

###

Tonight is the annual East Coast Advertising Awards and Jane and I have invites to join the execs as well as a few head of department big guns and their PAs. My personal stylist Lizzie picked out a knockout gown for me to 'shine in', as she'd put it. A backless, sparkly emerald green floor-length number with spaghetti straps and a deep plunging neckline, almost to my navel. She helped me style a half-updo, letting half of my curls fall across my back.

Jane wanted to ride together, so arranged for her Uber to drop by my place before taking us to the venue at the Ziegfeld Ballroom. As we stepped into the ballroom I just about tripped on my jaw as it hit the floor, blown away by the grandeur and elegance of the art deco-inspired space before me.

Holy hell, this is nicer than the Oscars.

There must have been a hundred tables in here, with even more people dotted in chairs and mingling around the room. "Oh my God Jane, I didn't realise it was this big of a deal. This is stunning," I gushed.

"I know," she giggled. "Doesn't it make you feel like a movie star? And I must say you look the part in that gorgeous emerald piece too," she waggled her eyebrows at me.

As if pulled by an invisible string, I turned to see Luca halfway across the room, chatting with Brad and a gorgeous man I'm assuming was his boyfriend. Jane followed my gaze, pulling me with her as she skipped towards the group of men, stopping by a bar to grab a glass of champagne for us both, before rushing ahead.

"Gentlemen, looking dapper," Jane beamed as she stepped into their circle. Their eyes roamed up and down, taking in her beauty before they shot back compliments for how beautiful she looked dolled up. I trailed behind, taking my time to approach, mesmerised by how striking Luca looked in his tailored black Armani wool mohair suit. I'd seen it hanging up in his apartment, but seeing it on him was breathtaking. A gorgeous dark emerald bow tie stood out against the crisp whiteness of his shirt. The same green as my dress.

I stepped forward, a smirk on my lips. "I've died and gone to runway heaven," I giggled. "Oh God, I didn't just say that aloud did I? I'm sorry, that was inappropriate," I gasped, trying to put the proverbial cat back in the bag.

Brad chuckled, "Not at all. No need for formalities when we're not in client meetings Charlotte. And besides, you're not wrong," he smirked, his hand snaking around the waist of Mr Pretty Boy next to him.

I smiled a warm thank you. "Then call me Charlie."

My gaze moved to the other man. "And this must be—"

"Nick, Brad's better half," he winked, reaching out to grab my hand, planting a sneaky kiss on my knuckles as I went to shake. "That's rich… Charlie, meet my *flirty* other half Nick," Brad joked.

"Nice to put a face to the name Charlie. And that gown… that gown is—."

"Stunning," Luca interrupted, his velvety baritone voice gliding over every cell in my body.

"Thank you," I choked, trying to clear my throat, feeling the heat rise up my neck.

More people piled in the room over the next half hour, all dressed to the nines. It really did feel like the Oscars, except I didn't recognise any of the faces. Luca sat to my right, Brad on my other side. Jane was opposite me, sitting in between Nick and Stephan. She looked in her element, glowing as she held the attention of anyone she spoke to.

Conversation flowed as a four-course meal was served throughout the evening, intertwined with speeches from each advertising agency present on current campaigns and the previous year's highlights. When Luca wasn't discreetly touching my knee with his, he was being more daring, gliding his hand against any body part he could get to. My thigh, my arm, the back of my shoulder as he walked around my chair to greet other partygoers. When others at our table were distracted in conversation, Luca would lean in whispering, and all but growling at me. Teasing me with promises of deliciously naughty things he was going to do to me when we left. He even begged to leave early half a dozen times, and I had to threaten a sex-ban for the night if he didn't stay until the award ceremony. And if that was going to happen, we were both going to suffer.

"Myyy goodness… Luca Crescent, it's been a second," came a lilting voice floating through the air from behind me. Luca's smile faded, muscles jumping along his jawline as his eyes went cold. I spun around in my chair, curious to see who owned that voice, and who made this powerful man look like he was being tortured.

A short, petite strawberry blonde stood just behind me,

daring to rest her hand on the back of my chair. "Cat got your tongue handsome," she drawled, seductively smiling at Luca. *My Luca.* "Well, aren't you going to introduce me?" she asked, turning to face me. She put out a hand, like the queen waiting for a kiss on the royal ring. "Hi, I'm Rose, I work at Lester and Co.," she grabbed my hand, shaking lazily. "But I used to work with Luca here. What's your name cutie?"

Wow, the cojones on this woman. How fucking patronising. But I'm not gonna bite. Keep your friends close, bitches who want your man closer.

"Charlotte," I replied sweetly. "I'm Mr Crescent's personal assistant."

"That's nice," she dismissed. "I was hoping to catch up with Luca here, you don't mind do you?"

Without waiting for an answer, she pulled an empty chair across from the next table, bringing it right in close between Luca and me. I wasn't able to get a read on Luca. He chatted with Rose and even smiled a few times, one of those real smiles that reached his eyes. But he seemed a little guarded. Rose ignored my existence, leaning in close to Luca to place a hand on his arm as she spoke. This woman oozed confidence, a female version of Luca, and she had me rattled.

Within five minutes she'd gone from asking how he'd been since they last saw each other and joking like old friends, to rubbing up his arm, grabbing his bicep as she laughed and flirted openly.

"I've been thinking of you lately," she teased, crossing her arms over her knees, bringing up a hand to rest under her chin, and raising a finger to bite the tip of it seductively.

Holy fucking fuckballs. Is this woman serious? And who the fuck is she to Luca?

I felt shocked, curious, hurt and my green-eyed monster was shaking the cage bars to get out. In that moment, Brad returned to the table, surprising me by placing a hand on my shoulder.

"Can I have this dance?" he smiled warmly.

Perfect timing, I couldn't watch anymore of that toying without either causing a scene to ask what the fuck was going on, or claw her damn eyes out.

I accepted Brad's outstretched hand and followed him away from our table. I wanted to look back to see if Luca even noticed, but I couldn't bare the thought that he wasn't watching me walk away. So I took a steadying breath and smiled back at the man holding my hand. He pulled me in closer to place his other hand on my hip and began spinning us around the dancefloor.

I kept silent for a while, staring at Brad's shoulder as we moved around.

"Everything okay Charlie?"

"Ah yeh, of course," I mumbled. "Why wouldn't it be?"

"Call it intuition if you want, but I can sense that something just shifted. Something's changed from earlier in the night where you seemed happy and talkative and at ease."

I considered keeping up the charade but have never been a good liar. "Who is that woman?" I asked quietly.

Brad looked towards our table briefly then back down at me. "Rose Tyler. She used to be one of our best creative directors."

"Why'd she leave?"

"Like they say, you don't mix business with pleasure. And when Luca and Rose ended things, she left the company. It was awkward as fuck in the office and it was better for everyone when she resigned. I mean don't get me wrong, it's been hard to find someone as talented as she is, but we have Yas now, and she is on fire," he chuckled.

They were together. And at work. I knew he had a fucking type, and he hired me just to have some fucking déjà vu. What an idiot, I played right into his hands. I should have listened to my gut.

I could feel the lump in my throat grow as I held back tears. I chanced a look back towards the pair to see Luca staring directly at me while Rose still rambled at his side. "Excuse me Brad, I have to use the restroom," I said, releasing his hold as I turned and dashed away. I didn't want to get trapped in the main ladies' restroom with prying eyes as I fell apart, so I headed up to the empty balcony area, knowing there were separate restrooms up there from my earlier exploration. I raced inside, my heart pounding in my throat, tears burning my eyes. Grasping onto the counter, I let a whimper fall from my lips.

"No, don't be that girl. Don't fall apart over a fucking guy," I sobbed at the reflection staring back at me. "You can't control him. You have no right to," I blew out. "He's not your boyfriend Charlie. Now calm, the fuck, down!"

I turned on the cool water, splashing some on my cheeks and rubbing it across the back of my neck as I took in some slow, measured, meditated breaths. The bathroom door swung open, stealing me from my trance. I shot around, leaning back against the counter with a gasp. Luca stood in the doorway, a frown creasing his perfect brow. I dropped my head, focusing all of my attention on the pattern of the tiles under my feet. Water dripped off my face, falling where I stared at the floor.

"Why'd you run princess?" he asked, a quiver in his voice.

What was I going to say, *'oh sorry, my stupid brain went off the Richter scale learning that Rose was your gorgeous ex and seeing her throw herself at you'*. Ha! Unlikely. He didn't need to see this side of Charlie. The side that had made a habit out of building mountains out of molehills. So I said nothing.

"Look at me Little One. Talk to me. What happened?" he hummed, moving inside the room, inching closer while I stood there frozen.

Fine. Fuck it. He wants to get to know me, well welcome to the good, the bad, and the ugly. "Where's Rose?" I questioned, looking up at him through my lashes.

He stopped a foot away. "Probably back with her work colleagues. Charlie, what's going on?"

"She's your ex, Luca. Or one of them," I whispered, digging deeper to find the strength I needed to get through this speech. "And it looks like she wants back in… and she probably stirred up some old flames in you too. You looked at home with her and she was ready to jump in your lap and take you right there in the middle of the fucking ballroom," I let out a bitter laugh.

His frown dropped into a crooked smile and he took a step back, pushing his hands into his front pockets.

"It's not funny Luca. Just be open and honest with me. She's your ex, if you feel drawn to her and you have a shared history, just tell me now before we start something," my voice cracked.

He swaggered forward, this time stepping right into my space so our foreheads were touching.

"Too late baby girl. We started something that very first night and you know it. This—" he said, gesturing between us, "is not a one-night deal." He cupped my face, gently kissing my forehead, then tracing little kisses down my temple and to my cheek where a tear had escaped.

"Charlie, Rose is my past, you are my present and my future. Tell me you don't feel it too?" he breathed, lifting my chin up with a curled finger.

"Yes, I feel it. I feel it in my mind, body and spirit. And that's what's freaking me the fuck out. I want you Luca, only you, and I want you to want me too."

"I do want you, all of you Little Lamb," he finished, pressing his hungry lips to mine. Our bodies pressed together, perfectly moulded to each other. His erection pushing hard against my pussy and lower stomach. His hands slid down my sides, down to my hips, landing on my outer thighs. He tugged my dress up to mid-thigh then lifted me, sitting me atop the counter as he stood in between my legs. "These lips are mine," he said kissing me firmly, diving deep with his tongue. He broke the kiss, "these tits are mine," he breathed, cupping them with his hands, lowering his head to playfully bite one through my dress. "These lush thighs are mine," he continued, bending down to kiss down one thigh, and lick up from the knee of the other, stopping where my dress was ruffled up. "And these panties and the pussy they caress are mine," he said, running his fingers up my inner thigh, so softly, so slowly, brushing the backs of his fingers up my pussy. Turning his hand to rub back down, he froze, his eyes going wide. "Charlie—"

"I didn't see a need for underwear tonight," I giggled, "and besides I would have had a VPL in this gown and no one wants that."

"VPL?"

"Visible panty line," I chuckled, throwing my head back at his expression.

"Oh no, we can't have a VPL, in fact, we don't want that in any of your outfits. New rule – no more panties. Ever," he growled, parting my soaking slit with his fingers and plunging two in with no hesitation.

My breath caught at the sensation and my need went from 0 to 100 in a heartbeat. I wanted to rip his clothes off, mark him, claim him as mine. "I want you now Luca, I need more. And I need it rough and fast. Fuck me Luca."

Our mouths collided, a mess of tongues and teeth. I unbuckled his belt and hurriedly pulled the zipper down, tucking my hands into his pants at his hips and yanking them down his thighs. I readjusted myself on the bench, pulling my dress out from under me. There was no way in hell I was going to walk out of this bathroom with a cum stain on this dress for all to see.

He grabbed his hard cock at the base, notching it at my entrance as I leant into him wrapping my hand around the nape of his neck, kissing up his collarbone and jaw. I bit at his pulse point and he ploughed into me in one motion, releasing a moan from both of us. I held on to his jacket as he fucked me senseless. He gave me everything I needed, riding out my frustration, my worries and my uncontrollable desire for him.

"Oh God, yes… yes! Fuck Luca, I'm close."

"Cum with me Little One. Let it all go."

We shattered together. A monster fucking orgasm ripping through my body, leaving nothing in its path. I swear my soul up and left my body. I held onto Luca, letting his semi pull out from me, then rested my head against his chest, feeling his breathing match my own. The green bow tie caught my eye again, this close I could see that it was the same material as my dress. The exact same.

"Luca, where'd you get this tie?" I asked, placing my hand over it.

His chest moved under my cheek as he laughed. "Lizzie."

That sneaky little meddler. "I'm gonna kill her," I said sitting up to look him in the eyes. "That could've been enough to give away our secret. What would the guys say?"

"I don't fucking care princess. Let them find out, I don't want to hide this anymore. Will you give this a shot with me? Will you give us a shot?" he asked, rubbing his thumb against my cheek.

I bit my lip, my brain racing off on its own again.

Pinch me, is this really happening? Is it too soon?

"Baby girl, you there? I lost you for a second."

I stared into his golden amber eyes, looking for a hint of doubt, but there wasn't any. "Yes," I hummed. "Yes, I want to be yours, and you mine," I smiled.

"Mine," he echoed.

CHAPTER 17

THE DAYS WERE warming up, marking the change of season, complete with trees beginning to change and grow, and flowers blossoming. I had been at Crescent Incorporated for almost two months and Luca had been true to his word, no longer hiding our relationship. Of course, being a couple out in public was great. Dinners out on the town, nights together at The Sparrow and even lunch at work together. But it also meant without sneaking around behind closed doors, we weren't fucking around at work with everyone's eyes on us. There were still corporate rules to follow and paperwork we had to sign to ensure legal knew this wasn't a breach of code of conduct with a boss using his power to sleep with a subordinate. And if the boss was having sex in-office with an employee, then what was to stop every other Tom, Dick and Harry from doing the same?

Jane had become a thorn in my side, insisting she knew all along, and we were just fooling ourselves to think no one could see what was really going on. I mean she wasn't wrong, but there's no way I was ever going to let her know that. But other than that, it was nice to have a girlfriend at work on this floor full of powerful men.

Brad had been supportive and warm about our coming-out, even Nick had visited to take me out for a 'BWags' lunch, as he'd called it, needing to elaborate that BWags *obviously* stood for Businessmen's wives and girlfriends. He was cooky, but I liked him. He made me feel at ease the same way Eric did.

But Stephan had distanced himself. He hardly made eye contact or acknowledged my presence in the same room anymore. It was difficult to get two words out of him, even after I'd spent time helping him with his pitch. And it was creating horrible fucking tension in the office. Brad had asked about it, as had Jane. I even took our Crescent Inc sisterhood to the next level, opening up a little and letting her know I'd helped Stephan out with some ideas. I told her we'd been getting along right up until the awards night, where without warning he did a 180 and decided that I no longer existed and wasn't worth his time. It was then that she admitted her office romance had been with Stephan and he was the master of hot and cold. After they had finished playing around, he had given her the cold shoulder for a full month before she told him to wake up to himself. Not that I was ever going to say that to him. I think you have to at least have sexual chemistry or a connection with someone before you can tell them they're being a fuckwit. But knowing this player had issues with not being the top dog that girls swooned over, that was an angle I could work.

Stephan had a meeting scheduled with one of his newer clients in an hour which meant the other execs would attend, but that Jane, as his EA, would be running admin support and I could sneak downstairs for an hour or so to watch the creative team work on a storyboard Luca had been working on last night while I watched *Below Deck* on catch-up TV.

"Charlie, I need your help," Jane whispered as she sat back at her desk. I turned to face her, noticing the paleness to her usually glowing skin and the line of sweat across her brow and top lip.

"Oh my God Jane, are you okay? You look—"

"Sick, I am. I can't hold anything down. It was just mild abdo cramps this morning and I was hoping it would ease. But now I can't stop vomiting. I think it was the fish I ate last night."

"Do you want me to take you to the doctors?" I asked, putting a hand on her cold, yet sweaty forearm.

"No, it's fine. I just need to go home and sleep it off. I'm supposed to be preparing for the client meeting and taking notes for Stephan. But I can't Charlie, I need your help," she sobbed, turning greener by the second.

"Jane, you don't even need to ask. Go home, I've got this," I said, grabbing Jane's bag and leading her to the elevators. "I'll let the bosses know. You just get better okay."

I set up the boardroom, preparing Stephan's presentation on the big screen, laying out the pitch briefs, and let Luca know about Jane when he came back from a lunch meeting. But Stephan, he could wait and get a surprise when I sat in on his meeting.

Once they arrived, I welcomed the clients, settling them in the boardroom with refreshments and sat with them, indulging in small talk while we waited for Stephan and Luca. Being raised in the advertising world and knowing the business ins and outs definitely helped me liaise with clients, and usually garnered a mutual respect easily. Today's clients; Liam, Rachel and Eliza, were no different. There was no air of righteousness, only authenticity and warmness. If I was an advertising manager, this would be the type of clients I'd bend over backwards for.

The glass door opened and Stephan walked in, exchanging pleasantries with the trio. He paused when he spotted me, nearly causing Luca to walk up the back of him. His eyes briefly moved to Luca before coming back to me.

"Is Jane on her way?" he asked, clearing his throat.

"No sorry, she's had to go home sick, so I will be filling in for her. Please let me know if there's anything you need," I answered in my sweetest voice.

The meeting went well with the clients pleased with the brief and only wanting to make a few additions to meet their needs. But there was still tension in the air and Stephan didn't look at me once. I just hoped it wasn't obvious to anyone else. I didn't want Luca or the clients getting the wrong idea. After they'd left, Stephan finally looked at me, offering a smile and a nod of his head. "Thank you for filling in Charlotte. If you pass on your notes to Jane, she can put it all together."

A little confused, and a whole lot of fucking annoyed, I bit back the anger and tried to remain professional. "No need Mr Hewitt, I took notes as we went along, so I will proof them to make sure I didn't miss anything and have them to you by the end of the day."

Shove that in your pipe and smoke it, you asshat.

"Right, great. Thanks," he stuttered as he walked back towards his office, leaving Luca and me in awkward silence.

"Have you got a sec Charlie, I need to see you in my office," he raised his chin, placing his hands in his front pockets and walking out ahead of me. I grabbed my notebook and laptop and followed Luca to his office, taking a seat as he closed the door behind us.

"Wanna tell me what that was about?" he narrowed his eyes.

I sighed, sitting back in the chair, crossing my legs. "To be honest with you, I really don't know. It's as if Stephan flipped a switch and now can't stand to talk to me, let alone look at me. Has he said anything to you? Have I done something to anger or insult him?"

Luca moved around, standing in front of me, leaning back against his desk, legs crossed at the ankles, arms crossed against his chest and a thoughtful hand playing at his chin. "It's not like him. From where I'm standing, it looks like a lover's spat. And if he has laid one finger on you, I will cut it off."

"Luca, you know I'd never do that. I am with you," I said, leaning forward to squeeze his arm.

"I know baby girl. But I also know Stephan and he's a fucking player. And worse than that, a hunter, who doesn't stop until he gets what he wants… he hasn't tried anything on you, has he?"

"No, he hasn't, well not that I'm aware of. And I might be a little like-struck with you so not really paying attention to any other man's advances. But I'm sure I still would have picked up on flirting."

"Ha," he frowned.

"Ha, what?"

"Just like-struck? Come on princess, surely you're a little fuck-struck if anything," he smirked, leaning down to kiss me, caging me between his arms on the chair.

"Don't you know it," I said, licking the side of his face playfully. "But seriously, what am I gonna do about this awkwardness between Stephan and me? I don't want to cause any issues in your company."

I grabbed Luca's hand, pulling him to the chair next to me. "You sure there hasn't been a time, a situation that he could have thought you were interested in him, and now he feels like I'm taking what's his?"

"That's not even funny Luca, I will never be his," I rolled my eyes. "The only time we've been together without others from work was a few weeks back before his SikBeatz headphones pitch when I sat in the boardroom brainstorming with him." I know I didn't want to mention it to Luca at the time, but if that was the cause of all of this stupid behaviour, then now was the time to come clean.

"Brainstorming. How did that come about?" he asked, curiosity electrifying the air.

"He was pacing one day looking like he was about to pull his hair out and I offered to listen and handball some ideas around. And he accepted," I said, shrugging.

"I knew that pitch and storyboard wasn't just his work," he huffed. "It was fresh, it was… different. And the bastard flat out denied it." The cogs were madly turning in Luca's brain and it was fascinating to watch his eyes flicker as he put the puzzle together.

"Please don't say anything Luca. It really doesn't matter. I just want him to go back to how he was treating me before."

"Breathe princess," he teased. "It's going to be fine, trust me. But I might just have to teach you a lesson about withholding talent like that," he leaned closer, squeezing my knee mischievously.

"Ooh, Mr Crescent, whatever do you mean?" I bit my lip at him, trying unsuccessfully to hide my grin.

"That sweet ass is going to pay for your deceit... in exactly three hours and fifteen minutes he said, examining his watch.

"But right now, Charlie, I'm interested in seeing some more of your work. And if you have ideas for our current campaigns, I want to hear them. No more hiding your talent."

Pinch me because I must be dreaming.

My heart swelled with gratitude. Thanks, and possibly a little love, for the man in front of me who didn't bat an eyelid at me helping a colleague with their creative ideas. For the man who got my foot in the door when every other company said no. For the man who now wanted me to share a whole other part of myself with him, and to help me take those baby steps towards my life-long career goal. There was no way this day could get any better... well unless Luca's promises included some spanking and a night of orgasms.

Guess I'd find out in a little over three hours... sooner if I had anything to do with it. But first things first. Time to show off my portfolio and maybe mention a few ideas I desperately wanted to bring up at that last meeting.

CHAPTER 18

LUCA SEEMED GENUINELY impressed with my portfolio, and my, how'd he put it? *'Tenacity to multitask and time manage like a woman possessed'*. He'd even made me advertising assistant on his latest project with *Laurent Leisure Wear*. As a trial, of course. But I found myself getting wholly wrapped up in that aspect of advertising again. And by God it felt good. I was spending more time on little tasks for that client, and possibly slacking off on some of my other EA jobs if I was being completely honest. But I didn't want to fuck it up, especially if this was my one-chance to prove my abilities.

All in all, it had been a fantastic few weeks and I was on cloud-fucking-nine! Work was going well, Lizzie had jumped into the Johnny pool with both feet, and Luca and my relationship was next-level orgasmic. He had started introducing me to a few of his fetishes and kinks, and there was no going back now. Everything I thought was wilder than just monotone sex in the past, was well dull, colourless and utterly boring. I was reborn. I had just taken my training wheels off and now I wanted to fly high, soar the wide-open skies with Luca. What more could a girl want?

Ding!

At the sound of the elevator stopping at the Penthouse floor, my head shot up, a welcoming smile plastered on it in habit. I felt the colour drain from my face, my heart sinking down, deep into my stomach. But I'm sure the smile stayed on my face, frozen in place by shock.

She can't be fucking serious? What the hell was she doing here?

Swaying her hips as if in slow motion, bright and bubbly Rose Tyler walked straight towards me.

"Hello again ah, Charlotte, right?" she smiled and I swear her teeth dazzled like a fucking *Colgate Ultra Brite* ad.

"Yes," I coughed, making my smile reach even further across my face. "How have you been Ruby?"

"Ah Rose, Rose Tyler... remember? We met at the Awards," she chimed, annoyance flickering in her tone, and a small frown trying to appear on her Botoxed forehead.

Ha! Priceless, Charlie 1: Rose 0.

"Sorry, yes, that's right. Rose from Lester and Co. Are you here for an appointment?" I answered, turning my attention to the computer to look through Luca's calendar.

"No," she giggled. "I'm on a personal errand today. Can you let Luca know I'm here please?"

My poise jumped out the window, boarded a plane for Paris and left me staring at Rose with my mouth wide open. Her face transformed as she turned away from the desk to sit casually on the chaise, looking like the cat who swallowed the canary.

Charlie 1: Rose 1. Goddammit.

I put the phone to my ear and dialled Luca's extension. Still looking towards Rose.

"Hi, Mr Crescent—"

"Mr Crescent, what have I told you about calling me that princess?" he interrupted, seduction swimming in his voice.

"I have a Rose Tyler here to see you," I continued flatly, peeling my eyes away from her to stare at my computer screen.

"What? Rose. Did she say why she was here? I don't have her in my scheduler. Are we supposed to have an appointment with Lester and Co.?" he shot question after question at me, sounding just as confused as I was.

"Ah no, she said she was here on a personal errand," I

lowered my voice, "should I send her in?"

Silence. "Luca?" I whispered. "Ah no, no that's fine. I'll be out in a few minutes," he coughed, and the line went dead.

I relayed the message to Rose and excused myself to pick up documents from downstairs. I needed to get out of there and had no desire to watch her flirt again. My head was spinning. I trusted Luca, but the look on her face sent shivers up my spine. She was like a dog in heat, and she wanted Luca back. I could feel it in my bones.

I waited for the elevator doors to shut and sent it hurdling straight down to the ground floor with a swipe of my keycard and its VIP ability to bypass every other level. No passing go and collecting two hundred dollars. Straight down to the bowels of hell. Well, the bowels of my own private hell in this fucked up, over thinking, catastrophising mind of mine.

I shut my eyes tight, breathing in long and deep, then blew out the panic. Slowly. Loudly, with controlled practice, one breath at a time.

"I am in control."
"I breathe in calm, I breathe out anxiety."
"All is well."
                              Breathe Charlie. Breathe.

I could feel the elevator car slow as it neared the ground. With one more big breath, I let my eyes open up, looking down to my outstretched hands, palms up, calm, not a tremor in sight. I spent the next twenty minutes walking around a few blocks, letting my mind trail with the 'what if' possibilities. But at least my inner voice was on my side this time, reminding me how amazing every second was that I spent with Luca.

When I returned to Crescent Inc., the Penthouse lobby was empty. I dawdled forward, noticing the boardroom was empty as well. "Jane?" I called out. "Just down here," she sang back from the direction of Stephan's office. "Coming."

"Hey, where have you been miss? I finished going over

Brad's appointments with him for tomorrow, and when I came back you were gone," she scowled, hands on her hips.

"I uh, just had to drop off a few things to the cleaners and wanted to get there before the lunch rush. Is Luca still in?" I asked walking around the desk to my chair.

"No, Rose took him to lunch. He said you knew," she hesitated at the last words, tilting her head to the side.

"Of course, that's right," I said with a smile, which I'm sure didn't reach my eyes.

"Well come on, no point in the two of us just sitting here waiting for our illustrious leaders to return, we deserve a lunch break too," she bounced forward, grabbing her bag and outstretching her hand for me to grab.

Luca didn't return to the office after his lunch date. But I knew he had a planned meeting out of the city, which would keep him late into the evening.

But I swear to the Gods, the circus must have rolled into town on the wind, because the shit show just kept on coming. I had a bunch of prank calls over the next couple of days to keep me appropriately annoyed, and I swear in one of them I heard the caller whisper "*fuck it*". Rose returned mid-week to take Luca to lunch *AGAIN*. And again, he didn't reject her offer.

Now I consider myself to sit above all the petty crap and as such I was trying my dang hardest to not go into full-blown meltdown mode. After all, he was still his usual warm self towards me. But you know what?… I wasn't born yesterday. And this ball of sass is no naïve little girl. Something had changed. The tectonic plates were shifting right under my fucking feet and my fight or flight was kicking in.

Was it just my own insecurities? Possibly.

Was my own baggage and colourful past making me doubt where I stood in this so-called relationship? You better believe it. But I'm not playing these games, not again. Nope, not even for a sexy-as-fuck millionaire.

I got deep in my head for the umpteenth time that week. *You just have to ask him what's going on Charlie. Tonight. You owe each other that. Stop pussy footing around.*

I'm not pussy footing around. It's just… it's just — complicated.

Ha, tell that to someone who isn't yourself. What would Lola say?

She'd give him a chance to explain. I can hear her now. 'Let's hear him out Charlie bear, but if I get even a hint of a lying, cheating bastard in there – off with his manhood! I'm not joking, I watch all the true crimes, I know how to bury a body, and get away with it.'

After a few hours of working on auto-pilot while my mind played endless reruns, reliving the chats, lunches, and sexcapades we'd enjoyed, I pulled myself back to the present and boosted my fragile self back up. I've gotta admit, I'm impressed with how strong my pre-game speech was. *Goooooo team Charlie!* A bit of internal dialogue and I was ready to play the bad cop, wear him down, maybe torture him a little, and find out the 411. No more tiptoeing around.

Ding!

Luca: Sorry Charlie, the deal with Rouchester is going south fast. I'm flying to their head office now to see if I can save it. I should be back tomorrow afternoon.

What the heck, can he read minds now? I make plans to sit him down and have a couples talk and he'd rather jump a plane. Seriously?! Stay calm Charlie.

Charlie: Sure, no worries. Is there anything I can do?
Luca: Cancel my meetings for tomorrow, but go to the appointment with Laurent on my behalf and present our recent updates for approval.
Charlie: Of course.
Luca: (…)

Goddammit, I hate those three little flashing dots.

Luca: Sorry princess. I'll make it up to you (wink face)

Well, fuck me. Just when I think I've got it all figured out, he goes and puts me into a tailspin. Again.

I don't want to jump to conclusions, but failing to return after two lunches with Rose can't be a coincidence. Alarm bells are ringing left, right and centre. And they're getting louder. And you know what? I think I'm ready to pay attention.

I was sitting at lunch the next day when Brad came and found me. "Hi Charlie, mind if I sit?"

"Of course not," I smiled back. "How's everything going?"

"I'm good, but I just got off the phone to Luca. Sounds like he is really struggling trying to talk the client off the ledge," he shook his head as he shovelled a forkful of some kind of exotic-looking beef salad into his mouth.

I looked back down to my plate, "do you know what the problem is? It's not something to do with the presentation or organisation for their campaign is it?" I questioned, worried for the first time that this drama could be because of something I had done.

"No, no, I'm sure it's to do with creative differences or something stupid like wanting to compromise on costs after

156

contracts were signed."

"What? They wouldn't—"

"You'd be surprised, happens more than you'd think. Fucking cheap skates. You pay for the product quality, plain and simple. And we provide services of the highest level," he smirked, raising his chin to the sky. I couldn't help but laugh, he definitely had a way to lower your walls.

"Anyway, I'm sorry to be the messenger, but since he's kissing a lot of ass right now, Luca asked me to let you know he won't be back this week. Needs to spend a few more days wining and dining Mr and Mrs pain-in-the-ass."

"Yeh of course. Thanks for letting me know Brad," I squeezed his hand before standing. "I better get back to it, see you up there."

I tried calling Luca when I got back to my desk, grabbing my phone and slipping into the empty meeting room. It rang, and rang, and rang. But no answer.

Charlie: Hey Luca, just checking in to make sure everything's okay. Feel like we've been worlds apart this week.

I left it a minute, hoping to see those three little flashing dots of an incoming reply. But nothing. Then I chanced one more message.

Charlie: Miss you.

I finished off organising the key people for Laurent's photoshoot after our meeting. Still radio silence from Luca. Then, like a pathetic little obsessed puppy, I tried dialling his number again. This time it went straight to voicemail. I dropped my phone on the desk, probably louder than it had to be and let out a sigh I'd been holding in.

"Everything okay?"

"Shit!" I jumped in surprise at the shock of a voice so close. "Sorry, I thought I was alone," I laughed nervously,

157

looking up to meet Stephan's eyes. I'd never noticed before, but they were the most beautiful mix of chocolate and honey brown. Framed by thick dark lashes and brows. Jane wasn't wrong, he was flipping gorgeous, and I bet he played it for all it was worth.

He leaned forward, half sitting on the edge of my desk. "Listen Charlotte, I wanted to apologise. I've been a dick—"

"Don't be silly," I interrupted.

"No, it's okay, I was. I can admit it. And I really am sorry Charlotte." Honey dripped off my name as it left his mouth. What a fucking smooth talker. I was thankful for his apology. I just wish it was Luca saying those words to me. "I should have given credit where credit was due. I wouldn't have received such a good reaction and had that light bulb moment on where to take the pitch without you. Thank you," he gave a crooked smile, giving my forearm a soft squeeze.

"Umm, thank you. That means a lot," I smiled back, confused that this A-grade douchebag had another side I hadn't seen before.

"Let me take you out for a bite, as a peace offering."

"Oh God there's no need for that, honestly you're forgiven," I chuckled. "Just don't do it again."

"Oh come on, you can't forgive me that easily. I've been ignoring you and making your life difficult here. Please let me buy you dinner. Strictly platonic," he begged with puppy dog eyes, raising his hands in jest. Then grabbed his white pocket square and motioned waving a white flag.

"Okay, okay. You can stop," I laughed. "Dinner sounds lovely. But let's make it an early bite – I'm starving," I exaggerated, rubbing my belly.

"Perfect, I'll go grab my things. Early mark approved by the boss. P.S. I'm the boss," he hummed, leaving a lingering smile as he turned and walked towards his office.

CHAPTER 19

"WOW, THIS IS cute. How'd you find it?" I asked Stephan, impressed with the homely little Italian restaurant tucked away down a Greenwich Village alley.

"I know right, *Nonna's Gnocchi* is one of my fave local spots. It's my little secret getaway where I can disappear out of the limelight and just enjoy being JoBlo," he smiled, a sparkle in his eyes. "Come on, you're gonna love the pastas,"

"Oh shit, I didn't ask if you're a coeliac or if you eat carbs?" he stopped in his tracks, looking at me with worried wild eyes.

"Only all the time," I chuckled. "It's one of my staples."

"You had me worried for a split second. I might've had to send you on your way and eat alone if you said no," he smirked, raising an eyebrow in my direction.

Stephan surprised me. Sure, he was a flirt first and foremost. But he was full of interesting conversation and wasn't afraid to ask questions. Seriously, the man had no filter. We chatted and laughed and ate at least four-courses while enjoying a couple of bottles of red. Without even realising I was letting my guard down. I didn't want to impress him, I didn't care what he thought about me. And it felt weirdly freeing.

"So what's going on with you and Mr Big Boss man?" He looked at me through his dark lashes, alternating between watching the wine swirl around the glass in his hand and me.

"We're…." I hesitated.

"Mmm-hmm"

"We're seeing each other. But we're still really just getting to know each other. Do you know what I mean? There are still so many things I don't know about Luca, and that he doesn't know about me. It's still very… fresh."

"Pray tell."

"Oh God no, I don't think I'm ready to spill any more beans to you Mr Hewitt," I admitted, suddenly feeling a little too warm in the cheeks from that last glass of Chianti.

"No, it's not like that Charlie," he shook his head. "I don't need to know how many different ways you and Luca are doing it. I mean, don't get me wrong, I'm not a prude and if you wanna share the dirty deets I'm all ears," he whispered, as if sharing a precious secret. "But it's not what I was after. I'm just curious what things you haven't shared with him yet. And I've been told I'm a good listener," he leaned closer, covering my hand with his.

"Wow. You're really going for it aren't you?" I grinned. "Thanks, but no thanks. Not tonight okay. I've had a surprisingly nice dinner out with you and you are without a doubt forgiven," I nodded. "But it's getting late and we should probably call it a night."

Without trying to convince me otherwise, he stood and led us out. Quickly paying before I'd caught up to him.

"Hey, I would have contributed towards that impressive banquet," I smacked at his arm.

"Nonsense. This was my treat, remember… my olive branch," he winked, grabbing my hand and moving us out into the alleyway. "You said you lived a few blocks from here. Do you want me to walk you home?"

"No, no. Think I'll grab a cab, my legs are feeling a little jelly-like," I giggled as we approached the street. "That Chianti just went down so easily and will definitely go on my regular drinks list now."

"No worries, I'll call you a cab."

"And they say chivalry is dead," I quipped.

Before I could recover from my wisecrack, laughter still caught in my chest, the look on Stephan's face dropped. He stared at me, a small crease between his brows, as though he was trying to read my mind and peel away the layers. He stepped closer, slowly reaching out to palm my cheek. My mind struggled to catch up to what was happening in the moment. Before I could react, Stephan lowered his head, his mouth covering mine. His lips were full and unbelievably soft against mine. The warmth and sweetness of his breath confused me, and I found myself relaxing into him when I should have been pulling back. He slid a hand to the back of my neck as his tongue licked along the seam until I opened, inviting him in. His gentle kiss found strength, becoming more passionate, hungrier and full of intent.

I pulled away in panic, placing my hands on his chest, creating some distance between us. "We can't do this Stephan," I exhaled.

"Why not? Tell me this doesn't feel good," he tempted, covering my hands with his.

"I—I, it's late Stephan and we've both had too much to drink. It's just some liquid courage spurred on by friendly banter," I assured him, pulling a hand free to flag an approaching cab.

"We wined, we dined, we became friends. That's all," I smiled, planting a quick peck on his cheek. "Goodnight Stephan." I dashed towards the cab, jumping in before he could say anything more to confuse me. I rattled off my address to the driver and slumped back into the seat. I blinked slowly, wondering how the fuck I'd let that happen.

What was that? I mean it was nice, but why didn't I pull away instantly? Shit, why did I let that happen or, worse, did I invite that? No. I wouldn't. Or maybe Stephan knows something more than he's telling me about Luca and Rose, and that's why he made a move.

Has Luca moved on? Why are things so fucking confusing?

I pulled my phone out of my bag, and absentmindedly

dialled Luca's number. My heart began racing, waiting for him to pick up. I wasn't even sure what I would say. "Hi, you've reached Luca Crescent, I'm not available right now. Leave your—"

I hung up, imagining him doing all the things he promised he'd do to me with his perfect Rose. "Fucking Rose," I whispered to myself.

Goddammit, why won't he answer my calls.

Luca turned up to work mid-morning on Tuesday. Storming into the office, phone to his ear, looking rugged and unkempt. Something was definitely up. He maintained his radio silence for the last few days, giving me way too much time to make some plans of my own. He was unravelling me and I had no intentions to fall back into the big black hole I knew too well. Just sinking, waiting to be rescued. Not again. Not ever. I needed to distance myself from him. Jump off the rollercoaster.

Luca locked himself in his office for most of the day. After lunch Brad and Stephan came storming out of Luca's office, heated words flying between them. "It's not the end of the world Crescent, just another fucking hit," Stephan said as he opened Luca's office door. "It's not just that and you fucking know it. Just go and do your job Hewitt and I'll sort this shit out," Luca growled as they walked out.

I spun away quickly, making myself busy with the filing drawers. Brad and Stephan mumbled to each other as they headed straight for the elevator. My phone rang, an internal call from Luca flashing on my display.

"Ah, hi," I whispered. "Can I do something for you?"

"I need all the files we have on Rouchester on my desk as soon as you can. I need to see what I've sold my soul for." The anger dripped off every word. And I didn't know how to soothe him.

"Not a problem," I said cheerfully, but spitting venom in my head.

"And prepare the meeting room for a four o'clock meeting with Lester and Co. please," he sighed, his voice cracking, somewhere between surrender and defeat.

This just keeps getting better and better.

"How many shall I set up for?"

"I don't know Charlie. Five, six. I don't have time for stupid questions right now. I'm sure you can figure it out," he snapped.

The phone went dead. And I'd just been put in my place.

Don't forget you're just an assistant Charlie.

Obviously, there were some issues happening with the client, but to be treated like the scum on the bottom of his shoe… *I don't fucking think so.*

I did as he asked, preparing the meeting room and pulling the files together that he asked for. I took some steadying breaths and knocked on his office door, determined to pull him up here and now.

"Come in."

I strode in, head held high and shut the door behind me. He kept his eyes on the papers in his hands, not bothering to acknowledge me, apologise for his absence or his behaviour, or jump my bones to take out his anger in some hot, cranky office sex.

"Luca," I said gently, not wanting to cause any unnecessary rage. Not even a flicker. I moved closer, putting a little more volume in my words. "Luca, look at me."

He lowered his papers, raising his head to look at me. He raised an arm, brushing a hand through his hair, by habit rather than to tidy up any unruly hair. His eyes lowered to the files in my hands and he automatically put his out towards them.

"Thanks for pulling those. I can't tell you how royally fucked up these clients are. I don't know how, but they've found some loophole to fucking take us for a ride."

I handed him the papers, taking a seat in the chair opposite him. "Luca, what's going on? Not with the client, but with you. With you and me?" I asked, sick of the last week and how he'd made me feel.

"I don't know Charlie. There's been a lot going on and I don't have time to play happy house right now," he shot coldly.

I watched, half in shock, half not surprised that I was being let down again. He stood up and began pacing back and forward behind his desk, not attempting to close the gap between us. "I've let a lot of business decisions and tasks fall by the wayside while we've been fucking around lately, and now my company is suffering. I need to focus on my work Charlie, not a relationship. Not now…. I'm sorry."

I bit my lip, tasting the subtle hint of blood on my tongue. I nodded, giving myself time to find the right words, words that weren't reactive.

"I'd never want your businesses to suffer for me, or because of me. Luca, I wouldn't want any part of your life suffering as a result of me. But I have never pushed for any commitment. Hell, I can't even put a label on whatever this is," I gestured between us, fire filling my belly. "But don't you dare blame me for any failing business deals. I've never asked you to spend every waking moment with me and ignore your duties. That's bullshit and you know it."

All the feelings were bubbling up and desperate to get out, sick of being bottled up. "Maybe you should question yourself on the time you've been spending with Rose, not me."

"Rose—"

"You know what, I actually don't want to hear it right now," I said, putting my hand up to silence him. "I just came to remind you that I have leave booked from tomorrow. I have handed over my upcoming duties to Jane and she will be at your beck and call."

His mouth hung open like a stunned mullet. Like he wasn't sure if he was going to say something. He straightened, hands coming up to rest on his hips as he nodded slowly.

"See you in a week and a half," I breathed, internally telling my heart to slow down and stay in my chest where it belonged, and walked out with a little more sass in my step than usual.

Lizzie and I had early flights booked for the next morning, a tradition we started when we met. Our birthdays were a day apart, well one year and one day to be exact, and we had made it a promise to spend our birthday week away every year, relaxing in some exotic place around the world. This year we were heading to Hawaii, and it honestly couldn't come at a better time.

We finished packing that night after dinner, and I listened as Lizzie rambled about the week that was. She was sure she'd found the next best-selling romance writer and couldn't put down her steamy forbidden love page-turner. She was seeing Johnny every other day now, and was completely smitten with the Southern cowboy.

But her little smitten kitten Scott was still in the picture and trying to win her back. And her self-defence classes were growing in popularity and the gym wanted her to teach a few more classes. Life was interesting. Life was good. Well good for Lizzie at least. With alarms set for five a.m., we called it quits at ten and headed for bed.

###

I stood in the middle of a long straight road, woods all around me and a bright moon in the sky. I could see my breath in front of me with every exhale. Wrapping my arms around my body trying to keep warm, I looked desperately around for any signs of life. A car, a house, a gas station. Nothing. 'Hello, is anyone there?' I called out. I ran down the road, squinting in the dark, straining to see something familiar. 'Hello. Anyone? Where am I?' I ran further, my feet turning over robotically, but nothing around me changed. Finally, I spotted a hut up ahead with a small light coming from one of the windows. I ran towards it, listening to the gravel crunch beneath my shoes. The hut looked familiar in its shadows, but I couldn't remember the deep dark woods surrounding it. Voices. Words drifted in the dark towards me as I approached. 'Ethan she needs us. She's all alone.' 'You know I wish we could, but we can't Maggie. We have to trust she'll find her way.' 'But she's our baby. Please Ethan, we have to find a way.' A tear rolled down my cheek and a lump caught in my throat. It couldn't be. But it was. I raced up the front step, twisting the door handle, letting the door creak loudly as I opened it. 'Mum. Dad.' I cried standing on the threshold. 'No Charlie, stop, you can't be here.' Ma sounded panicked, standing with both her hands up in front of her. 'Stay where you are. Don't take another step, you mustn't.' 'But why, I've missed you both so much,' I wept. 'My little Charlie Bear, you can't be here, but know we're always watching over you, sending all our strength to you and we love you so so much.' 'I love you too dad.' The tears were flowing as I was pulled back, a force sending me skidding in the dirt. Left on my knees, I stared up at my parents in the doorway. 'But why? Why can't I hug you? I need you—'

###

A warm hand was on my face, wiping the tears off my cheek. A soft whisper trying to get through to me. "Charlie honey, I'm here. I've got you. I'm here Charlie, please wake up. I need you to come back to me."

The blackness shifted, tugged away in a vortex. I blinked a few times, my eyes stinging from crying. I could see the early light of the Spring morning glowing through the blinds. And two bright blue eyes looking down at me, lined with tears of their own. "Lizzie," I whimpered. "I saw them. And they saw me. This was more than a dream, I swear," I cried, rolling into her, letting the waterworks take over.

"Oh honey, you know it wouldn't be a real vacay if it didn't start with one of us in hysterics. Just means this break was needed and it will be a healing holiday. Now let it out. Let it all out," she soothed, kissing the top of my head.

CHAPTER 20

THE SUN WAS shining, the sky glass blue and the holiday vibe was alive and well. After about 12 hours in the sky, plus a quick stop off at Arizona, we had finally made it. *Aloha Hawaii!* And you never would have guessed we'd been globetrotting and awake since five a.m. — well four, thanks to my little nightmare/out of body experience – with how hyped and alive we both were. And thanks to the time difference, we had stolen three hours back and some extra rays of sun. I know we'd eventually have to give it back, but for right now, it was a gift.

Just like this little yearly holiday tradition, Lizzie and I had incorporated our own take on a brief sun salutation to offer our thanks to light and life at the beginning of our vacay. Stepping out of the airport we moved off the path and away from the other travellers, parking our suitcases at our feet. Without a single word uttered we turned to face each other, then took a step backwards to rest hands on the other's shoulders. After a long, steady inhale and exhale, we stood in mountain pose and let our eyes fall shut. Leaning back, extending our arms over our heads we inhaled deeply again. Bringing our arms down into prayer hands we blew out slowly. Then with slow purpose, we moved our arms up towards the sun, still in prayer, inhaling as we went. I said my silent prayer, expressing my gratitude for life and all its experiences as I brought my hands back down to meet in front of my chest.

Opening my eyes, Lizzie stood there, a mirror reflection looking back at me with a big smile on her face.

"Ready?" I breathed, a goofy excited look taking over my face.

"You bet your bottom dollar," she said, leaning down to collect her suitcase and leading the way to the taxi stand.

"Aloha and welcome to Maui, Hawaii," our cheery driver greeted. "I'm Keona. Where to ladies?" he asked, lifting our cases into the trunk.

"Wailea Beach Resort," Lizzie sung back.

"Ah, nice choice. How long are you visiting for?"

The drive went by quickly with Lizzie and Keona chatting like lifelong friends. Keona gave us all the inside goss, letting us know which beaches to hit up to get away from other tourists, the best places to eat and some experiences off the beaten track.

"Thank you so much Keona, you have been an absolute gift to us," Lizzie kissed him on his cheek as she handed over our fare.

"Ah Miss Lizzie, don't let my ohana hear you say that," he chuckled.

"Why's that?" she raised her eyebrows.

"Keona means God's gracious gift and if they were to hear someone say that, there's no way they'll let me get away with my devilish ways," he shook his head, laughing to himself. "A Hui Hou Mizz Lizzie and Miss Charlie."

I smiled back at Keona, a small frown wrinkling my brow as I tried to work out what he had said to us.

"Don't frown pretty girl," he laughed. "Until we meet again," he winked as he drove off.

"Hawaii is ah-mayyy-zingggggg!" Lizzie sang, falling back

on the bed. "I'm moving here, honestly. I just need a little investment money to start up my own little boutique publishing house and a bungalow on the beach and I'm all set."

"I hear ya. Though I'm not sure I'm quite ready for the island life just yet. But make sure your little bungalow has a spare bed and I'll come visit all the time," I said, slipping on a little summer dress and some lipgloss for tonight's lūʻau.

So far we had relaxed in the resort pool, lounged in deckchairs on the beach, snorkelled around the reef and swam with turtles, made friends with a few local boys who shared a magical secret waterfall with us (or so they said), and drank our weight in cocktails. Life. Was. Good. And I'd hardly had a spare moment to think about Luca and the shit show that was my love life. Damn, okay, well right up until this second.

Sitting at one of the group tables at the feast, Lizzie sipped on a Maui Island Breeze Cocktail, while I enjoyed a Hawaiian Mai Tai, a little quicker than usual, since becoming a well-practised day drinker this week.

"Whoa, you inhaled that," Lizzie laughed.

"Hey, if a girl can't drink to her heart's content on vacay, then when the hell can she?" I hiccupped. My display of apparent early-onset intoxication was followed by uncontrollable laughter. "Sorry, I'm not tipsy, that hiccup just decided to happen exactly at the wrong time."

"No judging!" Lizzie smiled, putting her hands up in peace.

Once the giggling had died down, Lizzie's face became serious. She pursed her lips and furrowed her brow. "So are we gonna talk about it?"

"I don't know what you mean," I swatted her away. "Like I told you, Luca isn't interested in building a relationship or playing happy house. And he's made up his mind to go back to his skanky ex," I made a face.

I didn't give Lizzie a chance to try to make me feel better.

I liked the edge of this anger, it made me feel. Feel alive. And it pushed me forward instead of down a deep dark abyss. "Look, it was fun while it lasted, but I'm done Lizzie. I can't rely on a guy again only to be let down when I need them, because let's be honest, I'm a chaotic fucking mess after losing my family, and it's not going to change. Not now, and probably never."

"Okay. I hear you. Not gonna push baby girl. Especially not on your *birthday!*" she shouted the last word.

As if on cue, two of the dancers came up the aisle, pulling me from my seat and up on stage, tying a grass skirt around my waist and placing a flower halo atop my wild and out-of-hand curls. I pointed to Lizzie and told them it was her birthday too and in an instant she was up on stage with me. We danced, they sang, and the other guests cheered and clapped along. Before letting us go back to our seats, one of the fire dancers stood behind me, his ripped sweaty body against my back. He held my arms out and directed me on how to twirl a firestick down my arms. It was crazy, scary and exhilarating. At one point I could feel the hairs on my arms singe and *I loved it.*

We kept the party going into the early hours of the next morning, sleeping until close to noon. After a cold shower to wash off the morning humidity and the hangover from hell, I sat on our deck in an oversized t-shirt, sipping on an extra strong coffee. By the time I had my second cup in hand, Lizzie crawled out like a lizard, lying on the deck chair next to me.

"Happy Birthdaayyyyy!" I sung.

"Oh. My. Gerrdddd. I think this is a new PB for hangovers, but thank you," she scowled, opening and shutting her mouth tasting her furry tongue. "Ewwww. I need a shower, to brush my teeth half a dozen times and an extra-large bottle of mouth wash."

She stood to walk back inside, "and while I do that, can you pretty please make me one of those extra strong coffees of yours wifey?" She blew me a kiss and stumbled towards the bathroom.

I made coffee as requested and phoned the kitchen to get some lunch sent to the room. Thank God they served all-day breakfast here, because we were in serious need of a greasy breakfast with extra crispy bacon and soft eggs to soak up some of the booze.

I had it all set up outside before Lizzie popped her head outside again, looking and smelling a heck of a lot better. "Oh my God, you would make the perfect wife, have I told you that before? Honestly, Charlie, be mine," she begged, wrapping her arms around my shoulders from behind and peppering butterfly kisses across my forehead and cheek.

"Ha ha, you know I'm yours. I don't need a ring to prove it," I leaned my head back against hers.

We ate in silence, washing the food down with coffee first, then freshly squeezed OJ when that was gone. Now feeling a little closer to human than reanimated zombies, we popped on sarongs and hats and made our way down to the water's edge for a walk.

"I know we've been ignoring our boy problems, and I'm very aware that's my coping mechanism, so no psychoanalysing me, okay. But I think we have to talk about them or we're going to take the same issues back home with us," I admitted.

"I think you're right. Wanna go first?"

"No, you first. I already spilled most of my beans, but I'm curious what's going on in that head of yours Liz. What are you going to do about Johnny and Scott?"

"Johnny and I are going well. *Really* well. We are just getting to know each other, in and out, and it's fun, and freeing and fabulous," she grinned. "We connect on multiple levels. But Scott keeps calling and messaging saying he wants us to give it another shot. And I feel like I've hurt him," she said, brows furrowing. "He's a good guy and I wish he would move on and let some other woman treat him like a God. He deserves that. He doesn't really want me, he just wants a girl to settle down with. A Mary Jane that will love him and be content to live their lives on repeat. Gosh that sounds bitchy... but does that make sense or am I completely bonkers?" she shook her head, letting the ocean wash further up her calves.

"You are completely bonkers Lizzie Ryan, but not in a bad way," I joked. "People come into our lives for a reason, a season or a lifetime. See me, I'm with you for life. Sorry, I'm stuck like glue and there's no getting rid of me," I bumped her hip with mine. But I think Scott came into yours for a season, to offer something new and exciting for a short period of time. And as for Johnny—"

"Let me guess, a reason," she huffed.

"Maybe. Jury's still out, and it's still too new to tell, he could be any of the three. But you've had chemistry from day dot and I know you felt it, even if you laughed it off as innocent flirting."

"Mmm, there's always been something, I admit it. And now being with him makes me a little scared. Well scared's not the right word, maybe more nervous."

I spotted a nice shaded spot under a tree and diverted in that direction. "Nervous because this is different, or like that usual new-relationship nerves?" I asked, pulling Lizzie with me towards the tree.

"Different. Deeper. Exciting. Better," she sighed. "He lets me explore my desires with him at home and at House of Himeros. It is so easy to share the good and bad things about my life with him and he makes me feel safe. He feels like home, how cringe is that," she laughed, pulling a face.

"Not cringey at all," I smiled, pulling her in for a squeeze.

"Wow," Lizzie sighed. "That was cathartic. Now spill. What are you gonna do about Luca?" she said, sitting down to lean against the oversized tree out of Avatar that must have been thousands of years old.

I let out a heavy sigh, dropping down to sit beside her and

175

lay my head back to look up at the thick foliage. "He's been distancing himself from me for the last couple of weeks, and there was a moment in our last conversation where it felt so final. He blames me for taking him away from his work-saturated life and that's such a dick move," I answered, becoming a little louder as the frustration burst out.

"I get it, that's not okay on any level. I can't stand people who don't take responsibility for their own actions. Boils my blood," she said.

"Me too," I sighed again. "And there's something else... you know how I mentioned exec Stephan was giving me the cold shoulder after I helped him out?"

"Yeh..."

"Well he apologised and took me out for dinner and drinks as a peace offering."

"Yeeessss," Lizzie questioned, leaning closer.

"And he kissed me. I broke the kiss," I hurriedly added, "but I think I actually kissed him back first. We were tipsy and getting along and it just happened as we were saying goodbye."

"Well shut the front door. How did you keep that from me?" she mused. "Do you think that's got anything to do with Luca pulling away?"

"No, I don't think Stephan would have said anything and Luca didn't allude to knowing. It's not like I want to keep it a secret, but we haven't even spoken about the funk between us, let alone Rose or Stephan."

"Do you like him?

"Who Stephan?" I paused. "No, not like that. I think we would get along as friends and he is unashamedly gorgeous and might even be a good kisser. But I'm happy ending it before it begins. I can only foresee heartache with that player."

"And I love Luca. Or I was falling in love with him. But I'm not going to be a punching bag to take unwarranted blame for any man."

"A-fucking-men sister," Lizzie howled. "So, what are you going to do?"

"I'm going to see if any other agencies have an opening and create some space. I can't move on and find myself if I'm around him every day," I said, watching the leaves sway hypnotizingly in the breeze.

Saying it out loud, I knew wholeheartedly that's exactly what I had to do. If we got over this little bump in the road, there'd undoubtedly be another one down the track that would probably tear us apart. And by then I'd be completely head-over-heels and in need of saving, and he would leave. They always do.

CHAPTER 21

THE DAY WE returned home I made calls to a few people at other advertising agencies that I'd met at the Awards night. Bess from *Perception* had offered me an interview on the spot. Her agency wasn't as big as Crescent Incorporated, but it had been going from strength to strength for the past seven years since establishment and was now looking to expand. Thankfully, the last two months immersed in advertising had taught me a thing or two and sparked my creativity again. Enough so that I'd landed a new job *and* a promotion to boot. I, Charlotte Drake, was Perception's newest ad campaign manager. Someone up there must be watching over me.

After six drafts and a little help from Lizzie, I deleted the waffle and made my resignation letter short and sweet. Now I just had to hand it to the man of my previous dreams. The last few days in the office had been awkward as all hell. Luca had reverted to calling me Charlotte, and at times Miss Drake, as cold as ice, as though he hadn't seen me naked or fucked in every room in his house. But I didn't bite. I didn't get angry, in fact I was beginning to feel numb in his presence. Like I was having an out-of-body experience, watching on as I floated above the room.

So walking in on Thursday morning shouldn't have been any different, resignation letter in hand. But it was. Let's be honest, I'm not a cold fish and Luca means something to me, even if I don't to him.

"Charlie, are you okay? I've said your name like three times, and you've been miles away," Jane said, gently stirring my arm.

"Yeh, of course," I smiled.

Stop closing yourself off. Jane is a friend. Tell her.

"Sorry that was a lie," I blurted, turning my chair towards her. "I know you and everyone around here knows things have changed between Luca and me, and well, it's becoming difficult to work together."

"Mmm, I get it. When Stephan and I broke it off, it was awkward and uncomfortable. But it got better over time and now look at us."

"I know. But I don't think I can do that. No, I *know* I can't do that, nor do I want to," I breathed. "I'm handing in my notice Jane. I'm sorry, I can't stay."

"Oh don't. Please. We can make it work, maybe we can see if you and I can switch execs," she offered hopefully.

"No, no. It's fine Jane. I have another job to go to and this doesn't mean you and I won't still be friends. But I need distance. Clarity. And Luca shouldn't have to feel awkward to come to work. To his business, the company he grew from the ground up. That's not fair either," I shrugged.

"Agh. Why do you have to make sense?" she sighed.

"Thanks for understanding Jane, it's been a blast working with you and I'm so glad to have met you and become friends," I smiled warmly, squeezing her arms. "Now do me a favour, and don't say anything to anyone until I've had a chance to speak to Luca."

She mimed locking her lips and throwing away the key before leaning forward in her chair, knee-to-knee with me, pulling me in for a tight hug.

I looked at Luca's schedule and decided to make a beeline for him when he returned from his catch-up with the art department.

Knock, knock.

"Come in," Luca called out.

I took a deep breath in and held it while I entered his office, leaving the door open behind me. I breathed out slowly, moving towards his desk, stretching out my hand as I neared. He took the piece of paper in it and began to read. The silence was deafening. My blood whooshed in my ears, loud enough I'm sure everyone on this floor could hear it.

"Charlie," he murmured. "You don't need to do this." He looked up, his eyes finally meeting mine for the first time in what felt like weeks. There was a glaze to those golden amber pools and for a second I wanted to lean in and caress his cheek. Comfort him and tell him he didn't need to give me anything but I would be there for him, no matter how long it took.

Stay strong Charlie. You need a clean break. It's time to move on. Trust that you're worth more.

"I do," I whispered, "I really do. And you deserve to be happy at work and at home. This is your baby, and I don't want to make it uncomfortable for you to be the amazing boss you are." I smiled at him, but I could feel the sadness in my eyes and my heart.

He cleared his throat and stood from his chair. I took a step back. Then another.

"Princess, take a seat. Let's talk about this," he pleaded.

I shook my head, swallowing hard, wishing the big lump in my throat away. "It's for the best," I said, back against his office doorway. "I'm happy to train up my replacement if you find someone before my two weeks is up, otherwise we both know Jane can do it with her eyes closed."

I nodded my head before turning around to walk out.

"Charlie…"

I looked back, seeing sadness and confusion on his face. I smiled gently, feeling that familiar crack in my heart. Then I turned and walked away from the man I loved.

Goodbye Luca.

181

###

Spring had definitely sprung. The weather was warming up, the days were longer and the crazy weather meant I'd been caught out in the rain on more than one occasion. I loved watching the store window displays transform throughout the year, spreading warmth and excitement, and putting smiles on little faces everywhere recently with the Easter decorations and now gorgeous bright displays for the upcoming annual Sakura Matsuri cherry blossom festival.

I had officially finished my last day at Crescent Incorporated, cleaning out my desk and handing back my staff access card. Luca started office happy hour at four-thirty to give me a send-off, letting everyone clock off a little early. I stayed for a glass of bubbly, chatting with Jane and a few other coworkers I'd become close with these last few months. And although the execs never came to these drinks, they all farewelled me in the penthouse giving warm hugs and best wishes. Luca had even broken the distance for the occasion, waiting for Stephan and Brad to walk off before embracing me, his warm breath swimming over my shoulder and neck as he whispered in the shell of my ear, words only for me. *"You'll always be my Little Lamb."*

Dropping my keys onto the hallway table, I dragged my feet towards the lounge room. Johnny was lying on the couch, legs hanging over the end, his head in Lizzie's lap, lazily watching some reality show.

"And just like that, you're free," Lizzie hollered, swinging her arms out to her sides as I came into sight.

"Babe," Johnny moaned. "How 'bout a little tact, she just walked away from the love of her life."

"He's not the love of my life," I shot back, turning towards the kitchen and grabbing out a bottle of chianti and a chilled wine glass.

182

"Come on darlin', don't forget I know both of you. You two connected from that first moment. He would have taken out all of those drunk brawling yahoos that night if I wasn't there to take care of it," he smirked, bringing up his arms and planting a kiss on each of his biceps.

"What—, you never told me you knew what happened that night," I said, shock making my voice jump an octave.

He let out a low laugh, somewhere deep in his belly. "I was at the back of the club with Luca, giving him an update on the patrons who had one too many—"

"Oh God, did that include me?" I panicked, falling into the seat next to them, eyes locked on Johnny.

"Well darlin' I always keep an eye on my girls, and that includes you and Lizzie. But no, you weren't part of my handover to the boss. But I will say, he was watching the guys kicking off near you and before a fight even broke out he told me to take the guys down while he saved the *princess*," he finished with a wink. Making that last word sound dirty.

"He did not…" I gaped, mouth falling open.

"Oh my God," Lizzie giggled. "I fucking knew it. That's why he came on so strong."

"You did not. And that's not why he kissed me," I shot back as her words sunk in. "Oh God, Johnny, tell me she's not right."

"How am I to say what is in another man's mind or heart. All I know is he seemed to be in tune with you and his hackles shot up when those guys came too close to you."

That's gonna make my mind spin around like it's on crack.
Fuck me.

I was surrounded by ink black sheets. My hands and feet secured in place, tied to each of the four corner posts of the King bed. A fireplace crackled in front of me and the familiar smell of leather and musk mixed

183

with timber and flames took over my senses. Strong hands slithered up my calves, sliding over my outer thighs, then slowly gliding inwards, thumbs leading the way up my soft inner thighs towards the slick wetness pooling. The ache and need grew, but the hands moved away, grabbing onto my hips as a soft mouth came down. His hot breath blew across my stomach, followed by a slow, lingering tongue. I looked down, a head full of thick dark hair blocking my view of his face. My breath hitched as he licked up my stomach to my sternum, a gentle scrape of stubble driving my senses wild. His hands fisted my breasts, squeezing, moulding, thumbs drawing circles across my diamonds for nipples. His body crushed against mine as he sucked my breast into his hungry mouth, making my back arch. Forcing me further into him. His hard cock pushed against my sensitive clit and I felt my arousal grow. I opened my eyes again, desperate to see his face, to look into his eyes. His head moved from one breast to the other and I could see the strong outline of Luca's jaw. I moaned in pleasure, desperate for his hands to roam down south again. 'Luca' I breathed. He pulled back from my breast, planting kisses along my collarbone and up my neck. His lips claimed mine, his warm tongue sliding along my seam, dipping in while waiting for an invitation. I kissed him deeply, desperately. Full of desire and wanting. He broke the kiss and I pulled in a deep breath, opening my eyes once more, only to be met with the most beautiful mix of chocolate and honey-brown eyes framed by thick dark lashes and brows. Stephan.

CHAPTER 22

I HAD DISTANCED myself, unintentionally, from Crescent Inc and by association, Jane, Luca, Brad and Stephan. But Stephan had reached out, sending a few messages to check in and ask me to join him for dinner again, *strictly as friends,* he'd promised. But after the weird-as-fuck dream I'd had starring him, meeting up would be a bad idea. Way too complicated. And I couldn't do that to Luca anyway.

Bess had been very welcoming and super accommodating, considering I was still learning not only how her company did things, but also how to be an adult with an actual career. She had let me shadow her for the past few weeks and had now helped me land my very own client.

Shit just got real!

Johnny had a rare night off at The Sparrow and I'd taken up Lizzie's offer to tag along with the couple for a visit to House of Himeros, laughing off the flirtatious jokes to let loose and join them in a ménage à trois.

Not weird at all, thanks Lizzie.

Those two had made it a regular outing, but I hadn't been back since popping my BDSM club cherry.

I had put some effort into my outfit for the night, aiming somewhere in between successful businesswoman by day, vixen sex kitten by night. The navy jumpsuit was one of my faves. It hinted at sophistication with its long sharp lines, while the deep V-cut neckline would make

J. Lo blush and always brought a room's attention to the bust line, enhanced tonight by the delicate long gold necklaces that danced between my valleys, reaching down towards my belly button.

Pleased with the look, I headed out to show Lizzie.

"Ah ah. No way. You are not covering up that gorgeous body in a one-piece pant suit, and don't you dare try to fight me on it," she ordered, slapping me on the bum and sending me straight back towards my room. "This is the first time you've been out since your release into the wild."

My mood dampened, but there was no point arguing with Lizzie. She followed closely at my back, a hand pushing forward at my shoulder blade. I guess Johnny's dom nature was rubbing off on her. Then again, she's always been a little bossy firecracker.

"Fine, you pick. You know every piece of clothing I own," I sighed, stopping at my room door and motioning towards my robe like a grumbly teenager.

"I do, and that's why you're wearing something of mine. I have the perfect piece in mind," she sung, pulling me to her room instead.

Johnny picked us up just after ten. I was expecting to grab a cab together, but surprisingly he turned up in his car. Looks like he wasn't drinking tonight, which had me super curious and a little excited and giddy that they were going to play instead.

Am I ready to see my best friend bumping uglies with her man? Maybe. We'd seen each other naked plenty of times over the years. Just not getting hot and heavy. Guess we'd find out soon.

The club seemed busier than last time I was here. Every corner, every stage with an audience. The air was electric and drenched in desire. The butterflies in my stomach were going crazy and it filled me with renewed curiosity and a need to be part of this world.

Johnny turned to face me, Lizzie close to his side. "Want a drink Charlie?"

I hesitated, wondering if I'd have the confidence to get closer to one of the scenes tonight. I wasn't sure if I was ready to make a move with someone else just yet, or more than that, dive into exhibitionism. But if I said yes to a drink now, then my choice was made.

See where the night takes you Charlie.

"Ah, no thanks," I smiled back meekly.

"Well okay then," he grinned, his Southern drawl rolling along my nerve endings, as if setting off dozens of fire crackers. He grabbed my hand and pulled both Lizzie and I further into the room with him.

We moved around slowly, taking it all in, lingering on the kinks that stirred something inside. Lizzie was mesmerised, eyes glued to the man in leather chaps and nothing else. A gorgeous curvy woman knelt between his legs in her birthday suit, her hands and mouth filled to the brim with him. Her eyes never left his as she worked his hard cock like an extra large candy cane, bringing him to the edge of climax. He fisted her ponytail tight, taking control of her head and pulling her flush against him.

"How is she not gagging?" I whispered under my breath, eyes wide with wonder.

"Practice," a deep purr in my ear had my knees weak. But I didn't dare turn around. I kept my eyes on the woman on her knees, gulping hard as my breathing increased. In my peripheral I could see a man with light hair move forward, stopping at my side. "See something you like?" he hummed.

"Yes," I exhaled, finding the courage to face him.

He was about my height, his forest green eyes level with mine. As far as eyes went, they were gorgeous. A light green with brown flecks and a darker green around the iris. His sandy blonde hair was pulled up into a bun with the lower half of his head shaved close to the scalp. Complemented by the short beard, he was the vision of a Viking warrior. Only dressed better.

Fuck me. Well hello Ragnar. Tell me you're here to take me to

Valhalla with you.

My eyes roamed across his body, and I didn't care that he was watching me take every inch of him in. With a physique like that, he deserved to be admired. His built chest and biceps pulled tight in the charcoal-collared shirt, which was only just holding together with two or three buttons below his pecs. My gaze lifted to his face once more and the smirk was otherworldly. If he wasn't a Viking, then he had to be a demigod. Mere mortals don't look like that. And they don't exude so much... so much... power. My breath hitched as he leaned in, close enough to feel the electricity pulsing off him. "Careful princess, a look like that will get you begging to cum while screaming my name."

The blush climbed up my chest in an instant, and I dropped my eyes to the floor. He was definitely awakening something inside me, but hearing that word, *"princess"*, from another man's lips made my heart falter. I was Luca's *princess*, his *Little One*, his *Little Lamb*. *His.*

I *was.* But not anymore. So why the fuck was I hesitating?

"You okay Charlie?" asked Johnny, stepping into my space protectively.

"Yeh," I cleared my throat. "I'm good Johnny. I was just chatting with—"

"Leaf," he growled low, seductively.

"Yes, Leaf here, about the logistics of overcoming a gag reflex," I smirked, raising an eyebrow at the handsome Viking, before turning back to Johnny and placing a reassuring hand on his chest.

Johnny's eyes grew dark and he pulled Lizzie into his side. "What do you think babe, how'd you learn to deep throat like a goddess?" he teased, his hand playing over her ribcage.

"Practice," she giggled, standing on tiptoes to nip the corner of his lower lip. Her hand on his hip began to roam south, playfully flirting with his growing bulge shamelessly.

"Told you princess," Leaf hummed. "Wanna take a lap around, show me what piques your interest? Or you want to stay and watch your friends?" He offered a hand. As if there was even an option. Before my brain had caught up, my hand was already in his, finding comfort in his warmth and the callouses I could feel against my palm.

I smiled back at Lizzie, biting on my lip as he pulled me away.

So he worked hard with his hands... interest piqued.

I had just finished a client meeting when Bess popped her head around the corner, "got a second Charlie?" she asked, nodding her head back towards her office.

I took a seat at one side of the generous tan leather lounge in her office, tablet in hand ready to take notes.

"How are you going?" she asked, sitting down next to me.

"Yeh good. It's going really well with Marven & Myers. And I feel like I'm really getting in the swing of things. I can't believe it's already been six weeks," I smiled back, worried that maybe I wasn't doing as well as I thought.

"That's great, I've had wonderful feedback from the team and I can see you love what you're doing," she smiled. "But, I wanted to check in with you. How are *you* doing Charlie?" she asked again.

I stalled, not sure what to say. Did she really want to know how my personal life was going? Had she heard rumours? Did she know a certain Viking warrior? "I'm fine," I offered politely. The robotic answer rolling off my tongue without consciousness.

"Honey," she let her hand slide towards me against the leather, stopping before reaching me. "Please feel free to tell me if I'm overstepping... but I want to share something with you."

My stomach flipped and I felt like I was being blindsided. What on earth was she going to share that would be seen as overstepping with an employee. She was my boss and outside of these four walls, I didn't know a single thing about her, nor her me. That's how it had always been with previous bosses. Well except with Luca. But that was different. An isolated incident. I frowned, tilting my head to one side, waiting for Bess to go on. She just stared back.

"O—okay," I answered after an awkward silence.

"Do you know that I used to work with Luca Crescent?"

"No," I said surprised.

"I decided on a career change when I hit my thirties and we actually studied at college together and took an internship at the same agency. Of course, we don't have a lot to do with each other anymore. Different priorities and all that."

She shifted in her seat, crossing her legs and making herself a little more comfy as she opened up. "But we're still friends and every now and then we catch up for dinner. Chit-chat about the things that are going great, and the shit that's bringing us down. In this dog-eat-dog world we live in, he's always been one of the only people I can be completely honest with, and I feel like I'm the same to him."

"Okay," I said again, managing to keep my voice neutral.

"I know it's probably not my place to say so, but I like you Charlie, and I'm not into secrets, it's not my style," she said, oozing confidence. "I need to tell you that we caught up last week. And before you think there's some secret agenda or romantic tryst — there's not. But I wouldn't be me if I acted like I knew nothing."

"Sorry, now I'm a little confused. And I've got to be honest with you too Bess. I'm a woman who respects the truth, even if it hurts. So please, don't beat around the bush with me," I managed, my voice doing nothing to hide its shakiness.

She smiled, giving me a small nod. "He was down Charlie. He wasn't his normal self, you know. Almost a shadow of the powerful, confident man I know. A man that knows what he wants in life and isn't afraid to go after it. After some serious prodding he eventually told me that he had let go of the most amazing woman he's ever had in his life, and he didn't know how to get her back."

I was getting fed up with this little dance, and if she didn't get to the point real soon, I was walking the fuck out. "What are you trying to say Bess? Just say it already," I huffed.

"He told me he had fucked things up with you Charlie, and I have to be honest, I had no idea you two were together when you reached out looking for job opportunities. And I want you to know that either way I still would have hired you. But I digress," she waved her hands animatedly.

"In the last ten years of our friendship, I have never known Luca to fall for anyone. I mean it. *Anyone.* He has always put his career goals and business deals first." She let her outstretched hand reach a little further, gently grasping my twisted hands on my lap. "I think that man is heartbroken. And I think he loves you Charlie, or is fast on his way to falling. I don't know how you feel about him, and you don't need to tell me," she smiled tightly. "But I thought you deserved to know."

After my initial confusion and slight irritation, I was thankful Bess had shed some light on the man I hadn't had the chance to get to know yet. We chatted a while longer. Without giving away any specific details, Bess mentioned that Luca had lost his parents while he was at college. And it made a little more sense now why I felt like we truly understood each other deep down. We might even be kindred spirits.

Once she started talking about things outside of work, there was no stopping her. I liked my boss Bess, but I liked this Bess a little more. She brought up a couple of memories of college keg parties, how Luca had helped her pass her least favourite subject, and how his family losses drove him forward to succeed and leave his footprint on this world.

"He's just one of those genuinely good guys," she said. "It makes me sick," she laughed. "No, I take it back, not sick, just a little green that most other men aren't like him. I mean honestly, how many guys do you know that are loyal and faithful?" she asked.

"Maybe he once was," I argued.

Or maybe I was the first person to drive him to cheat.

"He still is," she shot back. "He has always been an advocate of loyalty and honesty, and he never had respect for the kids at college who would jump from bed to bed behind their partners' backs. He has always broken off a fling if he felt his interest wavering. Although I could count on one-hand how many times that happened," she babbled. "Actually, I don't think he had many serious relationships come to think of it. Too career driven."

"I must have been the straw that broke the camel's back then," I huffed under my breath.

"What? No. I don't believe that for a second Charlie."

"Well you mustn't know Rose then," I spat her name like poison on my lips.

"Actually I do, unfortunately," she pulled a face. "He told me Rose tried to slither her way back into his life. Little snake that she is. But Charlie, you do know that he told her how he felt about you and that he would only continue business relations if she didn't try to get between you two?"

I went silent. No more smart-ass comments were coming to save me now. But could I take her word as gospel? And if it wasn't Rose, then why did he pull away from me, so abruptly, so coldly? Why didn't he try to get me to stay? Why hasn't he phoned or messaged?

Fucking men! Can't live with them. Can't live without them.

I was stronger without him. I had survived the second anniversary of Lola's death without him. I had found the strength to continue building my career without him. And I had found the courage to keep living, without him. As much as part of me wants to dial his number and hear his voice on the other side, I don't think I can go backwards.

And if he were to smile at me again or glance at me with that look in his eyes, that, right there, is something I don't think I'd be strong enough for. Strong enough… to say no.

CHAPTER 23

I HAD CHEWED on Bess' words for a week, pulling up Luca's number on my phone multiple times, letting my finger hover over the call button. But sense had somehow prevailed. My inner voice and best friend had reminded me how he had treated me at the end, and how happy and confident I had become in the past month. Well, after I let myself wallow in self-pity for a couple of weeks after I left Crescent Incorporated and Luca behind.

Brrinnngg! Brrinnngg!

"Hey Lizzie."

"Hey gurrlll," she sang down the line. "Have you got plans after work?"

"I was going to buy a bottle of wine on the way home, then binge that series with that hot Aussie guy and that married woman who rekindle their relationship in all the fun naughty ways," I purred back.

"Oooh saucy. But… as fun as that sounds, let's make that our Sunday plans and instead let's go out to the opening of that new club. Come on, don't leave a girl hanging."

"I forgot that was this weekend. It's been a big week and I just don't know if I'm feeling it Liz," I sighed.

"Pleeeease, I'm not beneath begging. Johnny's working, and I was hoping you and I could test out the new club then drop by The Sparrow to pick him up when he finishes work. They're on the same side of town."

I stayed silent, considering the effort of getting dressed up, and how crowded it was probably going to be.

"Charlie, come on, you know you wanna. You're my ride or die. And if a handsome stranger catches your eye, I will be the *best* wingwoman you could ever hope for. Pleeeease," she begged.

"Okay, but we're binging that series tomorrow night if you and Johnny don't have plans."

"Deal. I'm all yours boo. See you after work," she said before hanging up.

The lineup for *Zest* twisted around the block, and then some. Guys and girls were dressed to impress, all dolled up and ready to mingle. We hadn't even entered the club when we were hit on by two guys that looked old enough to be someone's dads. Don't get me wrong, they were good looking, but that much of an age gap just didn't appeal to me in my early twenties. Maybe one day, but not today. Or any day soon.

An hour later we were finally inside. But it was so worth it. The décor was bling on top of bling. Think *Studio 54*. And the DJ had the room pumping. We found a spot not far from the DJ booth and danced until we were covered in sweat and high on endorphins, not a care in the world.

"I love this place. Thank you for making me come," I screamed at Lizzie, hardly making a sound over the buzz of the music.

Her signature red lips pulling into a wide smile, "I knew we'd love it."

After a few drinks and another couple of hours on the dancefloor, Lizzie grabbed my hand and danced us towards the door.

"You okay?" I asked, leaning close to her ear.

"Better than okay. It's midnight and Johnny should be finished work soon."

We decided to walk the few blocks to The Sparrow, laughing the whole way as we talked about the night so far, now that we could hear ourselves. Although, the ringing in the ears was always a strange sensation and we were probably still screaming walking down quiet sidewalks. The dads we saw making out with a couple of giggly girls fresh out of college. The pair dancing like no one was watching with the kind of dancing usually reserved for the privacy of your own home, preferably with the lights off. And the Sherman look-alike that was definitely on the prowl at Zest.

"Johnny," Lizzie squealed, throwing herself into his arms as we arrived at the club.

He looked around to make sure we were alone before dropping his head to Lizzie, hungry to eat her up, not afraid to let his passion take over.

"I'm almost done on the door," he moaned, slowly lowering Lizzie's feet back on the ground. "Why don't you ladies take a seat near the back bar. Eric will grab you a drink. I'll be in soon," he said, stealing another kiss from Lizzie before slapping her bum as she walked inside.

Fifteen minutes later Johnny joined us, and Eric strolled over for his break.

"So is Zest as good as the hype it built before opening?" Eric asked, letting his arm dangle off the back of the chair, playing with the curls that fell over the edge when I lay my head back.

"As far as opening nights go, it was pretty damn good," I laughed. "It was packed to the rafters and I've gotta admit, it was pretty nice."

"So, should I start looking for another job or do you think The Sparrow will live to see another day?" he joked.

"I think you're safe," I giggled, leaning forward to grab my drink, downing the last drops.

"Want another?" Eric asked.

"I shouldn't. And I think we're leaving soon anyway," I answered. Waiting for Lizzie to draw breath from her snogfest so I could ask if our plans had changed. Eric followed my line of sight, laughing as he stood.

"They'll be a while. Let me get you one more while you wait," he offered. "And some cold water to calm down those rosy cheeks."

"Thanks Eric. You're the best," I smiled, wriggling to get a little more comfortable in the booth. Now that I was looking around, The Sparrow didn't have anything to worry about. Zest was nice, but this place was better. The music, the layout, the lighting, hell even the air had a sweet smell to it.

I felt the weight of Eric sitting back down next to me without turning my head. A glass of iced water was put in my hand as I let my gaze linger on the people on the dancefloor.

"It really is a beautiful club, isn't it?" I said, taking a sip.

"Thank you," a deep honeyed voice answered.

My head snapped to the side causing a serious case of whiplash, and I was taken back by the gorgeous specimen sitting next to me. He was as beautiful as the first time our eyes met in this very spot. Our legs touching, his golden eyes staring into mine, in just seconds my resolve was wavering.

"Luca," I breathed. "It's good to see you," I admitted, letting myself give a small smile while my heart did flips under the surface.

Feeling eyes on me, I turned to see Lizzie and Johnny staring at us.

"You okay Charlie? Say the word and I'll beat his ass," Lizzie threatened. And by the look in her eyes, I didn't doubt she would give it a hot crack.

I shook my head, holding in a giggle. "I know you would. But it's not necessary, Luca and I need to talk. Too many things were left unsaid."

I looked back at him, hoping he thought the same. His face said it all. He did.

"Mind giving us a few minutes?" I asked, looking back to Lizzie and Johnny. With a nod, Lizzie grabbed Johnny's hand, standing to walk away. But not before pointing two fingers at her eyes then at Luca's. He grinned and nodded his head towards her in understanding.

"Charlie, I'm sorry. I let work come between us and I took out my frustrations on you, on our relationship. I pushed you away, and I wish I could take it back," he said, slumping his shoulders.

"You should have talked to me. We could have worked through it Luca. And if it was too hard working together you could have told me and we would have figured something out. I know I can get lost in my head and magnify things, but I'm not that breakable. I've been through hell and back and I've come out stronger for it."

He wrapped his hand around mine, rubbing familiar circles across my knuckle. "I know. If there's one thing I've learned this year it's that you are the strongest person I've ever met. You don't need all the money in the world or new shiny things to know you are strong, powerful and resilient."

"I'm not powerful Luca, and I've had to work fucking hard to drag myself out of the suffocating darkness time and time again," I confessed, emotions creeping to the surface. "But it has made me driven and determined. My family deserved to have so much more time on this earth, to do all the things they dreamed of. Without them, I have to keep going. For all of us. Life is short Luca, and I need to make every second count."

I was barely holding it together. Blinking hard against the growing heat at the back of my eyes, I drew in a long breath and felt a single tear roll down my cheek.

Luca's hand cupped my cheek, his thumb wiping away the tear before it reached my chin. "I miss you princess. I miss waking up with you in my arms and the smell of you on my pillow. I miss seeing you in the office. I miss how perfectly your body fits to mine."

"Luca—"

"I mean it Charlie. I was an idiot to pull away from you and an even bigger fucking idiot to make you think I would ever look at another woman. Because Charlie you are mine. And I'm yours. Only yours," he whispered, resting his forehead on mine. "Please forgive me, Charlie."

Another tear escaped, then another. "I missed you too," I breathed. His mouth hung so close I could smell the sweet whiskey and feel his hot breath against my skin. There were no more spoken words, just looks that promised the world. The hesitation I felt was dissolving, giving courage to my head and heart to take a leap. But fear still gripped me tightly.

'Grab onto every opportunity, every possibility — with both hands, and don't let go.'

Lola's words echoed in my head. She was right and I was ready to listen. Time is precious and the cards I'd been dealt had shown me we only live once. With renewed determination, I made up my mind. I couldn't let the fear of being hurt again stop me from living. I was going to grab onto this with both hands and not let it go.

I closed the gap between us, claiming his lips. He opened willingly, inviting me in, his tongue dancing with mine. His hands wrapped around my back, pulling me in deeper. Our mouths were desperate, warm and wet as our teeth collided and our tongues explored each other. He let out a low groan as I moved onto his lap, desperate to be even closer. To be one with him again. If we weren't surrounded by clubgoers I'd already be riding us closer to ecstasy.

"My office, now," he growled, lifting me off his lap. He stood hurriedly, readjusting his pants and grabbed my hand, pulling me with him towards a 'staff only' door.

God I missed this. I missed him. My Luca. He'd ruined me for anyone else. My body was meant for only him now. And I prayed he reminded me of it every damn day.

CHAPTER 24

THE LAST MONTH together had been so much more than I could have hoped for. I had spent most nights at Luca's place, which was music to Lizzie's ears with Johnny spending most nights at ours now. We melded his cooking style with mine. We lounged around, able to relax without uneasy silences. While Luca worked in his home office, I read or caught up on my own jobs curled up in his office chaise. It was as easy as waking up each morning and breathing.

And the sex — the sex had hit a new high. Luca made me feel listened to and completely safe to try new things that had been dancing around my mind for far too long. I mean, who would have thought flirting with ice and the heat of dripping candle wax could be such a fucking turn on. So erotic.

"Stop it," I warned with a smirk. I could feel the weight of his stare, even watching telly. He was staring and it hadn't even been an hour since he had made a quick meal of me in the kitchen, swiping the fruit bowl off the bench, and learning a new language with his tongue against my clit. *So. God. Damn. Hot!*

"What? Can't I spend time memorising every inch of my girl? Every curve of your body, every freckle on that nose, every goosebump that prickles your skin when I trace my fingers up your sides, or lick the sweet salt off your body," he hummed, the deep baritone of his voice bringing every nerve cell to life.

I bit my lip, giddy with how quick I was falling in love with him. "Well we can't get in the way of admiring perfection now can we," I giggled, rolling my eyes, before he pulled me into his side.

"Come back to work, it's so dull without you there and Mira couldn't organise an orgy in a brothel if she tried," he peppered butterfly kisses against my cheek and hairline. "Come on, I'll make it worth your while baby girl," he licked slowly up the shell of my ear, gently biting on the lobe.

"I can't Luca. I love my job and Bess has been great to me," I said, putting my hand against his chest and pulling back to look into his eyes. The golden pools drew me in, and if I didn't keep my wits about me, I'd agree to just about anything to be in his good graces.

I reached out, cupping his chin, rubbing my thumb across his stubble. "I will forever be grateful for the opportunity you gave me to get my foot in the advertising door. But I can't rely on you. I want to make my own way in this world, make a name for myself as not just the boss's hot arm candy," I gave him my best duck face, layering my hands under my chin in a cute-as-a-button Shirley Temple pose. "I like having my own clients. You understand," I half stated, half begged him to understand and not think I was being ungrateful.

"Fine," he huffed, throwing his head back against the lounge. "But how will I ever get over the heartache of losing the best EA in the country?" he feigned hurt.

"I can think of a few ways," I said, crawling onto his lap, grinding my hips against his. I dragged my nails through his hair before pulling him in and devouring his soft lips. Moving my body up his chest, I broke the kiss, pulling his face down to my breasts. He nipped at my nipple through my shirt. "This has to go," he growled, yanking my shirt off then diving back down to take one of my breasts into his hot mouth. Sucking, licking, biting, until I couldn't hold back a moan any longer. I rocked back and forward, rubbing his thick hard cock against my sensitive slit. Only his shorts and my panties stopping him from filling me up completely.

My phone buzzed on the lounge next to my leg, jerking me back to reality.

"Don't answer it," he breathed around the mouthful of tit.

"It could be something important," I sighed, reaching over to grab it. Lizzie's name flashed up on screen. I clicked the answer button, putting it on speakerphone.

"You okay Lizzie?" I said, sounding a little breathless.

"Did I interrupt?" she sang.

"Yes!" Luca shot back. "Now go and ride Johnny's fat cock so Charlie can get back to mine."

"Hey!" she laughed. "Johnny's fat cock is my business. But I've got an exciting proposition lovebirds… wanna hear it?"

"No," Luca spat.

"What could possibly come close to the feel of this man in between my legs," I flirted, pushing myself up against his hardness.

"Come to House of Himeros with me and Johnny," she blurted out. "Come watch, come play, or just cum," she giggled. "Whaddya say?"

Luca had released my boob and was gaping at me, as if staring hard enough would allow him to read my mind. The thought sent shivers across my skin and a shock of excitement to my core. I played with my lip between my teeth, waiting for an answer from Luca.

"Well," came Lizzie's voice.

I raised my eyebrows in question. "What do you want Little Lamb?" he purred, his hands finding my hips and massaging slowly.

I hesitated, my body freezing in place. Letting my nerves kick in and heart race as if sprinting. "I—uh, want… to go," I confessed.

"EEeekkk, it's going to be fabulous. Meet us there in an hour," Lizzie ordered. "Johnny, they said yes," she squealed before hanging up.

"You okay baby girl?" he asked, leaning in to give me a soft, sweet kiss. "We don't need to go if you're having second thoughts."

"I do," I interrupted. "I want to do this. I want to be your good girl and I want to make you feel amazing. In front of everyone. I'm ready. And I think I've been ready for some time now," I babbled. "I've just been waiting for an opportunity to fall into our laps."

"Well Merry fucking Christmas baby," he laughed. "Just remember though, if we get there and you change your mind, that's okay too. I'll whisk you off to the bathroom, or a backroom, or the car, or a back alley and fuck your brains out there instead," he promised, mimicking ploughing into me a few times to get the point across. If I wasn't wet before, I was a dripping mess now.

I giggled like a schoolgirl, leaning in to claim his lips again.

Luca swept me down on the couch, hovering just above me, his nose nearly flat against mine. "But if you keep doing that princess, I cannot be held accountable for tying you to the bed, naked, and never leaving this apartment."

My palms were covered in sweat when we walked into the club. Luca looked to die for in all black. The sleeves of his button-down shirt were rolled to his mid-forearm. His suit pants clung to his buns of steel. And he'd left his hair a little messed up from our earlier tussle. I could feel women's eyes around the room dart towards him. His dominating presence palpable. Whether he saw the stares or not, he held my hand tightly, pulling me possessively against his back as we made our way into the main room.

I scanned the room looking for Lizzie and Johnny, but I didn't have to try too hard. She always stood out from the crowd with her gorgeous blonde bob, ruby red lipstick and tonight; a floor-length shimmery red number with a thigh-high slit and low slinky neckline, caressing her perky tits.

She was sitting on Johnny's lap, moving ever so slightly like she was swaying to the music. Johnny's hand played at the dress slit while his other intertwined with Lizzie's hand on her thigh. They sat watching an exotic man, body covered in oil and leather shorts, and his hair tied up in a high bun. He was performing Shibari on a petite woman wearing nothing but crotchless harness panties. He masterfully tied intricate knots across her body. Every slow movement carefully thought about, as if he was in a state of meditation. The woman's arms were pulled tightly behind her back, pushing her small but perky boobs forward. One of her legs was tied at an awkward bent angle, her foot back near her bum, opening her legs for what was to come next.

Now that I was watching more closely, I could see she was suspended from a rope hanging from the rafters, her free leg balancing, almost on tiptoe. But the strange thing was that she didn't look like she hated it. Not at all. As he moved her around and tied her in place, her head fell back time and again, her chest heaving as she sighed, licking her lips and sucking them into her mouth on an inhale. Eyes filled with need.

I looked at Luca, an unspoken question on my face. "There's a fine line between pleasure and pain, and rope play walks that tightrope like no one's business. If the sub can relax into it, the dom can bring them to climax with touch alone, no penetration," he hummed in my ear. "But it's not for the faint-hearted sweetheart. It can leave marks on the skin. Bruises. And if the dom isn't skilled, it can be a death trap."

"Think I'll stick to handcuffs and ties on my wrists and ankles," I whispered back with a blush. I'd seen enough of the ropes and was eager to move onto the redhead being spanked by the rugged, tattooed giant across the room. I pulled Luca with me, making a beeline for Mr Grizzly and Little Red.

Voyeurism was definitely my thing because every scene in this place had me hot under the collar and wet between the thighs… and right now I wasn't sure if I'd made the best decision to go without underwear. I knew Luca was watching my reaction. I could feel his eyes on me long before his fingertips traced across my shoulders, up the nape of my neck and massaged at the base of my hair. I crossed my legs towards him in our seats, rubbing my foot up his calf. Wanting to climb on top of him and finish what we started on the couch at home.

"What are you thinking Little One?" Luca asked, dropping his hand from my neck to my thigh, working his fingers between my crossed thighs to squeeze the leg touching his thigh. His dark smouldering eyes never left my face.

"I'm thinking I want to make you cum," I mumbled, turning my head so my mouth grazed his jaw. "In this room, in front of these people."

"You want that control princess? Are you saying you want to dominate me?"

"No, not exactly. I want to make you feel good, but the way *you* want me to. The way you command me to, Sir," I confessed, butterflies igniting in flames deep in my core.

His jaw clenched and his gaze dropped to my mouth. "Come with me," he growled.

Pulling me towards an empty nook further into the club, he drew himself up taller, filling the space with his hypnotic power and authority. "Remove your dress Little Lamb."

I kept my eyes planted on him, slowly stripping away the layers. The dress fell to the floor and I stepped out of it, leaving it crushed on the ground next to me.

He widened his stance, eyes darting to my naked pussy. "Forget your panties princess?" he asked, looking up at me through his lashes.

"No Sir," I muttered.

"No?"

"I chose to go without them, for this moment right now," I smiled, lifting my head higher with fervour.

A smile pulled at one corner of his mouth. "Lose the bra."

I did as he said, unhooking the back and letting the straps fall down my arms as it fell slowly down my chest, hovering on the roundness of my breasts before falling next to the dress on the floor. I stood in front of him in all my naked glory, in nothing but high heels. And instead of feeling embarrassed or ashamed, I felt like a powerful goddess on full display to her lover.

He circled me once, moving closely, but not reaching out to touch. Instead, his eyes trailed across my body, as if mapping out every mountain and valley to explore. Stopping in front of me, he reached out to cup my jaw, his thumb rubbing along my bottom lip, pinching it between his thumb and finger. He took a step closer, and I mirrored. As if we were dancing. He stepped forward, I stepped back. He did it again and this time when I stepped back, I felt a chair against the back of my leg.

"Sit," he ordered, the deep rumble of his voice crawling across my body. He kept his hand on my chin, tilting my face as I sat so our eyes remained locked. "Now, be a good girl and play with yourself. I want to see you explore your cunt."

Fuck, I loved when he talked dirty.

I moved my hand across my thigh.

"Uh," he stopped me. "Do you consent princess? I need to hear it."

"Yes Sir." My hand fell between my gaping legs, and I ran shaky fingers up and down my wet slit before hitting that sweet little nub of electricity. No stranger to self pleasure, I knew what I liked and by muscle memory alone, my fingers moved to my clit, creating little circles with varying pressure. My eyes closed as I let my head rock forward. Clenching my jaw.

"Keep those eyes on me sweetheart… Good, now enter a finger into that tight pussy," he purred. "Now another and start fucking yourself — slowly." His thumb played across my lower lip and my mouth opened on instinct. He pushed in against my waiting tongue. I sucked on his finger, twirling my tongue around it, letting him see just how badly I wanted him.

He pulled his hand away and took a step back. Unbuttoning his shirt lazily, he shrugged out of it and threw it aside. His body was a masterpiece and lived rent free in my head. His chest muscles moved with his motions, and his six-pack was more ripped these days with all the sex we'd been having. What can I say? I liked making him work for it.

"On your knees, princess." My hand stilled and I dropped in front of him, lifting my chin to keep our eyes locked. "Take my cock out and suck it like you did my thumb."

"Yes Sir," I exhaled, eagerness taking over as I grabbed the top of his pants with both hands.

"But—," he stalled, "if you get carried away and don't do everything I say, I will deny your orgasms. Do you understand me Little Lamb?"

Fuck, I don't know how I feel about edging or orgasm denial. Not when I'm this worked up.

"Y—yes," I gulped. "I mean yes, Sir."

I slowed my hands, unbuckling his belt and fumbling with the zipper before releasing his beautiful thick cock. I licked from the base to the tip, savouring the soft velvety smoothness against my tongue. I licked the salty drop off his head and wrapped my lips around him. My cheeks hollowed as I worked my mouth and hand over him. I took him in deep, relaxing as I swallowed until he hit the back of my throat. Tears filled my eyes as I moved between long, slow strokes and faster movements, trying to breath around him and ignore my gag reflex. My mind went back to the girl deep throating and I tried to channel her mastery and focus on not gagging.

"Fuck that feels so good. Such a good girl," he hummed, fisting a handful of hair. "Cup my balls and suck me in, all the way to the hilt. Nod if you understand," he demanded. I did as he asked, feeling my need for him drip between my thighs. I was desperate for his touch, to be filled completely with him as he fucked me towards heaven. But having his desire, his climax in my hands made me feel like I ruled his world, even in submission.

I could feel him grow bigger as he neared climax. "Grab my ass and pull me in closer princess," he groaned.

I slid my hands around his hips to cup his firm bum, squeezing as much as my palms could grab. I pulled him into me, my nose tickled by the tight curls of his bush as he thrust his hips, increasing the rhythm. My jaw stretched as wide as it would go as his cock slammed against the back of my throat again and again as he fucked my face. Breath escaped me as he held my head still, his body shuddering under my touch as hot cum spurted down my throat. He released my hair, his fingertips lovingly caressing my cheek. "Good girl. That was perfect," he praised.

For the first time since walking away from Mr Grizzly and Little Red, I realised we were still at the club. Heat shot from the pit of my stomach to my cheeks. My eyes flicked around the room noticing we had a little audience of our own. There was no laughter, no judgement. Just looks of desire, and busy hands roaming needy bodies. I looked back up into Luca's eyes, a flush now covering my body. He offered his hand, pulling me to stand against the hard line of his body.

"That was fucking amazing," I giggled, resting my hands against his chest.

"Mmm hmm," he moaned, tucking himself back into his pants.

"But Luca, I want you every which way tonight and I want to scream out your name when I cum. And I don't think they could handle that much of me right now," I jerked my head towards our audience.

"Take me home and let's finish what we started," I begged.

"Your wish is my command," he gave a cocky grin, leaning down to kiss me softly.

CHAPTER 25

FOUR MONTHS LATER

WITH EACH SLEEPOVER, I had brought a few more of my things to get by. Not with a hidden agenda of course, but just out of necessity. First, it was a toothbrush, then my night-time skincare regime. By the time I had a book on the bedside table and more shoes in the closet than his, Luca insisted I move in with him. I didn't say yes on the spot. It took a few days to think over and even a hellish nightmare of my parents dying again in a fiery plane crash. But Luca had been there to pull me into his arms and wipe the sweat off my brow as I wept away the pain.

It was like popping the cork on your favourite bottle of champagne. Knowing the ever-expanding cork will never fit in the bottle again, and instead, you pour glass after glass, devouring it all in one sitting. Having a nightmare in Luca's bed had popped my cork. I opened up to him about my parents' death, and then my sister's. And I'd never seen him with so much regret lining his beautiful face than when he learned he wasn't around to support me for the second anniversary of my sister's passing. Of course, I forgave him a long time ago. But really there was nothing to forgive in the first place. We had broken up. There was no reason he should have been around to console me. But it didn't matter what I said, he still kept saying sorry, as though he could turn back time with those words and a desperate wish.

Since then, I had called this gorgeous penthouse my home. I can't believe we've seen each other night and day for two months now. And I've never felt so spoilt rotten. It feels like too much luxury for just one couple. Of course, Lizzie is just as in love with the place as I am. Hell, she begged to move in and make the downstairs guest room her own. It was only when Johnny promised to make her forget her name in all the naughtiest and nicest ways in *their* apartment, now that I was gone, that she dropped the pleading.

I was busy prepping dinner in the kitchen when I heard the familiar footsteps walking in from the entryway. "Charlie?" he called out.

"In here," I sang back. "Dinner's almost ready and the wine is freshly poured."

He rounded the bench, snaking his arms around my waist and kissing me hungrily. His two-day regrowth scratched just enough to make my desire for stubble rash between my thighs come to life. Just the thought of it made my stomach flip with anticipation and I wrapped my arms around his neck to deepen the kiss. He cupped my face, coming up for air. "God I missed you," he rumbled.

"Mmm me too," I said, stealing a chaste kiss, then leaned back against the counter to admire my man.

He walked back around the corner towards the front door, returning with a generous-sized gift box, complete with bow.

"What is that?"

"Now that I've seen *all* of your clothes, I figured you'd need something like this for our first holiday away together," he grinned.

"Holiday? Are you serious? Oh my God... when and

where? And how on Earth did you keep this a secret from me Mr Crescent?" I chuckled, accepting the gift and placing it on the kitchen bench.

"I'm taking you away for a white Christmas in the Swiss Alps. Complete with Christmas markets, sledding, Jacuzzi sex, mulled wine and don't forget the fondue."

"Christmas," I sighed, "Bess will never give me time off with such short notice."

"She already has. Pays to be friends with the boss," he winked, lifting a piece of sweet potato into his mouth.

I leapt into his arms, overcome with excitement and the prospect of visiting one of the top places on my bucket list. "I love you Luca," I smiled. "And not just because of the holiday. I mean the holiday definitely helps your case, but I do. I love you, with just the clothes on your back, or off if you'd prefer," I giggled. "You know that right?"

He smiled down at me. A smile that reached his eyes and softened every hard-lined feature on his manly face.

"Say something," I said nervously, shoving against his stomach. "And I don't mean you have to say it back, because well, you don't — need to, that is," I babbled, my heart racing a million miles an hour. "Not if you're not there. But I want you to know that I, Charlotte Drake, have fallen truly, madly, deeply in love with you Mr Crescent."

Luca dropped his head, sucking in his lips. He grabbed both of my shoulders, slowly sliding his hands down my arms to hold my hands. I'd stopped breathing, petrified that I'd said too much. Scared him off for good. But when he looked back up at me, his expression made my heart skip a beat. Like he was watching the first golden sunrise after being consumed by a three-month Polar Night in Antarctica. Like I was the centre of his world.

"You had me at hello," he whispered.

I rolled my eyes, pulling my hands free. Part of me was relieved that he hadn't run for the hills, the other part wanted to laugh at his joke. But I wasn't going to let him know that.

"You're an ass—"

He lifted me up against his chest, stealing the words right out of my mouth as our lips became one. "I love you too Charlotte. Always have, always will." He kissed me again. This time, a deep and long kiss, filled with promises. "You are mine, and I am yours."

The last few weeks had been nothing but pure chaos. Bess and I had worked late into the night all week, perfecting the finishing touches on a couple of jobs that needed client signoff so their ad campaigns could start for the new year. I was exhausted, but I'd do it a hundred times over to have this time away with Luca.

"I think that's it," Bess smiled, her hands splayed on her hips in triumph.

"Yeh, it's everything they wanted and more. Gotta say, I kinda love it too."

"I've said it before, but I'm gonna say it again until you stop brushing it aside. You've got the goods Charlie. You're smart, creative and seriously talented," she said, moving around the table towards me.

I uploaded the completed files to the server, shutting my laptop before turning to face Bess. "I'm no good at compliments," I blushed, "But thank you Bess. For everything. You took a chance on me and I've learnt so much. You're the real talent here."

"Now go, scat," she nodded her head at the door. "Enjoy Switzerland with that man of yours."

She didn't need to tell me twice. Scooping all of my things up in one arm, I gave Bess a hug before heading out of the boardroom. "Merry Christmas Bess," I turned back.

"Merry Christmas honey. See you for New Year's drinks when you're back in town."

###

"Pinch me," I said, shaking my head in disbelief. "I must be dreaming. I mean this view can't be real. How does anyone leave this magical place and go back to reality?" I gaped, walking off Luca's private jet.

Luca chuckled, "It is gorgeous, but I've got something more gorgeous at home, so there's no competition. Sorry Switzerland, but I'm only visiting."

After ten minutes mesmerised with the rolling hills and white peaks on our drive, we arrived at the most majestic hotel. No, that wasn't enough. Castle? Nope, more than that… a palace — a glorious palace fit for royalty. *'Gstaad Palace'.*

"Luca," I whispered, holding his hand so my legs didn't give way as I stepped out of the car.

"Just wait princess, we're only just getting started."

He checked in while I circled the grand foyer, taking in the grandeur.

"Come on baby girl," he whispered in my ear, leading me away.

"The Penthouse Suite… well of course," I teased, following him into our home for the next two weeks. "You do like being on top."

"And under, but just so long as you're riding my cock, or face," he smacked my ass as I walked passed him.

"Are you hungry, should we grab an early dinner?" he asked, shrugging out of his jacket.

I strutted towards him, swinging my hips, trying to channel runway model. And probably failing. "First, I think we need a shower from all that travelling," I flirted, gliding my hands up over his toned abs and muscly chest.

I stepped out of my heels, losing three inches as my feet stood flat. I turned, hoping I was walking in the direction of the bedroom. Slowly undressing as I went. First, I undid the zip at the side of my skirt, letting it drop to the floor and stepped out of it. I continued my strip, pulling my blouse up over my head, aiming for sexy but managing to snag a button in my curls for a second. I half-turned, tossing it over my shoulder at Luca. The desire in his eyes burned bright, giving me the boost to keep going. Keeping my eyes locked on his, I reached back, unclipping my bra, letting it slide down and dangle from a curled finger.

Luca groaned behind me, reaching to undo his shirt buttons. I watched his muscles clench as he yanked the shirt off. There was no slow burn to his striptease, and I was totally fine with that. His gaze roved unashamedly, taking me in from my feet to my curls. I raised an eyebrow, pulling the side of my lip between my teeth, smirking as I turned and began walking away.

I found the master bedroom and ensuite around the corner. Dropping my panties at the door, I walked towards the shower, flipping the handle and letting it warm up while I turned to watch Luca stalk towards me. A predator with his prey in sight.

I felt the spray of warm water, stepping under the stream, happy with the heat. I turned a full 360, letting the water fall over every part of my body. Luca stepped in, his body so close I could feel him buzzing with energy. He leaned in, his breath searing the shell of my ear as he vibrated, "fuck that was hot. How did I get so lucky?"

He licked and nipped at my ear, kissing along my jaw until he found that sweet spot behind my ear that always made me shiver. He pressed his body's hard edges against my soft ones. I leaned to the side, pumping body wash into my palm, moving around with him so his back was against the wall. "Turn," I ordered. He didn't resist.

I slid my hands and a soapy trail up his back, across his shoulders, and down his arms. Every part of him is beautiful. The breadth of his shoulders cutting inward to the taper of his waist. An athlete in peak form. I rubbed my soapy hands down his hips and across the firm curve of his ass. A growl rumbled from deep in his chest. "Baby girl—"

"Turn," I interrupted. He turned to face me, lowering his head as the stream soaked his dark hair and ran down the bridge of his nose. He looked up at me through lashes, his gaze now darker. I cupped the sides of his face, watching the water run over his plump lips, his heavy breathing spraying water towards me.

I rested my forehead against his chin, wrapping my hand around his impressive length. In answer, he groaned, lifting my chin to bite at my bottom lip. He kissed me with such passion, a raw need, as though his life depended on it. His hard dick pushed against my stomach. My pussy heated and clenched in response.

He moved us around, my back against the cold tiles. He lowered his head, his hot mouth closing around my peaked nipple. As if a man possessed, he flicked and sucked, driving me straight to the edge of that cliff. I sighed, stroking him from root to tip with an eager hand.

"Little One," he breathed. "I can't be slow and gentle tonight. I need you to come apart while I fuck the living daylights out of you. You're driving me fucking wild."

"Then don't. Help me ride that fine line between pain and pleasure. I want you so deep we don't know where I start and you end."

He speared his cock into me, driving straight to the hilt. I gasped, taking a moment to stretch to accommodate his girth. He filled me entirely, wall to wall, rubbing deep against my cervix. He pulled out to the tip before ramming in again, his hand cupping the back of my head so I didn't get a concussion from slamming against the wall with his movements. His teeth sank into the nape of my neck driving me close to climax. With his other hand he lifted my leg higher, wrapping it around his hip, changing the angle as he fucked us over the edge of the abyss.

Geezus fucking Christ. Oh God, yes.

"Oh God. Luca. I'm so fucking close," I whimpered.

"Cum for me princess," he growled, pumping so deep I could see stars.

My body trembled, my pussy clenching as my orgasm ripped through me, my nails digging into Luca's back as the wave crashed over me again and again. He slid in and out as I finished, his orgasm shooting through me soon after. And the growl he let out was something new. Something so fucking primal. So Goddamn sexy.

"Are you okay? I didn't hurt you did I?" he breathed, cupping my face.

I laughed. I couldn't help it. "No baby. That was next level amazing." I leaned up, taking his lips with mine, his cock slipping out of me as I stood on tiptoes.

"I can't say I've never fantasised about being taken like that. So ruthlessly. So primal. But that, my love, was life-changing. Being devoured by a man consumed with lust and need. That I loved."

CHAPTER 26

WAKING UP CHRISTMAS morning, wrapped in Luca's arms was the best feeling I've ever had. His strong arms cocooning me, protecting me from the world. His steady breaths hovering over my neck and shoulder.

We went skiing a few times and I got to wear the amazingly warm ski jacket he'd gifted me before our trip away. Sure, I spent most of the time on the sidelines, eyes glued to Luca as he carved his way down the slopes like a pro, but I didn't mind. Not at all. We drank mulled wine and ate fondue as promised. And we fucked like the world was ending. In bed, in the kitchen, the living room, in front of the fire, and he wasn't kidding about the Jacuzzi sex.

Ho—ly shit!

He spent every waking moment ravaging me with his eyes, his hands, his tongue. Learning what made me gasp, moan, and scream his name, begging desperately for more. And I took pleasure in finding the spots on his body that made his breath hitch, his muscles flex, and his cock grow two-fold.

We also spent days wrapped in the most luxurious blankets, talking about our families and what life was like before they left us. It was bittersweet.

"Do you want kids some day?" he asked, making me choke on the mouthful of wine I'd just sipped.

"I—uh, don't know. I can't imagine creating a happy life

as a family, only to die and leave them alone in this world. I know it sounds morbid."

He didn't rush to reply. Letting me sit in my thoughts. "Just because your parents and sister passed away too soon, doesn't mean you will too, baby. You can't live life afraid. Life's too short. You deserve to be happy in whatever makes you happy. Whether that's having kids one day or not," he smiled softly, rubbing reassuring circles on my arm.

"I know. It's just…" I struggled finding the right words.

"Scary, yes. But exciting. Hell yes," an easy laugh stirred in his chest. "Don't look at me like that, I'm not saying we should have kids. But I'm definitely up for the practising part."

"Ha ha," I rolled my eyes. "I think we're pretty Goddamn good at that part."

"Fuck yeh we are," he winked.

"So, while you mull that over in your head for the next one hundred years or so. I want to ask you to consider something else," he coughed, clearing his throat.

"Now you're scaring me," I said with wild eyes.

"Charlie, I want you to come work with me."

"Luca," I cut him off. "I've told you, I can't come back and work for you."

"With me Charlie. Not for me," he narrowed his gaze. "I want you to be my partner. I'm looking at expanding Crescent Incorporated and I want you to be my business partner."

I gaped at him, speechless.

"You have what it takes. I've seen it. I saw it when you were my EA, and I've seen it in the campaigns you've led at Perception. Some people just have the skills, the knowledge, the creativity. They don't need ten-plus years' experience to prove that."

"Luca, I don't know what to say," my eyes glistened as tears welled up.

"Say yes. Life is short Charlie, take the leap with me."

This was crazy. But life without him would be crazier. He was my anchor, my true north.

"Yes Luca," I answered, nerves spilling over every edge. I leaned in, planting light kisses against his lips. "Yes."

January came and went in the blink of an eye. We celebrated Luca's 28th birthday with a dinner party at home with Lizzie and Johnny, Brad and Nick, Stephan and his plus-one, I think her name was Katy, Jane and her new flame Mark, and Bess and her husband Tom. I relished in the warmth and joy it filled my chest with. Being surrounded by my rock Lizzie, and this group of amazing people I didn't even know just over a year ago. And now I couldn't imagine life without them.

Luca had been planning on expanding his advertising company for quite a while, so the plans were well in place before he asked me to be his partner. Now here we were, one week away from officially opening our doors. To begin with, we were starting off with a modest number of staff until we had a few clients on the books. There was no point in stealing his current clients from Crescent Incorporated, and this company, *our* company, *Mayflower*, had a different target group. We weren't aiming for big corporations or franchises like Crescent Inc. Mayflower was for the boutique business, the hidden gem, the multi-generation family business. We'd had a few local businesses we frequented reach out to set up meetings already. And I was pumped to think completely outside the box and let my imagination run wild. In the opposite direction of mainstream, if that's what the clients wanted, of course.

Ding!
Luca: I'm going to be pushing it tight tonight, meeting with Bill's

gone over. Can you drop my suit at the new office and I'll grab it on my way home to pick you up?

Charlie: I can wait there for you.

Luca: Now how could I be your Prince Charming if I didn't pick you up in a stretch limo and be shocked into silence when you walk towards me all dolled up for the ball?

Charlie: No stretch limo!

Luca: You're no fun.

I take that back.

You're the funnest person I know (wink)

Charlie: Funnest? Hahaha

Fine, I won't wreck your fun. I'll drop your suit off and you can pick me up later. Any requests for my outfit? Panties… no panties?

Luca: Surprise me (kiss face)

I put my phone in my pocket and moved towards the bedroom to grab his suit for the East Coast Advertising Awards night. It felt like only yesterday that we were there and he'd chased me into the bathroom. Talking me off the ledge, *'Rose is my past, you are my present and my future'.* And then he fucked me fast and hard right there on the counter, no thoughts for if anyone walked in and saw us.

Be still my beating pussy. Meow!

Ding!

Luca: No panties. You set the bar high last year princess.

I laughed aloud, loving the thought of Luca having dirty memories filling his mind while he sat through a boring business meeting.

Luca called up to the apartment two hours later, "Your pumpkin carriage has arrived my Queen."

"On my way my liege," I giggled, grabbing my clutch. I turned towards the hall mirror, looking over my reflection one last time. Ma's auburn curls and blue-green almond eyes stared back at me. I shut my eyes, filling my lungs with a slow, long breath. Smiling at the thought of her watching over me, and knowing she would have approved of the man I'd fallen in love with.

Walking out of the lobby, I stopped in my tracks as a blush raced over every inch of my body. There, standing at the open door of the stretch limo, that I said no to, was Luca with the biggest bunch of deep red roses you've ever seen. A smile pulled at the edge of his mouth, "you look beautiful baby."

I let out the breath I was holding. My face lit up with a smile just for him. I raced forward, landing in his waiting arms, squashing his lips with mine. I covered him with butterfly kisses before nipping at his juicy bottom lip. "Quite the grand gesture Mr Crescent," I teased.

"Only the best for my girl," he said, swatting my ass into the backseat.

"Thank you babe. These are absolutely beautiful," I said, burying my face into the heavenly sweetness of the bouquet in my arms. "And this limo is.. pretty damn nice too," I chuckled.

"To Ziegfeld Ballroom please Enzo," Luca called to the driver, before pressing the button to close the divider between us and him.

"I've gotta say, that suit looks like a second skin on you. Honestly, I don't know how I'm going to contain my desire all night," I fanned myself.

"I could say the same thing you naughty little minx. I don't remember seeing that dress in your wardrobe, he said, letting his eyes roam up and down my body.

"Funny story, I bought this years ago, but after being dumped the night before my friend's wedding, I zipped it back up in its bag and hid it in the back of the cupboard, hoping one day I'd be in the right frame of mind to give it the life it deserves. And I am, I can't even remember that loser's name," I laughed, scratching my head.

"I think this night is going to be full of unforgettable

memories that will create a whole new life for that dress of yours."

"That's exactly what I wanna hear," I smiled, adjusting myself to cross my legs towards Luca.

"And to kick it off, I have something I want to ask you."

"Because a stretch limo and all the roses in all of New York weren't enough," I giggled. "Baby, I can promise you, you are getting lucky tonight," I waggled my eyebrows playfully.

"Behave, Little One," he scalded seductively.

"Yes Sir," I answered, my heart hitching.

He turned his body towards me, his knees entwining with mine. "Charlotte May Drake. You are the most incredible woman I've ever met. You have overcome so much cruelty in your life and can still sit there smiling, laughing, and being vulnerable and powerful all at the same time."

I couldn't help but grin. No one has ever seen me the way Luca does. He's always reminding me how much he loves me, how amazing he thinks I am. It was a strange sensation, and somewhat excessive. But it was also so fucking intoxicating and addictive. He certainly knew how to work my praise kink.

"Charlie, you are my present and my future. You are mine—"

"And you are mine," I interjected.

He returned my smile, eyes sparkling with a brightness from within. "Baby, I never thought I'd know what love is. But I love you, so deeply, so madly it destroys me and makes me anew every damn day. I want to worship you, ravage you, and protect you forever. Will you do me the honour of becoming my wife?"

My eyes dropped to his hands, an open ring box staring back at me. A stunning platinum princess-cut diamond ring sparkled in the passing street lights. I looked between the ring and Luca, tears blurring my vision.

"Luca—, I, I."

He pulled the ring from the box, gently grabbing my hand and placing the sparkler at the tip of my ring finger. "Marry me Charlie. You know it'll be a crazy ride, but it'll be perfect and filled with love, happiness and top shelf sex."

His eyes gave everything away. He had no poker face tonight. He meant every damn word. And I felt it in my soul and returned every single sentiment, one-hundred-fold.

"Yes," I gasped. "Absolutely, 100% yes. I love you more than I could ever explain. And my words will never be as perfect as yours. But you saved me Luca. Pulled me out of the suffocating darkness and made me feel loved again."

He slid the ring down my finger and claimed my lips for the first time as his fiancée. Our tongues danced, caressing each other with raw, primal need. I wrapped my hands around his neck to deepen the kiss. It wasn't enough. He scooped me into his lap, desperate to devour the last breaths from each other's bodies. We stayed that way until the car slowed and came to a halt at our destination. I hopped off his lap, returning to my seat, grieving the loss of his heat and touch. This new feeling was overpowering. Luckily I had time to get used to it. Like forever, wrapped up in the beautiful man who would become my husband.

Husband. Holy shit, I have to tell Lizzie.

CHAPTER 27

AS FAR AS awards nights go, we knocked it out of the park. Crescent Incorporated took out six awards and I even landed one of my very own. The 'Up and Coming' Award. I felt like the belle of the ball as colleagues from Crescent, Perception and Mayflower rose together, giving a standing ovation. The night was indescribable. A black hole could have formed in the middle of the dancefloor, threatening to end the world and all that we know, and I wouldn't have noticed. Even seeing Rose there couldn't throw me off kilter.

Of course, she did try though. Strutting over to our table, just as she had done the year before, she put on the fakest of smiles to congratulate me, all the while eyeing Luca. It was quite comical actually, the way the words looked as though they left a sour taste in her mouth. And it was only sweetened when her eyes went wide, and her mouth dropped open at the sight of the ring on my finger when Luca grabbed my hand and brought it to his lips to kiss it.

I walked out of the venue on an all-time high. How could this night get any better?

"Can I get you a drink *husband*?" I asked in a husky voice.

"Mmm, I like the way that sounds rolling off your tongue," he smirked. "Whiskey on the rocks *wifey*," he stirred back.

"Ooh, I see what you mean," I giggled. "How can a single

word provoke feelings of truly belonging to someone? Being captivated. Protected. Owned."

I crawled into his lap on the couch, handing over his drink before settling my back against his chest. He wrapped his free arm around me, kissing my jaw then resting his head back. We sat there in candle glow, listening to one of my 'Booktok Dark Romance' music playlists and chatting about our plans for the next year. Building our company. Enjoying another getaway, maybe somewhere warmer this time. And starting to plan our wedding.

"So how hands-on do you want me to be in the wedding preparations? Do you want to hire a wedding planner? Or have you got a dream scrapbook from when you were a little girl with all of those big dreams of your perfect day?" he smirked.

I went quiet for a moment, a nostalgic smile forming on my face as I remembered the days when Lola and I would steal wedding magazines from our parents when they were working on one of those projects. Dog-earing the pages we loved. The dresses, the flowers, the pretty little lights hung around the trees at garden weddings and receptions. It was all so magical.

"Where'd you go princess?" he asked, tucking loose strands of hair behind my ear.

"No scrapbook. But I remember flicking through wedding magazines with my sister when we were younger. It was all so pretty, like a fairytale."

"Is that what you want for our wedding day? The big fairytale affair? Because whatever makes you smile like that, I'll make it happen," he kissed my temple.

"I don't know. But we've got plenty of time to think it through," I smiled.

He shuffled around me, pushing off the armrest to stand at the edge of the couch. Grabbing the empty glass from my hand, he placed it on the coffee table next to his and pulled me with him.

"Come with me Mrs Soon-To-Be-Crescent. I want to make love to my fiancée."

###

"Charlie you're going to have to make a choice," Lizzie insisted.

"It's too hard," I sighed. "How 'bout you hold up a picture in each hand, blindfold me, spin me around and I'll pin the tail on the donkey?" I suggested, getting an eyeroll from Lizzie in return.

She stood with lips pursed and arms crossed, tapping her foot like ma used to do when I'd drag my feet getting ready for school.

"Okay, okay. The Maldives. No, Japan. No no, hang on. Ummm, Portugal."

"Now you stop right there Charlotte May Drake. You can visit the whole world, one country at a time. But remember, this is a quick Spring getaway for the two of you to celebrate your engagement and the success of your new business. Not the last destination you will ever go."

I frowned, trying to come to a decision. "So here's what I'm thinking," I finally said. "Japan has cherry blossom season and a 14 hour flight to boot. Portugal or Greece will have beautiful, warm, long days and a 7-10 hour trip. Or we could explore Toronto less than an hour away, and they also have the cherry blossoms I love. And the Maldives, well my God is there anyone who doesn't have that on their bucket list," I snorted. "But that's about a 20 hour flight on Luca's Gulfstream jet," I finished, hands raised in challenge.

"Wow, you've put some serious thought into this week away. I'm impressed," Lizzie smiled. "Now, I'm just going to add my two cents, but you know you're going to have to decide soon."

I nodded, wriggling myself on Lizzie's couch to cross my

233

legs and give her my undivided attention.

"So Japan is amazing, I speak from experience. Although it was a brief trip to sign that stubborn author, it was breathtaking, *but* super busy. All those people, you just won't feel like you're really getting away on your own. Now Toronto, don't you make me come over there and smack you. You can go there any weekend it's so damn close. You're not going to waste a well-deserved break somewhere a stone's throw away," she teased, slapping me on the knee.

"Now if I was you and money was no longer an option—"

"Hey, that's not nice. I'm not marrying him for his money," I frowned.

"I know honey, I just joke because I'm green with envy," she laughed. "But in all seriousness, if it was me, I'd save the Maldives for your honeymoon. It's supposed to be heaven on earth and deserves to be taken in uninterrupted, unrushed, with oxytocin in the air."

"But have you considered the Greek Islands? Oh. My. Goddess. The romantic ruins, stunning whitewashed villages and jaw-dropping sunsets. Need I say more? And take your pick of 200 islands, all with golden sunsets and clear blue ocean views. Mmm, mmm, mmmmmmm," she closed her eyes, squeezing her shoulders as if savouring the thought.

I smiled wide, knowing she knew me inside and out. "Lizzie Ryan, what would I do without you?"

"Hmm," she scratched her head. "Probably holiday in Florida with all the retirees."

I gasped, feigning shock and hurt, bouncing forward to tackle her on the couch. With Lizzie in a head lock, as if she even had a chance, we laughed until tears were lining our eyes. "I take it back, I take it back," she screamed, trying to squirm free.

I let go, grabbing the sides of her head and planting a kiss on her forehead.

"Love you Lizzie."

"Love you Charlie Bear," she giggled. "Now, finish packing your bag woman. You and I have a birthday weekend away to get to. And we better get going before Luca changes his mind about being able to survive a few days without you."

"Havana here we come," I sang.

FOUR WEEKS LATER

Luca and I were booked into our little Greek Isle getaway tomorrow, in the most perfect little villa looking out across the Mediterranean Sea, with its own pool right outside the bedroom doors. And now here I was, sick as a dog. A fever had taken over my body in the early hours of yesterday morning, and I was covered in sweat and shaking uncontrollably. Luca stayed home, catering to my every whim as I drifted in and out of sleep. He even pushed back our holiday for a month to fit around project deadlines, taking care of all the bookings.

What a keeper! If I didn't already have a ring on my finger, I would have taken the first opportunity after I felt human again to propose to this unicorn of a man.

"We made it princess. And I've got to admit, having the extra time to sort out a few loose ends on Blaire's campaign wasn't a bad thing," he smiled, raising his arms out to his sides and falling back on the bed. "Now I can enjoy our time away without thinking about work. In fact–," he said reaching into his pocket. "Phone's already off!"

"This place is beautiful. Look at that view, it's stunning. It looks like a beautiful Monet painting," I breathed, pushing the doors open to take in the expansive view. I walked out,

235

letting the warmth prickle across my skin, dipping my toes into our private pool. "Oh Luca, it's nice, let's go for a dip before finding somewhere to have dinner where we can watch the sun drop over that horizon."

I changed into one of the bikinis Lizzie had made sure I packed, even when I insisted a one-piece swimsuit would be just fine, and threw my hair up into a loose messy top knot.

"Stop right there. Let me look at you," Luca purred, already leaning back against the pool's edge as I walked out. My cheeks coloured, similar to the rosy suit I wore. I did a little spin, laughing as I entered the water. "You look perfect wifey," he said, pulling me in for a kiss.

"So do you Mr Crescent. You look like you belong here. Honestly, your skin is too golden for someone with an office job. It's not fair," I huffed, wrapping my legs around him, covering his lips with mine. He took my breath away, figuratively and literally. His warm skin against mine, and the coolness of the water sent shivers across my body. It was the perfect combination. I stayed in his arms like that, tasting and breathing him in, feeling his hardness grow against my stomach.

"Baby girl, does that exhibitionist want to come out and play again?" he breathed against the shell of my ear.

The dominant tone laced his words, power rolling through every syllable. "Yes Sir. I want you inside me," I sucked at his lip. "Out here in the open, so anyone around can hear how much pleasure you bring me."

His fingers hooked into the sides of my bikini bottom, pulling the knots that held the piece of material in place. His hand slid down my stomach, tracing patterns across that sensitive spot below my belly button. He continued to stroke south, his palm rubbing my pussy as he ripped away the bikini. With his other hand, he pulled at the strings at my back, freeing my breasts so they rubbed against his chest. He continued to explore my needy body, pushing two fingers inside. In and out. In and out. Slow and deep. His thumb focused on my clit, building the heat in my core.

The European sun warmed my skin, glowing across my shoulders as the cool water pebbled my nipples. I moaned into his mouth, sucking at his tongue, letting my teeth scrape and nip at his juicy lower lip. Luca lifted me up against his body, drawing my nipple into his mouth, alternating between flicking his tongue against it and sucking at my heaving breast. I could feel my excitement coating his fingers, mixed with the cool water every time he moved back inside me. Reaching down to his waist, I pushed down his shorts, fisting his long, hard cock. I circled his head with my thumb, then stroked the length of him. I could feel the veins and blood pumping under my hand as he squirmed between my legs. He pulled his hand away, gripping onto my hips. Shifting myself with my hand on his shoulder, I lined him up, teasing his tip at my entrance. With one hand I held onto the nape of his neck while the other guided him deep inside. We moaned in unison, welcoming that feeling of completeness. Our bodies fitting together perfectly.

Being weightless in the pool, Luca easily controlled my body, moving me with him, then holding me firm while he thrust in deeper. My head rolled back as he slowly increased his pace until we were both breathing heavily with the pleasure. Bringing my eyes back to his face, I was mesmerised by his beauty. A deer in the headlights. His wet hair curled at the nape of his neck. Water dripped down his cheekbones, beading on his chiselled jaw. His muscly arms and shoulders flexed at the workout. And his golden eyes had a new shade to their charm, lightened from the glow of the sun, yet darkened by his growing desire.

My growing orgasm coiled tight in my core, striking out as though it was lightning beginning at my centre. Spreading that warm feeling to every limb and organ until my whole body was humming, ready to explode. I closed my eyes, letting myself feel every sensation, in and out of my body. Luca mirrored me perfectly, our bodies as one. My pussy clamped down on his dick as I cried out in ecstasy, my release tearing through me like the creation of a new star. Luca sped up, chasing his own climax, biting down on my neck as he growled out his orgasm.

I wrapped my arms around his neck, laying my head against his shoulder, allowing my breathing to slow down once more. Luca's chest heaved with his breathing as he held me against him. I opened my eyes, letting my gaze wonder across the vast ocean, surrounding mountains and several boats spotted across the water. This truly could be heaven, right here in the home of the Greek Gods. I sent up a prayer.

> *Dear Goddesses Gaia, Alectrona, Elpis, and Aphrodite.*
> *I thank you for bringing this man into my life.*
> *For watching over us as we join mind, body and spirit.*
> *And I pray to keep him.*
> *To keep this happiness.*
> *This love.*

On our fourth day holidaying along the Mediterranean Sea, I woke up as the first rays of dawn lit the sky, sickness rolling through me. Luca slept soundly as I tiptoed to the bathroom to wash my face and wait for the wave of nausea to pass. But it didn't and I retched up whatever was left in my stomach from last night's dinner. I sat on the cool bathroom tiles, wiping a damp cloth across my brow. With eyes closed I prayed that slow, rhythmic deep breaths would help me find my balance again. It took about ten minutes, but I started to feel better.

What the heck was that? A wave of nausea and vomiting. Gross.
It's as if—

I shot up straight, eyes wide as the thought settled where it fell.

"I can't be," I whispered against my hand.

My mind flapped around, trying to recall the last time I had my monthly visitor. But I'd lost track with how sick I'd been last month. And now that my thoughts were flying a million miles an hour, I couldn't recall it clearly.

Was it in winter? Fuck-a-duck. I think it was after Luca's birthday. Shit! Did I have a period before my birthday getaway?

Panic pulled at the threads, unravelling me at record speed. My breathing became erratic and I felt like I was hyperventilating. About to pass out or... nope not pass out, just vomit again. I hugged the toilet bowl, dry heaving when there was nothing left to bring up. When I could breathe again, I stood up, washing my face and stared at my reflection, letting the water drops fall onto the countertop.

"I can't be," I whispered again. "It's not possible, I'm on contraception," I shook my head.

Breathe Charlie. Don't panic. Hormonal contraceptives can play around with periods, you know that. Just breathe, take a pregnancy test and then figure this all out.

I turned off the bathroom light, silently making my way back to the bedroom where Luca still lay where I left him. I picked up some clothes and snuck back out to the living area. I dressed quickly, leaving Luca a note on the kitchen bench.

Morning baby,
Needed to stretch my legs. Gone to grab us some breakfast.
Back soon. Love you. x

I walked slowly down towards the town centre, lost in my thoughts. The what-ifs. The worry that this would ruin everything between Luca and me. I didn't know if I wanted kids. Maybe I was too damaged to be a parent. Would I ever be able to get over the fear of losing them or leaving them alone in this world if the death reaper got its icy fingers around my neck? Because sure as the sun rises every morning, that fucker was always waiting in the wings, ready to destroy me again.

The warmth of the sun was starting to crawl across the streets and I could see other early risers beginning their day. I found a little pharmacy on the main street, ducking in to buy a test kit, and popping it in the back of my shorts when I was outside.

Out of sight out of mind, right? Wrong.

I skirted my way back towards our villa, diverting down a little alley I'd seen yesterday with a cute little bakery and café to grab the breakfast I'd promised. Luca was lounging in bed when I returned, a sheet haphazardly strewn across his lap, just managing to cover his manhood, and nothing else. The man was beautiful, there was no denying that. His arms were crossed behind his head as he looked out at the view.

"Mmm, there you are," he smiled as I walked in.

"I come with gifts," I gave a cheesy grin, handing him a coffee and koulourakia pastry. "I'll be right back, just need to pee."

My heart was hammering in my chest, but there was no point in talking about it if there was nothing to worry about in the first place. I peed on the stick and set it aside, counting down the minutes until I'd know my fate.

"You okay princess?" Luca called after I was missing far too long.

I stared at the two pink lines on the test in my hands. Tears welling up and a lump the size of a golf ball in my throat.

"Charlie?" he asked again, a hint of panic in his voice.

"I, uh. Yeh, be right out," I cleared my throat.

I couldn't stand lies or hiding the truth. So there was no other option than to just come clean and see what Luca had to say. We'd chatted about having kids. Well, I had skirted around it every time he brought it up. But Luca had described multiple possible futures in our late-night talks this year, and many of those possible futures included a kid or two in tow.

I opened the door, surprised by Luca standing there

waiting for me.

"I was worried when you didn't answer," he said. Taking a step forward to hug me to his chest.

"Ouch, what's that?" he said, pulling his chest back, my arms still held in front of me with both hands wrapped around the little white test.

"Luca—"

"Is that a pregnancy test?" he jumped in.

"Ah, yeh," I whispered on shaky breath.

He slowly wrapped his hand around mine, raising them to look at the test. Concentration pulled at his brow as he looked at the two lines. His eyes returned to mine as he pulled me out into the hallway with him.

"Two lines. Is that—"

"Positive," I said, holding my breath, sucking in my lips.

"Positive," he repeated. There was an air of silence when I couldn't even hear the birds outside or the gentle breeze blowing through the curtains.

"We're pregnant," he said, a smile pulling at the corner of his lips. "I didn't think it was on the cards with your contraceptive device, but how?" he said, pulling me to sit on the bed with him.

"I don't know Luca. I still have it in. And I know they're not 100% foolproof, but I'm not sure what's happened."

"How long have you suspected?" he asked, his thumb rubbing up and down my thigh in habit, the way he did when he knew I was on edge.

"Just today. I woke up sick and I was thinking to myself how the sudden onset was crazy and then it hit me and I couldn't remember the last time I had my period," I said in disbelief, shaking my head.

"I've heard that severe sickness, like you had last month, can throw out hormones and lower effectiveness of certain contraceptives. And if that's the case, then this is a little miracle," he smiled. He wasn't angry, or confused, or judgemental. His eyes held such warmth and love that I felt my shoulders relax and panic subside.

"But we're not ready."

"Charlie, who's ever ready?" he asked. "I love you with all of myself and I've always pictured raising a family with you someday. Someday just might have come sooner than we thought."

I stayed silent, processing what was happening.

"Charlie, do you love me?" he asked.

"Unconditionally," I said, a tear rolling down my cheek.

"And how does the idea of having kids with me sit with you?"

"I'm scared. You know that. I have so much fucking baggage, it's hard to let go of and picture everything being perfect for us," I murmured with an agonised frown.

He pulled me onto his lap, stroking my back reassuringly. "Charlie, whatever happens, we're in this together. I love you... and I will love this little nugget," he smirked, placing a gentle hand on my belly.

"Why are you so good to me Luca, when I'm clearly unhinged?"

"Because we were made for each other, by the Greek Gods themselves," he declared. "It's serendipity princess."

He raised an eyebrow, bouncing me on his knee and making me chuckle. And then he kissed me, and the world melted away, leaving just Luca, me and our little nugget, as one.

CHAPTER 28

"YOU KNOW THIS changes everything," Lizzie said, stalking back and forth, hands on her hips.

"Wedding planners will be all booked up for the next six to twelve months, so we're going to have to do it all, which I'm totally hyped about by the way," she rounded the kitchen, grabbing her third cup of coffee since coming over this morning. "Seriously, if I didn't go into publishing, I was going to be an event planner, can you just imagine?"

"Lizzie, slow down," I laughed. "You are seriously over-caffeinated right now. You're going to have a heart attack. Now, put the cup down and step away from the coffee," I warned, rising off the couch to lean over the kitchen counter and reach for her hands in gentle negotiation. "I'll make you a nice cup of camomile tea instead."

"Shoosh you," she squinted her eyes, bringing the cup up to her mouth in defiance. She patted the side of her head with her pointer finger, "these cogs need to be spinning in overdrive if we're going to pull off a fall wedding in a little over two months."

"Do you think that's too late? How much do you think I'll be showing?"

"If you want to plan it for the beginning of September so you're not competing with hectic heat and humidity, and your due early December, that will make you what, about six months?"

"Yep, end of second trimester."

She opened her mobile, tapping away with her fingers.

"You'll definitely have a bump. According to this source," she said, holding up her phone to my face, "your uterus will be about the size of a basketball. Oh my gawdddd, how cute will that be," she gushed.

"And I have some ideas of perfect wedding dress cuts that will enhance your gorgeous curves," she went on, bouncing on the spot.

Luca, Lizzie and I had caught up a few times each week since we got home from Greece and planned the non-negotiables. The dress and suit, flowers, and plans for a small intimate gathering. The idea of a big do with hundreds of guests made me queasy just thinking about all those eyes on me.

Luca was happy to take lead on organising the venue and photography, although if you ask me that was an easy way out considering he was using in-house creative talent for the photographer and event decorator. But he really did go above and beyond when he said he'd take care of the venue. I don't know who he had to torture or kill, but he said he 'called in a favour' to land us a beautiful spot in Central Park that we had spent many a day relaxing around together. A spot that usually wasn't offered for any events. *Ever.* It was one of my all-time favourite spots in all of New York city, and now it was going to be ours, forever tied to a magical moment in time.

SIX WEEKS LATER

"It won't do up," I panicked. "This is ridiculous Lizzie, I'm growing by the week, whatever fits right now won't come close on the day. And I'm getting married in six fucking weeks."

I slumped down on the bench in the dressing room, head in hands, hot tears lining my eyes.

"Damn these stupid pregnancy hormones, I'm a fucking mess," I sobbed, wiping the tears away with the back of my hand.

Lizzie embraced me tightly, pulling me into her body, cocooning around me, shielding me from the big scary world. "Shhh, sshhh, shhh," she tutted. "It's not all that bad. Obviously, this is not the dress for you. But—," she exclaimed, "I have the perfect one in mind. And I've asked Cindy to prepare it for you to try on. I think you'll love it," she tried to convince me. "This maternity bridal gown is romantic, graceful and will sit beautifully over your little bump," she squeezed a little tighter, her tone warm and reassuring.

"Will you try it on, for me?" she batted her eyelashes.

And you know what? She wasn't wrong. It really was the one. Like you know those romantic movies you watch and the bride-to-be tries on the umpteenth wedding dress to finally exclaim, 'this is the one'.

Well, this is the one. It's perfect. Simple yet stunning. It's... me.

The empire line enhanced my full, and growing, breasts, and draped over my belly. It didn't make it look like a watermelon or pull tight, making the material struggle with the stretch. It was so delicate, with a vintage romance vibe, and an intricate lace overlay and three-quarter length sleeves completing the vision.

"Luca's going to love it," I whispered, voice shaking with emotion.

"Yeh he will... But I'm pretty sure that man would love you walking down the aisle in a paper bag. So long as you say 'I do'."

###

I stood in the middle of a long straight road, woods all around me and a bright moon in the sky. I'd been here before, but my brain was a little slow to process it. I squeezed my eyes shut trying to make the memory focus. It glitched behind my eyelids, flying around in blurry snapshots. A feeling of dread and anxiety filled my chest. But a second later, it was gone, replaced by excitement and a desperate need. Mum. Dad. My eyes shot open and I spun around, finding the familiar hut up ahead. Last time it had been all but hidden in darkness, with the exception of a small light coming from one of the windows. This time it looked different. Warm. Welcoming. Lived in. Golden fairy lights adorned the front porch pillars, hanging from the roof eaves like a Christmas display. There was movement inside and a familiar melody on the breeze. Excitement filled my belly and I felt myself push forward, floating closer to the front door. Ma's favourite record was playing, Sia's melodic voice filling the air. As far back as I could remember, it always made her smile. I stood on the porch, hand hovering mid-air, ready to knock. But before I could, the door cracked open. 'Charlie Bear' dad hummed, his eyes smiling warmly. 'We've been waiting for you.' He swung the door fully open so I could see ma standing in the living room. 'I must be having one of those weird pregnancy-induced dreams,' I said to myself, running my hands up over my face. I rubbed at my eyes, letting them slowly focus. He was still standing in front of me, a gentle smile in place. 'It's not possible for me to actually be here,' I laughed in disbelief. 'And the last time I allowed that black hole to swallow me up and dream this place, you told me I couldn't be here... and I was thrown out, left to comfort myself from the loss of you again,' I muttered, shaking my head as I drew my clenched fists against my chest. Ma moved towards me, reaching out to grab my hands. 'We don't have a lot of time, but we had to see you again. To see you in your beautiful wedding gown and tell you how proud we are.' Confusion wrinkled my forehead. But as I swung my hands out to object and look down where my pyjamas pulled across my belly, I stumbled back. My ivory lace gown stared back at me. 'You look gorgeous Charlotte,' ma smiled, a tear rolling down her cheek. 'Now Maggie, this is the happiest of days, no need for tears. We promised.' They each grabbed onto an arm, pulling me in for a hug. 'If we could change the past, we would in a heartbeat,' ma whispered against my hair before pulling back to look into my eyes again. 'But everything happens for a reason. And you, my angel, were meant for great things. For the career you've worked so hard for, the man that loves you so deeply, and that little one you have given life to,' she choked out, placing a hand on my baby bump hesitantly. I couldn't swallow. The lump in my throat was ready to burst into uncontrollable ugly crying. 'Just know we are always with you, and we will be right there with you on your big day,' dad said, planting a kiss on my temple. I blinked away the tears as I looked back up from my belly to my parents. A sudden glint further back in the house caught my eye, and my gaze followed it. There standing as though not even one day had passed, was Lola. My mouth dropped open, but I couldn't form a sentence, not even a single word. She smiled at me, a smile that wrapped itself around my heart and filled me with such warmth. She spoke in whispers, but it rang in my ears as though she was right beside me. 'I love you Charlie Bear, to the moon and back. And I'm so proud of you. Don't ever stop shining.'

THE WEDDING DAY

I'd already thrown up twice this morning, and I wasn't sure if it was morning sickness rearing its ugly head again, or if my nerves got the better of me. Don't get me wrong, it wasn't a case of cold feet. No way in hell. This man was mine and I knew it deep in my bones. That, and it was sweltering outside and only ten in the morning.

Luca had kissed me farewell this morning before heading to Brad's place. I know, I know. Tradition forbids the bride and groom spend the night before the wedding together or see each other until they've proclaimed their everlasting love in front of witnesses. But there was nothing traditional about Luca and me. How we met. How our relationship started. And how we had somehow ordered a new business, marriage and baby, express delivery.

After my visit to mum and dad, or dream, hallucination or whatever you wanted to label it, I had insisted fairy lights be added to the venue. Particularly around where I would be walking towards my future husband. Although Lizzie and Eric had both offered numerous times to walk me down the aisle, it just didn't feel right to say yes. But knowing those little fairy lights would be flickering around me, glowing as dusk approached, gave me a sense that my parents and sister would be watching over me. Holding me up and settling my nerves. And I was ready to walk alone, for the last time.

I had a few hours to myself before Lizzie was set to arrive with a little help to do our hair and makeup. I decided on a bubble bath to release some of the tension and some honey, cinnamon and ginger tea to settle my stomach. I flicked off the lights, lit a couple of candles and turned up my relaxation playlist. By the time my hands and feet were pruney, I felt like myself again. And the thought that I would be Mrs Luca Crescent tonight had me a little too excited to be in a sensual bubble bath on my own. Honestly, no one tells you about the crazy sex drive that comes part and parcel with pregnancy. I shook the thought away knowing I had way too much to do still, and hopped out of the tub, ready to begin preparing for the moment I said I do.

I stood near a big American Elm, taking slow, measured breaths as I watched Lizzie walk off towards the makeshift aisle. The deep red of the small rose bouquet she carried matching the aisle runner she stepped onto. I shut my eyes, picturing a ball of glowing light below my sternum, and focused on finding my centre, my balance, before taking a step forward. And whether it was their spirits whispering, or all in my head, it didn't matter, because I heard the steadying, reassuring words I needed from my family.

'Are you ready Charlotte? One foot in front of the other. You've got this. You are ready for the next chapter in your life. We're here every step of the way.'

A warm gush of wind blew across the park, ruffling the curls that fell around my shoulders and I felt at ease. Cool, calm and collected.

'It's time Charlie.'

I held my rose bouquet, gently resting at the top of my belly. As the music changed, I stepped around the large tree, meeting Luca's gaze. And for a passing moment I had a vision of him holding a little bundle in his outstretched arms, swinging around a little girl with pigtails, right where he stood now, a little boy not much older sitting atop my shoulders as I watched on in awe. It was brief, and it was probably the afternoon heat creating a mirage, but I didn't care. That was the future I wanted, and in this very moment, I knew it with every single part of my being. Every cell of my body. And deep within my soul.

My eyes roamed across our gathered friends. And if love and support were tangible emotions, I would have felt each and every one of them reach out and wrap around me. I looked back at Luca and everyone else became a blur, a sea of tears and smiles. Everything stood still. Frozen in time. The music, the singing birds in the surrounding trees, the whispers from the guests. Luca was all that remained. His golden eyes locked on me. The muscles in his jaw working as he sucked in his lips. And then, as God is my witness, I swear the gates of heaven opened up as he shot a crooked smile at me, making the ball of light in my chest explode into a million pieces, lighting me up from the inside out.

He grabbed my hand, leading me to stand in front of him. Massaging his thumbs across the back of my hands, he mouthed 'you look beautiful'. I smiled back, 'you too'. I could see Stephan and Brad standing at Luca's back and I glanced over my shoulder to see Lizzie and Jane grinning behind me, blinking away the tears threatening to ruin their makeup.

I didn't hear much of what the celebrant said, but I didn't take my eyes off Luca. He was the centre of everything, the rock who held me strong. I followed his lead and read my personalised vows aloud through glossy eyes. Hesitating only once to clear the lump in my throat. When asked if we would love, honour and cherish one another, you can bet your bottom dollar we said 'I do'. And when the celebrant spoke those six little words I'd been waiting to hear since waking up this morning, I felt myself ascent, no longer a lonely 20-something year old, plagued by a history of loss and grieving. I was something more. Something greater. A partner, an equal, the half of a whole.

"You may now kiss the bride."

CHAPTER 29

"I LIKE HER," I said, after Luca closed the meeting room door.

"Yeh, she's got a good track record, already has some solid contacts, and a dash of that sass of yours. She'll fit right in," he smirked, leaning in and kissing the corner of my mouth.

"Mr Crescent," I scolded lazily, holding back a smile. "Not at work."

"Too late to play that card Mrs Crescent," he winked. "But back to business, you're about to pop and we're running out of time."

"I am not," I slapped his arm. I know it doesn't look it, but this little one still has two months of growing until they're ready to come out. Well, at least I hope so, because you're not done cooking yet, are you little nugget?" I cooed at my belly, rubbing my hands over the spot that had become a favourite for practicing kicks. Right on cue, nugget stretched and kicked under my hand. "He understood," I laughed.

"He?" Luca shot. "Do you know something I don't, because if you've been holding out on me princess, there's gonna be hell to pay." He playfully squeezed above my knee, "or at least a light spanking," he narrowed his eyes.

"No, I swear," I giggled. "It just popped out. I don't know why. I mean I've pictured a handsome little mini-you in my arms, but you know I'll be over the moon with whatever the Gods give us."

I lifted his hand to my lips, kissing over his knuckles and the wedding ring I'd placed there. "Let's get back to my replacement for maternity leave," I straightened, picking up her portfolio. "I agree. I think Heidi will be the perfect fit as campaign manager," I said, flicking through her resume. "Assuming her references are good, and I don't doubt they are, then we can bring her in the next few weeks, and I'll have some time to bring her up to speed and handover my clients before I 'pop', as you so poetically put it," I scrunched up my nose, making a face at him.

"Agree. I'll get the backgrounds done then get her onboarding organised so you can tie it all up in a nice bow before this little one makes an appearance," he said kissing my belly.

He rolled his chair closer, so our knees were intertwined, and rested his hands on the outsides of my thighs. "Now, I've got another proposal for you to cast your eyes over."

He reached on the desk behind him and placed a file in my hands.

"Where'd this one come from? Word of mouth, a previous client, or did they seek us out?" I asked, flipping the folder open. I stopped in my tracks, my eyes focused on the picture in front of me.

"Oh my God Luca. It's beautiful," I gushed. "And it's in that neighbourhood we love."

"I know. One of dad's old buddies is still in the realty business, and we bumped into each other recently. I told him what we were looking for and he's been keeping an eye out. He sent this over first thing this morning, to give us first dibs if we want to have a look, before it goes on the market next week."

"Yes," I exclaimed excitedly, fingering through the other images and glancing over the specs. "Set it up as soon as he can show us. This could be the one baby. It has everything we've been looking for."

I couldn't help the stupid smile covering my face. I don't know what it was that had turned the tables and persuaded the universe to finally smile upon me. But it felt like I was getting everything I wanted deep down. Even if I'd hidden those thoughts from the light of day since I was a teenager. After crawling out of the all-consuming darkness, could I really have it all? A friend as true as a sister, a husband as loving and protective as my parents, a child of my own to cherish, a job I'd always dreamed of. And now, the perfect house to raise a family and grow old in?

If you believe it Charlie, you'll achieve it.

But part of me, the damaged part was waiting for the other shoe to drop. Waiting for it all to be taken away. For the waves to crash over me, dragging me down into the drowning abyss that would surely be the end of me if it ever got its cold hands around my throat again. I could feel panic clawing at the edges of my happiness and my breath hitched.

"Baby girl," his honeyed voice reached out and soothed my heart and soul. "I've got you. There's nothing to fear anymore."

I took a deep breath in, lifting my gaze to meet his. The warmth in his eyes melted away the growing doubts and corrected the abnormal beating in my chest. The back of my eyes burned, and I swallowed against the emotion rising up my throat. His presence and essence rolled off him, flowing out to wrap protectively around every pore in my body. Caging the monster that had plagued my life for too long. It was as if Luca could feel it all. Understood every turn in the road that had shaped my life and was able to calm the storm battling within.

"We create our own destiny," he reached out, placing a hand over my heart. He pulled one of my hands to his chest and did the same thing. "You and me Charlie. 'Til the end of time."

255

After Bill had taken us through the house, spouting all the features that would make it a quick sale, we signed the papers that same day. But it wasn't the number of bedrooms, or the open plan family areas, or even the dreamy pool that had us hooked. It was so much more than that. How many places could you find where you felt safe in the neighbourhood, had enough privacy to raise your children out of the limelight but still close enough to civilisation for work and school, where you didn't have to spend hours travelling to and from the office and missing precious time with your family. Time you could never get back.

Luca negotiated a quick settlement to move us in before this baby arrived. Luckily, the previous owners had already moved on and our new home was empty, ready for a little family called the Crescents to make it their own.

I might have been a month away from giving birth to what was starting to feel like a little giant, but that hadn't dampened the desire for my husband. The man I affectionately referred to as *Mr Hot Sex* a lifetime ago. As if he'd written the book on 'how to make a pregnant woman orgasm into oblivion', sex had certainly not lost its lustre after marriage, or with a round belly in the way.

I was relaxing in the glider rocking chair in the nursery, feet up on the footstool, eyes closed and a smirk tugging at my mouth. The moans and curses coming from Luca, as he wrestled with the side of the cot that didn't want to slide into place, were entertaining and so bloody human. I cracked an eye open, seeing Luca sitting on the floor frowning at the instructions in his hand. A peek wasn't enough. I tilted my head forward slightly, focusing both eyes on the vision in front of me. I licked my lips, desperate to rid them of the parched feeling that struck suddenly, and I bit my bottom lip as my heart da-dumped like a girl crushing on the high school hottie.

His chest was bare, the shirt stripped off and thrown aside hours ago. The muscles in his back rippled, tensed from building the nursery furniture for the past four hours. His bicep bulged as his arm sat bent across the top of his knee, fingers brushing through his hair absent-mindedly. He hadn't changed out of his grey sweatpants from last night and I was still trying to figure if he'd purposely done that knowing how wild I found the sight of him. Especially when those sweatpants hung so daringly low on his hips, inviting me to trace down his V-lines and fist the cock that those pants always outlined to perfection.

Right now, they were sitting just below his hips and from my vantage point, his lower back dimples were stirring up all sorts of feelings. Butterflies were fluttering right out of my belly and heading south, straight for my pussy. "Need a hand?" I hummed, seduction lacing every word.

He threw the instructions to the floor, leaning his chin atop his bicep as he turned to look at me. "I know that look," he raised an eyebrow.

I kept my eyes trained on him, pushing up against the armrests to adjust my position, opening my knees ever so slightly, rising on tiptoes in anticipation. My tongue darted out again to lick the dryness away. His gaze roamed down towards my legs, stopping at the hem of the oversized shirt I was wearing as it scraped the tops of my thighs. My hands traced my thighs, skimming from the outside, working their way inwards to the building ache. My thumbs scratched the edge of my panties and my chest rose as I inhaled deeply. He spun his body, crawling towards me. Slowly. Seductively. Eyes on fire as he stalked forward.

Waves of desire shot through me when my eyes met his heated stare. He stopped at my feet, his hot tongue licking from my knee up across the top of my thigh. His strong hands followed, gripping just above my knees and opening me to him. I reached out, cupping his cheek, my thumb tracing his lip, dipping down to his jaw as I leaned forward, dropping my head to his. I hovered my lips just above his, letting my eyes flick up from his lips to his eyes. The golden pools were flushed dark with desire.

He dragged his fingernails down the outside of my thighs, breathing heavily into my mouth. His unique smell filled my nose. Woody, spiced rum taking over my senses. "Is there something I can do for you, my Queen?" his warm voice was tinged with roughness.

I nodded, moaning in agreeance. I closed the small gap between us, licking across his lips, my tongue persuading him to open to me. He leaned into me, wrapping his arms around me as he kissed me back, our tongues wrestling with the building need. His body was against mine, the thin material of those teasing grey sweatpants unable to hide that he wanted me as much as I wanted him.

He broke the connection, planting kisses down my body. Across my collarbone, down my breasts and pebbled nipples. Across my perfectly round belly and down my thighs. His fingers hooked into the top of my panties at my hips and dragged them down my legs. He positioned himself kneeling at my core and pulled me closer to his face, his strong arms wrapping under my thighs.

He planted a kiss at my entrance, slowly licking against my lips. I breathed out a ragged breath I didn't realise I'd been holding, sinking into the chair and against his hungry mouth. My fingers dug into the armrests and I pushed up on my arms, scrunching my shoulders up to my neck. His tongue slid inside me, darting in and out as he unwrapped a hand and pressed his thumb against my buzzing clit. He licked and sucked, and fucked me with his tongue while his thumb matched the rhythm, changing the pressure and the intensity of circles as he drew me closer to climax. My breathing increased and I could feel the wave getting closer and closer.

"Fuck Luca," I groaned. "I can't. Hold. On."

He pressed two fingers in me, his tongue replacing his thumb and working double time against my clit. I arched my back, hands fisting the armrests. "Oh God, oh God, Luca—," I panted as I tipped over the edge. Every part of me vibrated as the waves of my orgasm crashed against me. Wave after wave as my body clenched. Shaking as it came apart under his touch.

When colour had returned to the world and my heart stopped racing, I looked down at my husband. He lay his head against my thigh, staring up at me, watching every emotion cross my face and body. If I could see myself reflected in his eyes, I was sure I was glowing. Every inner ember now burning bright because of him. For him. And only him.

"I love you baby," I breathed, running my hand through his growing hair, gently playing with the curls that sat at the base of his neck.

"You will never want for anything Little Lamb," he promised, and I knew he meant every word.

EPILOGUE

LIFE WAS PERFECT. Busy. A type of organised chaos. But perfection.

Luca was everything I could ever have hoped for as a father. He was doting, comforting, protective, soft but firm when needed, and absolutely in love with our little nugget.

"Daaaada-dada-dada," Eli giggled as Luca bounced him on his leg like a pony. His squeal became more and more high-pitched the happier he became, and it set my soul on fire. I watched on from the kitchen, finishing up a call with the office to set up an introductory meeting with a possible new client. After hanging up, I stayed where I was, mesmerised as the two loves of my life played without a care in the world.

"Where's mama?" Luca hummed. "You tell her we can see her watching us and if she doesn't come here toot sweet we're going to cover her with kisses and cuddles, and a generous serving of teething drool," he joked, a lilt in his voice. He raised Luca up to his face, blowing raspberries on his belly, filling the room with the most beautiful sounds of pure enjoyment.

Luca's bare upper body was fucking magic, and still filled my core with butterflies every time I laid eyes on him. Even covered in baby drool.

"I'm coming," I giggled. "Just let me grab little mister a

261

bottle for bed."

"Oh no, don't listen to her Eli. We can stay up all night partying. Sleep is overrated anyway," he said, standing and bringing Eli to his chest. It's funny how the minute you have a baby in your arms you bounce on the spot, rocking from one foot to the other. Watching Luca do that with his son in his arms made me beam, and I'm pretty sure I felt my ovaries explode a little.

I walked towards them, warm milk bottle in hand. "Well if you boys want to keep the party going, you do it in the pool house," I pouted. "Because this mama needs some under the cover care tonight. But—," I let my voice drawl. "If she has to do it by herself, then so be it."

As quick as a flash, Luca wrapped his arm around my waist and pulled me into his side. I laughed at his superhuman reflexes and the way my body reacted, wanting to bow down to his every command.

Luca nibbled at my shoulder as Eli clapped his hands, giggling in excitement. "Don't you dare," he growled. "That's my job. More than that baby girl. My reason for existence," he breathed against the shell of my ear.

I claimed his lips, the same way I did every day. With love, lust and a raw fucking need to be one with him.

Eli jumped into my arms, snuggling under my chin and against my chest. He stole the bottle from my hands and began drinking. I looked between my two boys, still shocked how alike they were. Luca's eyes had been reborn in our son, long dark lashes and all. His beautiful soft hair was dark like Luca's, but it curled more like mine. But the way his cheeks filled and his face glowed when he giggled was different. In his smile, I saw Lola.

It had been a rough week. I felt completely drained both

emotionally and physically. I had worked late two nights this week to make changes for one of our clients before the set deadline. And today was the anniversary of Lola's death.

Last year was hard. Eli was only five months old and I was still dealing with unstable hormones, lack of sleep and was struggling to balance how to deal with the joy of my present with the loss in my past. This year it felt a little easier, but only just. My heart still ached, and I knew the parts that my sister and my parents held would never completely heal. But the wounded edges didn't feel so sharp and raw this year. Instead, they felt like the soft, rounded edges of sea glass that's been washed up on the beach with the ebb and flow of the tide a hundred times or more.

Luca came with me to visit her grave. After placing Lola's favourite flower, oriental lilies, on her headstone, Luca took Eli for a walk, leaving me to talk with my sister. I sat there for what seemed like hours, chatting as if she sat beside me. Telling her about everything that had happened in the past year. And when we returned home, I felt like I'd run a marathon. Luca ran me a bath and insisted on looking after me, drying me, brushing my hair and dressing me in pyjamas. Then he settled me in bed, kissed my forehead and left me to sleep while he looked after our son. Before I could hear his footsteps disappear down the hallway, I fell into a deep sleep. The best sleep I'd had in over a year.

I woke to little hands crawling across my chest the next morning. A sloppy mouth covering mine. I laughed with my mouth closed, trying not to suck in the drool Eli covered me with. I rolled with him to my side, snuggling into his neck, peppering him with baby kisses as he squirmed in my arms.

"Good morning baby boy," I sung, planting a kiss on his nose. I reached out to Luca with my free hand, squeezing his forearm as he watched us. "Morning babe," I smiled. "And thank you. Seriously, I slept like the dead. Crass I know, but I feel reborn."

"You needed it," he hummed, rubbing his hand over

mine, letting his other hand play with Eli's soft hair.

In moments like this I knew my true purpose in life. It wasn't to suffer alone, or hide away and let life pass me by. It was here, as a wife, mother and one helluva advertising exec. And I was finally whole again.

"We better get a move on," Luca hummed gently. "We promised Lizzie and Johnny we'd meet them for brunch across town."

"Oh crap, I nearly forgot," I sat up, passing Eli to Luca and giving them both a kiss before running for the shower. "I'll be ready in twenty," I called back. "Then I'll get Eli ready while you shower," I finished as the spray of water warmed enough for me to dive in.

"Sorry we're late," I said, pulling Lizzie in for a hug.

"You're not late, we just got here ourselves," she smiled. "How are you doing Char?," her eyebrows pulled in concern. "I was thinking of you all yesterday. I'm sorry another year has passed without Lola here with us."

"Thank you. Yeh life can be cruel and don't we know it. But you know what? I'm okay. I really am. I am surrounded by so much love and for that I am the luckiest girl in the world," I smiled through tight lips, pulling her in for another big hug. We stayed like that longer than was probably acceptable in public, but I didn't care. I finally let her go and Lizzie stepped to my side, moving to give Luca and Eli hugs.

"What's cookin' good lookin'?" Johnny flirted stepping forward, pulling me in for a tight squeeze.

"Still as charming as the day we met," I teased.

We found our way to a reserved table on the terrace, a highchair was already set up for Eli. We caught up on what had been happening in each of our lives for the last few weeks since last chatting. Johnny kept Eli entertained, picking up his toy from the ground every time he threw it off the edge. The cheeky little monster finding happiness in his own version of playing fetch. And it made him cackle and drool like a demon child.

"You don't need to keep doing that Johnny," Luca said, taking the toy from Eli's hand, replacing it with a piece of banana to smoosh.

"You know I don't mind. The little guy's really grown on me, and I don't care how many times he makes me reach for his toy."

Johnny and Lizzie exchanged looks. Something unsaid sitting between them. My eyes flicked to Luca, and I know he noticed it to.

"What's really going on here?" I asked, raising an eyebrow at Lizzie.

Again they just looked at each other, Lizzie's bottom lip disappearing into her mouth.

"Lizzie Ryan, don't you sit there in silence. There are no secrets between us. You know that," I said, a little hurt that there was hesitation on their faces.

"Of course not," she said, grabbing my hand in between hers. "It's one of the reasons we wanted to catch up with you both today."

She let go of my hands, dropping hers to her lap and fiddling with her purse. I narrowed my eyes at her, flicking back to Johnny who looked like he had stolen the donation plate from a Sunday church service.

"Lizz—"

My exclamation was cut short as Lizzie held up her hand, a serious sparkler now on her ring finger.

"We're getting married," she giggled nervously as she showed off the beautiful new addition to her jewellery collection with spirit fingers.

I gasped, my hands shooting up to cover my mouth. The burning feeling behind my eyes hit home again, and tears lined my eyes for the 27,000th time since I'd met Lizzie all those years ago.

"Oh my god," I said grinning, "I am so incredibly happy for you both."

I leaned forward, wrapping my arms around her for a congratulatory hug before pulling back to examine the whopper on her hand. "It's stunning. Johnny, I'm impressed," I gushed, smiling between him and Luca.

"Charlie, you have been my family, my rock for the past eight years and I need you by my side through this and everything after," she said, eyes locked on me. "Will you be my maid of honour?"

"Oh Lizzie, you are my sister from another mister, and you are stuck with me forever," I sung. "But I would be truly honoured to stand by your side on your special day."

For the first time that week, I felt completely at peace. With Lizzie, Luca and Eli by my side for whatever the universe threw at us, I knew I'd get through it all. On my best days and worst. Wild horses couldn't drag me away from being part of Lizzie's life, and by extension, that now included Johnny.

Life was perfect. Busy. A type of organised chaos. But perfection. And I was happier than I ever could have imagined I was deserving of. Lola was right. I was meant for big things and I was never going to stop shining. In this life or the next.

The End

###

ACKNOWLEDGEMENTS

When I set out to write down my thoughts and dreams, the stories that have been living inside my head rent free for way too long, I never could have imagined actually getting to the finish line. It has been exciting, and nerve-racking, and a wild journey.

Thank you first and foremost to my family. To my husband and sons, Paul, Isaac, Jacob and Lucas. You have put up with me being distant, wrapped up in my own world, busy in thought, fingers madly tapping away on the keyboard. Dinner has been late on many occasions, and missed on others. I would never have finished this story without your patience and ongoing support. Thank you so much. I love you all with my very being, with my heart and soul.

Thank you to my parents, Michelle and Tibor. You have been an incredible pillar of support, even if your first reaction was of complete shock when I told you I was writing a smutty romance novel. But you always make me smile and laugh, and I'm so unbelievably thankful to call you mine.

To my beautiful supportive friends. Mel, Janet, and Elle. Your words of encouragement have kept me going. And I couldn't have made it as schmexy without being able to soundboard off you. My beautiful tribe of women. Thank you. And a big thank you to my Beta Readers, you're the best!

Thank you to each and every reader who has picked up this book, with the name of an unknown author on the cover, and given your time, your imagination and maybe even a naughty thought or two into Charlie and Luca's story. I thank you from the bottom of my heart.

And if you fell a little bit in love with Charlie and Luca, I hope you're excited to dive into Lizzie and Johnny's story next. So stay tuned!

Until then, keep dreaming, keep reading and live out those sexy dreams!

Justina xo

LEAVE A REVIEW

If you enjoyed this story, I would love if you would consider leaving a review! Reader reviews, both official and unofficial, are the lifeline for an indie author's success. No matter where you feel most comfortable – Goodreads, Amazon, wherever's your fave review spot – your honest review means the world to me. And every review helps me on this writing journey. I write for everyone, like me, who is looking for that escape from reality, if only for a magical few hours.

ABOUT THE AUTHOR

Justina Staniforth is a new indie author, taking her love for contemporary romance and smutty escapades and letting them fill the pages for all to enjoy. The soul-crushing love, the dirty fun, and the happy ever afters. She currently lives on the sunny Mid North Coast of Australia with her husband and three sons. She loves thrillers, sweet wine, candles and always has music playing, even when reading and writing. Honestly, go check out her Spotify playlists, including her *Controlled by Desire* bangers! While pursuing her dream of becoming a full-time author, a girl's gotta pay the bills and her career as a midwife and educator do just that. Well that... and feed her soul.

You can find Justina on these social platforms:
Facebook -> @justina.staniforth.author
TikTok -> @authorjustinastaniforth